BINDING THREADS ON BEAMER STREET

SHEILA RILEY

Boldwood

First published in Great Britain in 2026 by Boldwood Books Ltd.

Cover Design by Colin Thomas

Cover Images: Colin Thomas

A CIP catalogue record for this book is available from the British Library.

Paperback ISBN 978-1-83678-866-9

Large Print ISBN 978-1-83678-867-6

Hardback ISBN 978-1-83678-865-2

Trade Paperback ISBN 978-1-80656-136-0

Ebook ISBN 978-1-83678-868-3

Kindle ISBN 978-1-83678-869-0

Audio CD ISBN 978-1-83678-860-7

MP3 CD ISBN 978-1-83678-861-4

Digital audio download ISBN 978-1-83678-862-1

This book is printed on certified sustainable paper. Boldwood Books is dedicated to putting sustainability at the heart of our business. For more information please visit https://www.boldwoodbooks.com/about-us/sustainability/

Boldwood Books Ltd, 23 Bowerdean Street, London, SW6 3TN

www.boldwoodbooks.com

1

MAY 1930

'Mam, will you please sit still.' Twenty-three-year-old Daisy Haywood stood behind her mother, seated at the dark oak dressing table, which had stood in the same place between two sash windows for as long as anybody could remember.

'I'm sorry, love,' Molly said, eyeing a lethal-looking hatpin being poked into her new sky-blue, crushed-velvet cloche hat. As this was a special day, Molly had opted for the hat with a side feather in shimmering peacock blue, which the milliner said would enhance any mother-of-the-bride. Fifty-year-old Molly hadn't the heart to tell the bustling assistant that she was the bride. 'I'm just nervous, that's all.'

'What are you nervous about?' asked Daisy. 'You've known Percy since Adam was a lad.' Percy Pierce worked alongside Daisy and had had a soft spot for her mother since he'd joined Mary Jane's coterie of bakers after coming home from the Front twelve years ago. He'd been lodging in her mother's parlour and back bedroom for the last three years.

'Well, you never imagine yourself getting married for a second time when you're my age,' said Molly, hoping the hat didn't crush her new hairdo, which her youngest daughter, Bridie, had ironed into deep S-shaped Marcel waves.

A newly qualified stylist at Madam Fontane's Hair Salon, Bridie had spent most of the morning perfecting each ebb and flow, to the point Molly was sure she'd taken root in front of the bedroom mirror.

Daisy smiled, remembering her mother's astonished expression when Percy had got down on his arthritic knee and asked her to marry him on the stroke of the brand-new decade.

Daisy could not think why her mother had been so surprised, she and Percy had been 'walking out' for years. He'd started by taking her mam to the pictures every weekend, then, after seeing their first talkie, *The Jazz Singer*, they went every night and were still inclined to break into a rendition of Al Jolson songs around the piano in the parlour.

'The only thing that mystifies me is why it took him so long to ask you,' Daisy said, failing to hold back a chuckle. 'After all, it's not like you two are getting any younger.'

'Cheeky mare.' Molly laughed easily. She knew it wasn't Daisy's intention to sound rude. Her eldest daughter didn't have a mean bone in her body, but she could be a bit thoughtless in her wording. Molly didn't have a clue where she got that from. 'Nothing is going to spoil my big day,' Molly said, knowing she had waited far too long for Percy to broach the subject of matrimony. 'He was worried I would turn him down. Knowing how much I missed your father, God rest his sainted soul.' Molly said those five words like a mantra every time she mentioned her late husband, Bert, who had been killed on Flanders Fields in 1916.

'Maybe Percy thought you weren't ready,' Daisy said drily, wondering what hope poor Percy had against such a hero in

Molly's eyes? Anybody would think her father won the Great War single-handed.

'I don't want Percy to think he's second best,' said Molly as if reading her daughter's thoughts, 'because even though he's going to be my second husband, he will always receive the same love and affection as your dearly departed father once did. *God rest his sainted soul.*'

'I don't doubt it, Mam,' Daisy said, looking out of the window when she heard the front gate open. 'It's the flowers.'

Her daughter's bright smile cheered Molly, who suddenly felt she had a stampede of horses thundering through her chest.

'I'll just go and see how everybody is doing downstairs, Mam. Can I get you anything?'

'Send me up a nice cherry brandy to calm my nerves,' said Molly, 'just a small one.' She held up a two-inch measure with finger and thumb.

'You're not getting that much.' Daisy's eyes widened. 'Percy will run a mile if he sees you zigzagging up the aisle with your hat skew-whiff.'

* * *

'Here, let me do that,' Daisy told her brother, nineteen-year-old Freddy, who was holding a pin and looking a bit lost at the bottom of the stairs. Taking a white carnation from the box, he rested his backside on their mother's pride and joy, the latest in art-deco consul tables, a wedding present from Mary Jane and Cal Everdine, as Daisy slipped the stem of the flower into Freddy's blue serge lapel and fixed it with the pin. 'Men are useless when it comes to flowers.'

'Is she having a canary yet?' asked Freddy, looking up the wide staircase towards their mother's bedroom.

'She'll be right as ninepence when you take her a small cherry brandy,' whispered Daisy as some of the guests began to arrive, knowing her mother liked to have her family around her. 'It won't be long now,' she said, peering out of the semicircular stained-glass window in the front door that was never usually closed during the day.

'Is she doing the right thing, Daisy?' Freddy asked, taking in a lungful of his untipped Senior Service cigarette, letting his older sister do what she loved doing most. Fuss.

'Well, it's a bit late to worry about that now, Freddy,' said Daisy. 'We're all off her hands and grown up, now's her turn to please herself, she's looked after us all long enough.'

'She won't stop, just because she's married, surely?' Freddy's dark brows pleated into a quizzical frown and Daisy shook her head, knowing Freddy liked being coddled by his mam. The youngest of her two brothers, she suspected Freddy was Mam's favourite, not that Mam ever said as much, but because he looked so much like their father. 'Not that it will make any difference to me.'

'Oh?' Daisy's dark brows almost met in the middle of her pleated forehead, her puzzled expression matching his.

'I'm going away to sea after the wedding.' Freddy had decided to join the navy. 'I want to see the world before I settle down to a life of married bliss.'

'Good idea,' said Daisy, suspecting her mam would be heartbroken when her youngest son revealed he would soon be off into the wild blue yonder.

'She will want you to do what you think is best,' Daisy said, assuring him that what he was about to do was the right thing, even though she knew their mother would not agree.

'She'll probably cry her leg off,' Freddy laughed. 'Anyway, I don't have any choice in the matter, I've already signed the papers.'

She noticed Freddy's tie was crooked, and she straightened it. 'There, that's better.' Daisy stepped back to view her handi-work before patting her younger brother's chest. Then, looking around the hallway, she noticed the table flowers. 'They need to go in water,' Daisy said. 'Here, pass them over, and don't drop ash onto them.' Her dependable tone barely carried over the babble of voices coming from the other room, where guests had gathered before the cars arrived to take them to Saint Patrick's R. C. church.

Daisy, along with her mother Molly, and her sister, Bridie, had been up till way past midnight, scrubbing every room in the house until they gleamed. Then it was up at the crack of dawn to prepare food for the wedding recep-tion being held in the large front parlour. She was glad her mam had agreed to settle down with Percy. Molly was still a fine-looking woman who held herself well and had single-handedly raised four fine, upstanding offspring. She deserved a good husband in her autumn years, thought Daisy, making her way to the back kitchen, where their neighbours were preparing the sit-down wedding breakfast of hot soup, a cold meat salad, with sherry trifle to follow, unprepared for the conversation that stopped her in her tracks.

'Daisy Haywood is the most finicky person I know,' complained Ina King, a neighbour. 'Twice she told me I hadn't got the place settings right.'

'That's Daisy,' replied Peggy Tenant, a friend of her mother who had come to help with the wedding arrangements. 'She's been the same since she was a little'n. Rounding up the kids and looking after everyone when poor Molly lost her husband in the war.'

'Don't mention the war to me,' said another neighbour. 'The way things are going with that Charlie Chaplin lookalike, I'd say he's spoiling for another one.'

'Not a chance,' replied a voice near the sink. 'They said the last one was the war to end all wars.'

'What they say and what they mean are two completely different things,' Ina replied.

'Aye, well, don't let Molly hear you talking about war today,' said Peggy. 'She'll have a fit of conniptions. And we can well do without that.'

'Where's our Davey?' Molly asked, holding on to her prayer book over the banister and waving her corsage of pink and cream coloured tea roses, expecting her daughter to pin it on the brand-new navy-blue dropped-waist costume.

'He's gone to get change of a ten-bob note, he said,' Daisy called up the stairs. 'And you can believe that if you like.' She stood in the doorway of the back kitchen to see the women working away. 'Half an hour to go before the cars turn up and he nips out for a sly pint in the Tram Tavern!' Davey, next in age to Daisy, was their mother's best man, and in need of a bit of courage, he had told her.

'Daisy, can you fix my corsage?' Molly called downstairs over the chatter of guests.

'I'll be with you in a tick, Mam.' Daisy needed to put the table flowers in a vase. And although grateful for the help from her neighbours, who banded together to help with the wedding reception, she knew some of the Beamer Street neighbours were always eager to muck in and do their bit, while others like Ina King came to see what they could glean from the situation.

'I thought she'd be the first to wed,' said Ina, and Daisy

raised an eyebrow, knowing her neighbour was not aware of her presence. She'd wondered how long it would be before somebody got around to mentioning her lack of a spouse and Daisy's heart dipped. Other people's business was always the favourite topic of conversation in this street.

By Beamer Street standards, she knew she was considered an old maid. But she would rather walk barefoot over broken glass than hotfoot it down the aisle to matrimony and mother-hood with the first man who asked her. *Unlike some* – she looked to Ina, whose nine assorted offspring ranged from ten to twenty-five.

No, thought Daisy, marriage was not for her. Even though Max had hinted that he would like to marry one day, he hadn't asked her. They were two halves of the same soul. Both ambitious and independent. She couldn't hold him to marriage. She had an empire to build. But that was not to say she hadn't thought about it when he said he was going overseas to work.

* * *

In the fading light of the summer's evening, the well-dressed young man gazed with fixed intensity into the beautiful dark eyes of the girl he had loved since he'd first set eyes on her. However, neither could deny their ambition.

As the sun dipped below the horizon of the dockside, casting a warm, amber glow over the small north-Liverpool town, Max Galant gently took her hands in his as Daisy Haywood's eyes brimmed with unshed tears, reflecting the ache in her heart. Though they both knew this moment was inevitable, it did little to ease the pain of parting.

With a tender smile, he reached into his pocket and retrieved a small velvet box. Opening it to reveal a sapphire

pendant, its deep glow reminiscent of the summer night sky –
calm and reflective. He placed it around her neck, his fingers
lingering for a moment longer than necessary.

'Keep it with you,' he whispered softly, 'a reminder that
even when we are apart, my heart is with you always.'

Her breath hitched, and she clutched the pendant close,
feeling the cool stone against her skin. Yet, despite the gift and
his words, the ache of his departure lingered, like a shadow
over her heart.

As he prepared to leave, she watched him walk up the gang-
plank of the ship, the weight of impending separation heavy
upon her. Though the sapphire symbolised hope and fidelity, it
could never erase the sorrow of their parting. Daisy didn't like
goodbyes. They always brought her out in tears. It was the same
when their Bridie said she wanted to work in one of those posh
salons in London.

She knew Max and her love would be tested in the coming
months, or even years, by distance, but the memories they
shared, and the pendant, would serve as a beacon of their
enduring friendship.

2

23 DECEMBER 1935

Twenty-eight-year-old, Daisy Haywood lifted her head as she passed Mary Jane Everdine's bakery and confectioner's shop – the shop she had worked in until she had started her successful Silver Service Events catering business, after Max Galant went away.

Gazing up at her office window above the bakery, she could hear the ringing of her office telephone and, fumbling in her swing coat pocket, Daisy hurried around the corner and unlocked the side door, before hurrying upstairs to her first-floor office – the heart of her business, where she organised the fundraiser events she had become renowned for.

Her training in Mary Jane's shop below had been the springboard to Daisy's success as one of Liverpool's most sought-after event organisers, catering for rich clients.

She had been asked many times why she didn't operate from one of those upmarket offices overlooking Bold Street or Rodney Street in the more affluent part of the city. But Daisy's heart and her business belonged to Beamer Street. The address kept her grounded, as well as keeping her locally placed staff in a job without having to pay a fortune in travelling costs every day.

She had experienced the poverty that pervaded the surrounding streets, especially in these economically depressed times when jobs were still scarce on Merseyside since the Wall Street crash of '29. But her determination to better herself had allowed her the prerogative to employ only locals, who would otherwise struggle to find work. Daisy offered higher-than-average wages, and she was never short of workers. There was always a willing queue of locals ready to start work at a moment's notice.

Mary Jane had taught Daisy the finer points of catering to the upper classes, and Daisy had come a long way. Her unstinting work ethic and excellent attention to detail had propelled her towards some of the highest echelons in society... But by the time she'd got to the tastefully decorated office, the candlestick telephone had stopped ringing.

'Bugger!' she breathed.

Crossing the floor, she went over to the long sash window on the other side of the office and rested her knee against the low sill, gazing across Beamer Street to the home she shared with her mother, Molly, stepfather Percy and, later this afternoon, her sister Bridie, who was returning from London and the posh salon she had worked in for the last five years.

Daisy knew she should be at home, getting ready for the party to celebrate her engagement to Harvey Harris. But just thinking about it made her heart sink. As it had done several times today, and she wasn't naïve enough to wonder why. Harvey was a nice enough chap. But was 'being nice' enough to promise the rest of your life away?

As always in quiet moments, her thoughts turned to Max, a roving reporter on the *Liverpool Daily Post* whom she had loved and lost five years ago to the big wide world she had never seen. Max wanted excitement. Reporting on world affairs would do that, he'd said. Taking particulars of local weddings and christenings would not.

The recollections brought that familiar surge of bewilderment within her, a reaction to what should be long-forgotten memories of Max. Instead, they left her perplexed, causing an uneasy wave of guilt to rise inside her. Daisy knew that today, of all days, she should not be thinking of Max.

He had gone abroad in search of those exciting stories, while she became one of the northwest's most successful event organisers. A broken heart could do that to a girl, she supposed.

From the other side of the office, the tall sash window overlooked the Mersey dockside, its cranes, and ships clearly visible. Daisy gazed with unseeing eyes, lost in her own deep thoughts of the day Max had boarded the ship. She hadn't seen him since. Yet, the question still troubled her. Would she give all of this up if Max came back and asked her to? As Harvey had asked of her yesterday.

The shock of his casual expectation had shaken her to the core. And set her thoughts reeling. She didn't want to cease the business, which she had worked so hard to make the success it deserved to be. She couldn't. She wouldn't. Not for anything.

Her despair over losing Max had muted over the last five years by long hours of doing the work she loved. The events she hosted were lavish, often exclusive to the elite, and always bespoke. Daisy refused to believe the effort was but a distraction from a broken heart that had never properly healed. She had been moving closer to this, her chosen career, since she was fourteen years of age.

She suspected her business was only one of the reasons she and Max were two halves of the same soul. They were ambitious. Driven. They wanted to grab life by the shoulders and shake everything they could out of it. She understood Max had to move away to make his dream a reality.

Shrugging her shoulders, Daisy knew she should not be thinking this way. But she couldn't help it. She should never have agreed to Harvey's proposal. But it was too late to back out now. When she'd voiced her doubts to her mam, Molly had looked pensive.

'He's a good worker,' Mam had said. 'He's got a steady job on the docks, he'll never be out of work.'

Was that the be-all and end-all around here? With so many men out of work, Daisy supposed her mother was right. But Mam didn't know Harvey Harris like she did.

Harvey showed the outside world a genial, good-fellow-well-liked disposition. Nevertheless, since she had agreed to marry him, Daisy had seen cracks in his character, the ongoing effort of being a loving suitor seemed too much for Harvey to endure, and lately he could be snappy, especially if she talked about her work. Belittling her efforts by saying she was little more than a glorified waitress. How wrong he was!

Older than Daisy by seven years, Harvey had never been married. At thirty-five, he was still living in the same house he was born in, with his ailing mother. Her mam said Harvey was a traditionalist who believed a woman's place was in the kitchen. Daisy suspected he was looking for a woman to cater to his every need. As his doting mother had done all his life.

Set in his ways, he did not believe married women should go out to work and said so, often. And no matter how many times she tried to tell him she would not give up her business until she was good and ready, their *conversation* inevitably turned into a row.

Would she endure Harvey's unreasonable demands? Or

would she, like so many women, be forced to cave in to her husband's wishes. Especially when he had the backing of his mother. Because Daisy knew Harvey was not the kind of man who would leave the comfort of the house he had always known, to find a place for himself and her. But, Daisy wondered, why should she have to give up the business she had worked so hard for just to keep the peace – in his mother's house? Because, as sure as hens laid eggs, Daisy would never be mistress of her own house while his mother was still alive.

Momentarily turning from the window, her gaze fell upon the staff photograph on the office wall, and framed letters of gratitude from satisfied clients, pleased with the service she provided. Her staff, impeccably uniformed in black and white, their hair hidden beneath starched white caps, would be out of work if she gave in to Harvey's demands and sold her business.

And for what? Daisy felt an unusual surge of rebellion rise inside her. She hadn't come this far, only to look after his cantankerous mother who was never satisfied with anybody or anything. *You think you're something, lady. Well, let me tell you, a girl from Beamer Street never rose to owt, never mind run their own company.* Harvey's mother's words, whispered on the sly on their first meeting, were the spur that now drove her.

Daisy recognised that breaking through the class barrier to achieve a position of equality with the elite was the result of that devious remark two years ago. So, with sheer determination, talent, and hard work, she had made Harvey's mother eat her words.

While it *was* unusual for a working-class girl to reach the heights she had climbed, Daisy proved it was possible. She refused to be scorned by Harvey's mother. And she refused to give up her business now.

Silver Service Events was aimed at the powerful, richest,

most successful clients in England, but Daisy prided herself on the fact she never forgot those less fortunate, giving her service freely to local charities. Her modest upbringing had been no different from every other family in this close-knit dockside community. Raised single-handedly by her widowed mam after her father, like so many others, was killed on the battlefields in the Great War. Daisy was independent before she even knew the meaning of the word. She never worried about money and riches because her family didn't have any.

Nevertheless, lack of money did not diminish her ambition, or her opportunity. Which was why she vowed she would never go back to the old days when she would be beholden to anybody. As the day of her engagement drew closer, Daisy realised if she agreed to Harvey's suggestion, to give up her business and settle down to be a housewife, or even a mother, he would use her loss of her independence to dominate her.

In that moment, turning her attention back to the window, the silhouette of cranes and ships brought her firmly back from her contemplation, Daisy knew she would never give up her business to do a man's bidding. Silver Service Events meant far too much to her.

Daisy gave a quiet smile as she watched Percy, her stepfather crossing the street. Her heart secretly burning to find the same kind of love her mam and Percy shared. A love that allowed each to be their own person. There was nothing selfish or demanding about their love. And in that moment, it was as if the scales had fallen from her eyes; she doubted she would receive the same understanding from Harvey.

She reached for the letter she had received this morning from Max. He wrote sporadically. His letters, filled with news you would never hear on the wireless, were kept in the top drawer of her dressing table. He wrote of the growing unrest in

Franco's Spain. And of the rising victory of that ranting little man with a Charlie Chaplin moustache, whose furious tirades drew thousands in colossal rallies.

Herr Hitler was being hailed as a national saviour, who had founded the National Socialist German Workers Party, now known as the Nazi Party. Ensuring there was no unemployment in Germany, like there was here, at home. Yet, according to Max, the work was in munitions factories, building weapons in case of war. The news, while unsettling, didn't affect Daisy in the same way as the unemployment crisis here.

Max believed a woman should do as her heart told her, and not what was expected. With much effort, over the last five years, she had done just that, while trying to bury her dreams of marrying him. Then, this morning, completely out of the blue, she had received the letter and heard his voice on a BBC news broadcast.

She couldn't help herself, even though she knew it was wrong, but in that moment all the old familiar feelings came flooding back, his deep, soulful voice echoing in her thoughts. She couldn't get his words out of her head. She didn't want to.

'...With no other leader able to command sufficient support—' Max's voice now filled the office as the news repeated his overseas report '—President von Hindenburg had no choice but to appoint Adolf Hitler Chancellor of Germany in 1933. Now, as leader of the Nazi Party, he believes that people could be separated into a hierarchy of different races, and that some races are superior, and others are inferior. Herr Hitler believes the German race to be superior. An "Aryan" race, as he calls it, will be a blonde-haired, blue-eyed society.'

'Shouldn't you be getting ready for your big night?' Twenty-year-old Ailish Cavanah, Daisy's right-hand, lowered the office wireless, obviously more interested in the forthcoming shindig this evening in the Tram Tavern.

'I was listening to that,' said Daisy, turning up the volume to hear Max speak again. 'This news is what your father and my father fought for in the war. It is also something we must be aware of, if our clients choose to converse about world affairs whilst waiting for their dessert.'

'I'm usually a bit rushed off me feet by then,' said Ailish, deliberately slouching her words.

'*My* feet,' Daisy corrected, and Ailish smiled.

'When I'm rushed off *your* feet, then,' she answered, and Daisy tried but failed to suppress a smile.

Ailish was a tonic. Daisy had known her all her life. She was competent enough to assist her in everything she did and was able to speak on any level, to prince or pauper. Not that they had any of either on the books.

'Now, if you were discussing the affair of the woman in number twenty-two, I'd be interested,' said Ailish, tidying the office desk. 'Well, flabbergasted actually, seeing as she's got eight kids and a husband who hasn't worked a day since 1929. So, I doubt there's much in the way of naughty shenanigans going on in that quarter. But I would be *extremely* interested all the same.'

'I don't doubt it for a minute,' Daisy laughed. She liked a bit of local gossip herself, which was why, in rare quiet moments of peace and quiet, she liked to stand looking out over the same old street in which she had grown, remembering the days when she helped her widowed mother raise three siblings.

How could she even contemplate giving up all of this? Daisy knew in her heart that she had to call the engagement off before this charade got out of hand. Harvey wanted to reduce her to the realms of a domestic servant, curb her dreams, make her subservient to him and his mother. That was not how she saw her life panning out in future.

The sudden shrill ring made Daisy jump, catapulting her out of preoccupied thoughts and, crossing the floor to her desk, she cleared her throat and lifted the black Bakelite earpiece from its cradle and spoke clearly into the telephone mouthpiece.

'Good afternoon, Silver Service Events, how may I help you?' Daisy's calm, authoritative manner proved the elocution lessons had paid off. Her perfectly enunciated diction was a boon in this business, giving nothing away regarding her dock-side upbringing.

'Good afternoon,' said the confident female voice on the other end of the line, 'I was given your number by a mutual friend who told me you cater, amongst other things, for charitable causes.'

'Certainly,' Daisy answered in an equally confident tone, 'Silver Service Events is a high-class catering service.' As she spoke, she unconsciously watched Ailish draw the specially embossed paperwork from the in-tray and expertly slip it into a high-quality envelope. 'We specialise in elegant soirées, opulent weddings, and exclusive corporate and charitable events. We have a reputation for culinary excellence, impeccable service, transforming ordinary events into extraordinary occasions.' Her expert promotion, honed by years of repetition, was not glib sales patter, Daisy believed totally in the service she provided. The framed letters of recommendation that graced her office walls proved it.

'I am calling with regard to raising funds for local hospitals.'

'A service very close to my heart,' said Daisy. 'Let me pop a brochure into the post. Rest assured you will not be disappointed... May I take your name and address, please.'

'Certainly, I am Miss Treadwell, Lady Almoner of the Mersey Infirmary...'

When Daisy concluded her phone call, she looked at the clock on the wall. It was time she wasn't here.

'I can't leave Mam and the neighbours to do all the work,' she said, her heart dipping into her highly polished shoes at the thought of the engagement party.

'I'll see you later,' said Ailish. 'Big smile, best foot forward.'

'We'll see,' said Daisy, knowing what she had to do.

3

'She's very particular is Daisy,' Agnes Cavanah said as the local women worked, preparing food for the later party, when everybody came back to her mother's house after the pub closed at ten o'clock. 'That's as it should be, now her catering business is doing so well.'

'You're only siding with her because your Ailish is working in Silver Service.'

Daisy listened at the door into the back kitchen, even though she knew she shouldn't.

'I'm doing no such thing,' Agnes sounded impatient, which was understandable, thought Daisy. Ina had that disagreeable habit of saying the first thing that came into her head, whether it be true, imagined or a downright invention. 'I think it's marvellous what she's done with that business. It takes guts for a woman to go it alone. Not to mention owning one of the top catering firms on Merseyside.'

'It's been five years since she started the catering lark,' said Ina. 'Surely she can afford a swanky set-up somewhere like Bold Street?' Bold Street was a thoroughfare for high-class shops in Liverpool's city centre, a place where Ina and those like her could never afford to shop.

'It's none of our business,' Agnes answered, and Daisy, standing on the other side of the kitchen door, smiled. Agnes, always pragmatic, was never going to side with Ina. 'She's done well for herself,' said Agnes.

'Makes you wonder what she sees in Harvey-the-plodder,' said Ina, never one to mince her words.

'That's none of our business either,' said Agnes, knowing Ina delved into everybody's life, but was shy about anybody knowing much about hers.

'I thought she had her heart set on Max,' Ina continued unabashed.

'That's the thing,' answered Agnes, 'he had to follow the stories – wherever they led him.'

'I know.' Ina sounded like she knew him personally. 'He had that look about him. Couldn't keep still... Pass me the butter, please.'

'Don't put it on and scrape it back off again, like you usually do.' Agnes sounded irritated.

'I mean to say, what man of thirty-five still lives with his mother?' Ina asked, ignoring Agnes's remark about the butter, imagining Agnes had never seen a poor day, what with her only having the one daughter and no sons. Unlike Ina, who had popped a new baby out every year. But those days were behind her now.

'A girl like Daisy, with her striking looks and shapely figure, could have any man she wants,' Agnes continued. 'She reminds me of the American actress, Louise Brooks, with her bobbed hair and dark eyes.'

Even though Daisy knew she shouldn't listen, she could not pull herself away from the jangling neighbours, knowing they were speaking the truth as they saw it. But they would never know the despair she had suffered when Max had left.

How could they? She always wore a ready smile, inclined to make a cheerful quip. As far as anybody was concerned, she was carrying on as she always did. It was a sham, of course. But life had gone on day after lonely day until she'd met Harvey, who'd invited her to the church hall dance. She had felt it churlish to refuse after he had asked her on numerous occasions. Max had been gone for three long years then, and it didn't look like he was coming back. So, when she and Harvey had started going dancing two years ago, she was inclined to wonder what, exactly, was she saving herself for?

'I'd have put a penny bet on her walking down the aisle with Max.' Ina sounded wistful.

'And you'd have lost your penny,' answered Agnes.

By the sound of it, thought Daisy, Agnes was doing most of the work as her voice travelled around the kitchen, whilst Ina's voice stayed in the one place.

'This Harvey chap,' said Ina. 'Well, it's not for me to say, but...'

'That's right, less saying... and more doing.' Agnes sounded like she'd lost her patience with Ina, which was quite easy. 'We don't want to go troubling Daisy today of all days, do we?' Agnes's tone held a warning note. 'She's put a lot of money into this celebration, so we don't want to go mentioning Max.' Daisy heard the plates rattling. 'Anyway, Harvey's a pleasant enough chap.'

'Harvey's a bit... well... set in his ways, a bit staid. Not like Max, he was a mile a minute that one... But you never can tell.'

Daisy knew she should interrupt Ina, if only to stop her dissecting her love life. But her neighbour was right. Harvey was a plodder. He had his opinions, and he stuck to them, no matter what anybody else thought.

He was safe. Stable. He'd been in the same job since he left school at fourteen and, unlike her brothers, Harvey had never chased any kind of promotion. But he was dependable. Her mam, Molly, was always saying she needed someone dependable. Unlike Max, who was always sniffing out the next big story, leaving her dressed up with nowhere to go.

At least you always know where Harvey is. Her mam's words rang in her head like Saint Patrick's church bell on Sunday mornings, and she gave a long silent sigh. She had agreed when he'd asked her. But even as early as the following morning after promising to marry Harvey, Daisy was sure she really didn't want to.

She knew she would never have such doubts about Max, but Max, a master of words, could never form the four she longed to hear. *Will you marry me?*

He could tie her in knots with the notions he came out with. But he was never dull. Never boring. Daisy had to contend with reading his headline articles, from a disgruntled Europe, in the evening newspaper. She had even cut out his newspaper columns and stuck them in a large scrapbook. Tales of fighting between Spanish nationals and Republicans, which he said was heading towards civil war. His heart-stopping devil-may-care attitude set Max apart. Nothing fazed or worried him. He rushed in where angels feared to tread.

She missed him with every beat of her heart. Nevertheless, staying busy helped ease the heartache. It was something she had always done. Keeping her hard-working hands occupied controlled her runaway thoughts.

'Aye, Max is a hard man to forget, I imagine.' Ina's voice brought her out of her deep thoughts and stopped the creeping guilt that was her daily companion when her mind drifted to that secret place of memories, where only she could go.

Daisy opened the kitchen door, deciding she had heard enough from her mother's friends and neighbours. *A listener hears no good of themselves,* Molly was often heard to say, and Daisy knew she was right... Although, if truth be told, so was Ina, she had spoken the words Daisy had kept buried deep down since Max left.

Was she doing right by Harvey? Allowing him to believe she wanted to be his wife? Was she being fair to him? Of course not! He deserved someone who loved him wholeheartedly. Someone who wanted to spend the rest of her life with him. Not someone who suspected she was only getting engaged to keep her mother happy. Or someone to look after his ailing mother. The thought sent a shiver of dread through her body.

But she could not break Harvey's heart. She could not cancel their engagement, which was galloping towards her at a terrifying pace. Harvey was kind, he brought her mother flowers every Sunday. He listened to the Saturday football results on the wireless and enjoyed checking Percy's coupon from Littlewoods Pools. Even though he rarely gambled, Harvey was a safe bet. Hurting him was never her intention.

He got on well with her family, he thought her brothers were dependable chaps – he said so. Often. He never tried to force himself on her. Sometimes he even forgot to kiss her when he brought her home from the Saturday night dance. She respected that at first. But in her heart she knew she needed more than Harvey was expecting to give. If that made her sound like her reckless sister, Bridie, then so be it.

'Is everything all right?' Daisy startled the two neighbours, whose deep conversation stopped as soon as she entered.

At least Agnes had the grace to look uncomfortable, obviously embarrassed at being caught out, if that pink flush creeping up her neck was anything to go by. But both neighbours recovered quickly, giving exaggerated smiles.

'Oh, you look nice,' said Ina, who was not usually one to exert herself in the overuse of compliments. 'You really suit that colour, and the pendant sets it off a treat.'

'Thank you, Ina.' Daisy smiled. Her fingers resting on the precious blue sapphire nestled in a broken heart on a gold chain.

'The colour sets the dress off beautifully,' said Agnes, seizing a plate of sausage rolls made fresh that morning and turning to the sink, hurriedly wrapped the plate in greaseproof paper and a tea towel.

'Isn't that the one Max gave you before he went away?' Ina deliberately ignored Agnes's darting flash of irritation when she turned to glare. Then, turning back to the table, Ina threw the words over her shoulder when she said, 'I don't suppose Harvey will notice.' Backtracking, she quickly put her foot in it again when she said, 'It's a shame Max couldn't have been here. Mind you... if Max were here, I doubt you'd be marrying Harvey.'

'Ina!' Agnes exclaimed.

Daisy knew Ina could not hold on to one thought when another was elbowing its way to her tongue.

'Well, maybe it's for the best, after all...'

'Put down the shovel, Ina,' Agnes murmured, rolling her eyes, 'before you dig yourself into a hole you can't get out of.'

'Mam's been looking forward to this for weeks.' Daisy knew she couldn't let her mother down at this late hour. She was just having an attack of nerves. Understandable... considering...

'What time will Harvey's lot be turning up?' Ina covered her embarrassment with another question as she poured milk into two teacups for her and Agnes, motioning to Daisy, who shook her head. She was sure she couldn't keep anything down.

'They'll meet us in the Tram Tavern at half past seven,' Daisy told the two women. 'Queenie's putting on a cold buffet.' She wanted to keep the party on a more local footing than the ones she usually organised. Most of the residents of Beamer Street would not thank her for putting on canapés and caviar when homemade sausage rolls and ham sandwiches were more to their liking.

The food being prepared by Agnes and Ina was for the table in the front parlour when the pub closed, and everybody would return to Molly's for a good old knees-up and a feed.

'A little bird tells me that Bridie's been rubbing shoulders with royalty and stars of the silver screen in her London salon.' Ina could not abide a silent pause and did her best to fill it.

'That little bird's got a beak the size of the new Mersey Tunnel,' murmured Daisy, knowing her mother could not resist boasting about her talented offspring. Nevertheless, she worried about Bridie, knowing her younger sister was fun-loving and gregarious when the mood took her.

4

Max Galant knew today was the beginning of a brand-new chapter. This new adventure would bring him closer to someone very special. A girl who had stolen his heart the moment he had set eyes on her. As the train came to a juddering halt, he placed the Agatha Christie novel he had finished reading onto the seat beside him.

Standing up, he lifted a heavy canvas duffel bag with ease, before collecting a gift-wrapped box that had sat beside him throughout his journey and beyond. The gift was too big to fit into the canvas bag he was now slipping onto his shoulder, so he tucked the present under his arm. Heading towards the exit, he recognised Bridie Haywood immediately. She was reading a woman's magazine; hardly aware the train had reached the end of the line. He made no attempt to speak to her as he opened the carriage door, to leave the train. He didn't want to bring attention to himself. Not yet...

* * *

When Bridie stepped from the railway carriage onto Liverpool's Lime Street Station, she felt a wave of dread wash over her. Not usually given to deep thoughts, the pull of buried memories did nothing to confirm she was doing the right thing.

Home for her sister Daisy's engagement to a chap called Harvey, Bridie knew as soon as she'd bought her ticket at Euston Station that she was never going back to London. She couldn't go back. It was more than she dare do.

Clutching a crocodile skin vanity case, she had not let it out of her sight on the long journey home, filled as it was with brand-new white five-pound notes. A fortune. She could not take that risk.

Suddenly her mother's maternal, yet curious tone, rang in her head.

How long will you be home this time, lovey?

Bridie had no idea.

Where's that dashing chap from the Metropolitan Shipping office?

Bridie couldn't care less. Nor would she tell Mam that Karl had never worked in an office.

Is he still coming to visit as planned, my dear?

Not bloody likely! Bridie clamped her teeth together so hard her jaw ached.

Making her way through the crowded station, her mind wandered back to the year before, when she was last home. She had been with Mam and Percy to watch King George V and Queen Mary open the new Mersey Tunnel. The event had done her ambitious sister, Daisy, the power of good, according to Mam's frequent letters that gave chapter and verse about the daily goings-on in Beamer Street, not only in her own family, but the whole of the street. According to her mother, Daisy had a major role in organising a huge luncheon for most of Liverpool's leading bigwigs after the opening of the tunnel. The event was so successful, Daisy was now a celebrated organiser of many social and corporate gatherings.

Scanning the crowded train station, desperate for a cup of tea, Bridie knew nobody was ever going to know she hadn't walked the length of the Mersey Tunnel, as so many did before it was officially opened, but the information impressed the free-spending clients back in London. Not the kind of rich women her mother thought she pampered, in an upper-class Knights-bridge hair salon. No, that job had never materialised as Karl, her boyfriend, had promised. Instead, she served the rich husbands from behind the bar of the Cranford, a gentlemen's club owned by Karl's father and managed by Karl. And Bridie had a sneaking suspicion not everything was as it seemed.

Nevertheless, the tips were lucrative, the chat banal and it was work, albeit in an exclusive all-male club for the old boys, the aristos, the landed gentry, and allowing rich businessmen and professional gamblers.

She enjoyed the change from hairdressing for a while; her quick-witted chit-chat was a great source of entertainment to the members. Outsiders were temporarily admitted for amuse-ment, work, conversation or even romance. But the upper classes were serious about their status. Bridie did not, for one second, believe she could ever truly belong.

Dodging rushing passengers eager to get on to their train, people hurrying along the platform, was a fleeting distraction for Bridie. The stationmaster held his flag aloft and blew a piercing whistle clenched between his teeth, warning passen-gers to alight a locomotive about to leave the station, as another chugging steam engine rolled in on the other line, adding to the smoke-filled air of the busy station.

The local familiarity cancelled the promise she had once

made, when she vowed never to return to this congested port city, where families of ten or twelve, living hand-to-mouth, could rub shoulders with the cream of Liverpool society. Yet the place still had a way of pulling her back.

Bridie recalled wanting to talk privately to her older sister to get another viewpoint about Karl, who, she was sure, was involved in some kind of underhand dealing. However, in Daisy's determination to create the perfect business, she had developed a tendency to push others away when they most needed her.

Gripping the handle of her fashionable vanity case tightly, Bridie smoothed the stylish kiss curl under the wide brim of her hat and swallowed the shame that threatened to over-whelm her.

The lucrative salon work Karl had promised last year had turned to dust. Instead, she mingled outrageously with the elite for cash. She earned more in one night than she could have done in a salon. But the novelty soon wore off, being a hostess in a *gentlemen's* club was not what she had trained for.

Humiliation burned within her. Why did the so-called gentlemen assume her work meant they could openly paw and leer without restraint? She was initially scandalised when she realised what they were after. She had imagined Karl, her so-called boyfriend, would have something to say when she told him she had been propositioned so outra-geously. But he had laughed and said it was just a bit of fun – she shouldn't be so gorgeously corporeal. She didn't know exactly what that word meant and was never going to make a show of herself by asking Karl to explain. But she got the gist.

Then, to put the top hat on the whole contemptible situa-tion, she had arrived home last night to find Karl straddling her housemate on the kitchen floor. The pan of potatoes boiling dry. The girl was supposed to be her best friend!

Until she saw the evidence with her own eyes, Bridie had refused to believe the lies about Karl being a womaniser. But they weren't lies, were they. She knew that now. The bastard couldn't wait long enough even to use the bedroom. The money in her vanity case would only go some way to make him pay for his reckless indiscretion. She'd left him a note, telling him not to go bothering her mother because she wouldn't be there. Then she'd reminded him that she had two older, strapping brothers who would soon see him off if he deigned to darken her mother's doorstep. Whether the threat would work or not, Bridie was uncertain.

Tightly gripping the handle of her hastily packed suitcase, she knew her older sister Daisy would have seen through Karl's two-timing talk in a heartbeat. And she did play with the idea of telling her, but then that little voice that sounded so like Daisy admonished her.

You brought it on yourself, Bridie. You never could resist a naughty boy!

Tell Daisy? Not likely!

Deep in thought, Bridie headed towards the railway station's refreshment room. She needed a chance to line up her thoughts before being bombarded with questions from Mam and Daisy.

Why leave the high life of London when you have the rich and famous at your feet? She could hear Daisy's suspicions, as if she were standing right next to her.

Home last summer, she had entertained her mother with fictitious tales of film stars, wives of the rich and famous, even royalty. Molly had revelled in open-mouthed amazement as the lies had tripped off her tongue like butter from a hot knife. Her mother would never visit London, Bridie knew, so would never discover her youngest daughter worked in a gentlemen's club serving overpriced champagne to rich punters who openly discussed their right-wing tendencies and thought nothing of demeaning the girls who worked there.

Bridie recalled her mam thinking her ever so daring, when she'd discovered Bridie had taken up smoking exotic cigarettes in long holders, like Claudette Colbert, Jean Harlow, and Carole Lombard. Preening when her family oohed and Ahed at her deep S-shaped Marcel waves, hennaed to a rich autumnal red like Bette Davis and Marlene Dietrich. Daisy didn't seem to be as taken with her numerous changes of hair colour, but then again, Daisy had worn the same Louise Brooks bob for years. The neighbours had all but dribbled over her crimson talons and toenails, gasping at the daring of wearing her skirts above her silk-clad knees, and giving off an air of worldly-wise sophistication.

If only they knew.

Balled fists dug deep into the pockets of her camel-coloured cashmere overcoat that covered wide-leg trousers, a white blouse and a V-necked Fair Isle jumper, Bridie made her way across the platform, putting her worries to one side to secretly enjoy the gaping stares of flat-capped porters, who probably thought it was outrageous for a woman to wear trousers in public, whilst ignoring the side-eyed glances from curious women who were unaware that beneath the surface of her very modern apparel lay the quivering wreck of a woman who carried a dangerous tangle of secrets and lies.

So deep in thought, Bridie was startled when a young woman tripped, tottered, and tumbled in front of her onto the concrete platform. Her hand shot out instinctively to catch the young woman before she slipped onto the railway track into the path of a terminating train.

Audible gasps surrounded her as people surged forward to help, but Bridie was there first. She bent to assist the young woman, whose pale, freckled skin turned ashen. Obviously confused, she scrambled to gather her belongings.

'Here, let me to help you,' said Bridie as she gathered the woman's handbag. 'You're as white as a sheet.' And the helpless expression in the mournful dark eyes told Bridie the woman, no older than herself, needed a shoulder to lean on.

'I'm fine... Thank you.'

Bridie, undeterred, nodded to the milling crowd of onlookers, silently letting them know she had the situation in hand. 'They say a cup of hot, sweet tea is the best thing for shock. Whoever "*they*" are.' Her quick remark did the trick when the woman managed a wan smile. 'I'm Bridie. Bridie Haywood. I was about to get a cup of tea in the refreshment room. I'm sure you could do with one too.'

'I... I just need to sit down for a wee while,' the woman emitted a precise yet almost sing-song articulation of an Irish accent, her large eyes darting in all directions, as if searching for someone.

5

'I'm Mara. Mara Foy.' Mara swallowed the lie. Her birthname was not Foy. She was born Mara O'Murchu. The daughter of a well-known physician and Irish Republican branded an outlaw.

He had vanished in 1922 during the last chaotic weeks of the Irish Civil War and Mara was desperate to know if her beloved pa was murdered before or after he was taken to Kilmainham Gaol, which closed in 1924 after one hundred and fifty years housing the most famous political and military leaders in Irish history. It was the main reason she was here in Liverpool. To find the last man to see her father alive and finally get to the truth.

Her beloved pa was said to be executed by Black and Tans acting on their own initiative, who swore black was white that her father was smuggling arms. Although no official record confirmed the allegation. Her poor mother was shamed and impoverished and had sent Mara to live with distant cousins, changing her name, to shield her from retaliations and scandal.

'Here, take my arm. That cut on your knee looks deep.' Bridie discreetly nodded to the blood dribbling down Mara's leg.

'Oh no, these are my only pair of stockings, and I've got an important meeting this afternoon.' She had come to Liverpool to bury the ghosts of her past, and, catching sight of the bloody gash through fearful, half-closed eyes, she was immediately haunted by conflicting memories of her father, the kindest, most loving man, who had kissed her tears away when she was young. The man who sang her songs to help her sleep. Her hero. His untimely death when she was just nine years old had plunged herself and her mother into exile. But she could not dwell on that now. 'I have an appointment with the hospital's lady almoner.' Mara's move to Liverpool was not only to seek out Seamus O'Flanagan, the man who held the truth about her pa's last day, who was rumoured to have escaped to here in Liverpool after the war. She was also here to take up a calling to care for the poor.

'I've got a new pair in my suitcase.' Bridie hooked her hand through Mara's arm. 'There is a ladies' restroom. You can change in there.'

'Thank you, that's very kind of you.' Mara's quiet words shook like a leaf in a swift autumnal breeze as she took her handbag from Bridie. Dressed in a tweed jacket and matching skirt, her beret was a little skew-whiff on her auburn hair, and one of her sensible brown lace-up brogues had come undone and landed across the platform.

Bridie went to retrieve the shoe. It was not something she would be seen dead in, she thought as she bent to pick it up, but it wouldn't do for everybody to be the same.

'So, you're here for a job? You've come a long way.' Bridie, aware of the crisp Irish accent, knew jobs were still hard to come by. Liverpool welcomed the Irish, unlike some places where they were given short shrift and moved on with force. The Depression had hit towns and cities all over the world. And Irish people were hit harder than most.

Bridie helped Mara as far as the restroom, allowing the lady attendant to fuss over the injured young woman, while dabbing powder on her face with a silk-backed powderpuff, and freshening her lipstick in the mirror overlooking a green marbled sink.

'Come on, let's get you something sweet and sticky,' Bridie said after Mara had changed and came out of the cubicle dressed in a new pair of stockings.

'I've never worn silk stockings before.' Mara's eyes were wide as they entered the station tearoom. 'They feel lovely on. You must let me pay you for them.'

'No, there's no need,' said Bridie, waving away the offer. A friendly, outgoing girl, she could easily afford a new pair and, unabashed at her reckless thoughts, pulled the vanity case a little closer. 'So, where are you heading? If you don't mind me asking.' Sitting at a table near the door, Bridie raised her hand to summon the waitress and ordered two teas and two iced buns.

'I've come over for the position of assistant to the lady almoner, at the Mersey Infirmary,' Mara answered from the other side of the square table. 'This is my first time away from home. Mammy says I'll never stick it.' Nevertheless, Mara knew she had no choice. She had to find the truth.

'You'll be fine,' Bridie encouraged her new friend. 'My mam said the self-same thing to me when I got on the train to London.'

'So, is this a holiday, to see your family?' asked Mara a while later. She didn't seem as timid now, finishing the last of her tea.

'No, I'm home for good. Mam was right after all,' Bridie smiled and then, pausing for a moment, she laughed. 'Listen to me throwing out advice like confetti!'

'I feel much better about going for the post now,' said Mara, loving the feeling of silk on her legs, whilst admiring this outgoing girl willing to help her. 'I got off the boat this morning and wandered around like a lost thing.' Mara felt she had walked through Liverpool with two shadows – one from the foggy dockside, the other from the misty hills of Mayo – knowing the tension between past and present defined her secret turmoil.

'The Mersey Infirmary?' Bridie wanted to know more. 'I was there a few times as a kiddie.' They were quiet for a moment, then Bridie continued conversationally. 'You sound just like my mother's next-door neighbour, Mary Jane Everdine. Do you know her? She owns the bakery in Beamer Street and a few more dotted around the north-west.'

Mara shook her head and suppressed an amused smile, refraining from telling her new-found friend that she didn't know everybody in Ireland.

'I could tell by your accent. You're from Ireland.' Bridie had already told Mara she was a ladies' hairdresser. And was comfortable asking questions. It was part of her profession. Or at least that's what she told herself. Although she was sure it would be considered prying in any other situation. Bridie, like her mother, loved to know the ins and outs of other people's lives.

'My father had a farm in County Mayo before he passed away last year.' Mara was surprised to find that inventing a new past came quite easy to her. Although, that did not mean she was happy with her ability to lie on demand. 'Mammy was headmistress of the village school.' She could never tell Bridie the truth about her father. She could not tell anybody.

'My dad had relations in Cashalree, you might know him, Albert Haywood. He died in the war,' Bridie told Mara. 'I don't remember him, but Mam keeps his picture on the mantelpiece even though she remarried five years ago, to Percy – he's a master baker at Mary Jane's shop in Beamer Street, where our Daisy trained and we grew up.'

Mara's thoughts were spinning at the amount of information Bridie could squeeze into a conversation. 'Is it just you and your sister, then?' asked Mara, who didn't think she would make a new friend quite so easily.

'No, there's our Davey, who's in the merchant navy, away at sea a lot of the time, then Freddy, a former electrician at Beamer's Electricals near the docks before he decided to go away to sea too.'

'I wish I'd had brothers and sisters.' Mara sounded wistful. 'Maybe then, Mammy wouldn't lavish all her attention on me.' Mara hid more secrets than just her name.

'I'm the youngest, and love the attention, can't get enough of it, if truth be told.' Bridie laughed. 'Our Daisy says I'm spoiled rotten – she's like another mam. Mind you, I still couldn't wait to get out of Beamer Street.' Having been smitten by the glittering lifestyle Karl spoke of, she couldn't wait to taste the high life when he'd suggested she go to London.

He'd promised her riches beyond avarice. Provided her with her own flat. He'd filled her head with tales of modern living, triggering no end of excitement. She had never lived in a flat, just a big, old house in Beamer Street. How could she refuse?

'Things didn't turn out as I expected, though,' she explained. 'The *luxury flat* turned out to be a shared house with two other girls...' Bridie rolled her eyes. 'Girls who were living life to the full, in varying degrees of what Mam would call "indecency".' Bridie threw her hennaed head back and laughed again. 'The only riches I received were those I earned.' Bridie deliberately omitted to tell Mara, she'd emptied the contents of Karl's office safe into her vanity case before she left. Some information was best left unsaid.

Determined to appear successful and not come home empty-handed, she vowed Karl must pay for the way he had treated her. Strengthening her belief that she only took what she had been promised. And, if she gave the matter any thought, she knew the money would mean less than the humiliation, which gave her a reason to pray he did not come looking for an explanation.

The private gentlemen's club he had persuaded her to work in was owned by his father, Honourable Lord somebody or other, and was managed by Karl, who fawned over the clientele and pushed his sticky fingers into some unsavoury pies. Nevertheless, stowing this information to the back of her mind, Bridie delighted Mara with the virtues of her family.

Mara, listening intently, knew she could never divulge her true family circumstances, like Bridie did, and pondered the stark contrast between her own risky, nomadic lifestyle, and the high glamour, which Bridie had left behind in the capital city. The harsh realities of the poor people she would help, and the champagne lifestyle of Bridie's high-class world were miles apart. Yet they were getting along like lifelong friends over cups of tea.

'I met lots of women, some of whom were not quite what they seemed.' Bridie's mysterious answer caused Mara to shiver.

'I couldn't do what you do,' she said. 'I've always been destined to serve.'

'Women don't have to serve any more.' Bridie had learned a

lot in London. 'Haven't you heard? We're emancipated now. For the first time, we can do anything we want to do. Even buy our own house and open our own bank account.' She intended to do just that, first thing tomorrow when the bank opened. 'We don't need to depend on a man to save us from penury. We can go anywhere. Do anything we want to do.'

'Crossing the Irish Sea is the most outrageous thing I have ever done,' said Mara, 'but I need to follow my heart.' Mara's commitment to helping those less fortunate went to highlight the difference between the two. Yet, even though they were so different, Mara felt she had made a staunch and genuine friend in Bridie.

'Thanks, luv,' Bridie said cheerfully to the waitress who came to clear the table. 'Here, let me help you.' Collecting their empty cups, saucers, and side plates, she put them on the tea tray. 'Can I bother you for another pot of tea please.' Bridie wasn't in the mood to face a barrage of family questions just yet. 'And this is for yourself.' She gave the waitress a silver sixpence.

'Much obliged,' the waitress said, gladly depositing the money into her apron pocket.

Mara could see Bridie was not afraid to talk to anybody and listened as she spoke of her ambitions to open her own salon and make it one of the best in Liverpool. Mara, taking a slow, deep breath, didn't doubt it for a moment.

'You must be very well-to-do, what with your mother being a headmistress?' Bridie never believed in keeping a question to herself when the need-to-know took over.

'Poor as a church mouse, if you'll pardon the expression.' Mara smiled, giving Bridie cause to think she looked younger than she initially thought. A haircut would give Mara's mane of thick red hair a much-needed boost, instead of having a hatchet-straight middle part snatched back in a tight chignon at the nape.

'Mammy was the force behind the throne.' Mara's tone was low, hesitant, she did not wish to reveal too much. 'After Pa died, the land agent gave us a day to move all we possessed and find another place to live.'

'There's no loyalty in some quarters, is there?' Bridie's tone was tinged with a touch of bitterness as she wiped the rim of her cup with her handkerchief, although her lipstick still left a ruby-coloured stain on the white railway-issue cup. 'Some men think they own the world.' Bridie tried to sound light-hearted, but it was a stretch.

'Were you and Karl engaged...?' Mara soon realised that Bridie's favourite subject was Bridie, and she was only too pleased to let her speak, knowing that if Bridie talked about herself she wasn't going to ask awkward, personal questions.

'He asked me to marry him,' Bridie lied, trying to put on a brave face to soften the humiliation that still burned within her, knowing she had given herself to a man who cared nothing for her in the end. 'My home and my family are here. Karl would never leave London and move to Liverpool.' Nor the company, the secrets, the coded telegrams he received on behalf of a club member. The mysterious visitors with foreign accents, with whom Karl fluently conversed. Italians and Germans were regular visitors to the club and Bridie knew Karl held Oscar Beasly, a high-ranking fascist leader in elevated regard for his intimidating standards. Bridie did not agree with the extreme doctrines that did much to create social instability among the poorest people of London. She wanted no part of it.

She had listened to the after-hours, brandy-fuelled meetings, which loosened the tongues of Karl and his 'friends.' They didn't care that she was within hearing distance. Nor did they mind revealing their intention to take their militant beliefs around the country. They understood that in these days of hardship and unemployment, people could be persuaded to listen to their enraged, entitled principles, which seemed to favour the desperate and downtrodden. But Bridie knew the reverse was true if anybody took the time to look close enough.

'Karl's father is a member of parliament,' she told her new friend. 'He gripped his son with tales of biased entitlement. Karl considered him a shrewd observer of political affairs, following him obsessively. His aim mirrored his father's – to persuade the people how much their poor lives would change if he were voted into power. But all Karl wanted was power.'

Bridie soon understood, men like Karl and his father had never seen a poor day, not like the hand-to-mouth existence she had endured as a child, no matter how hard her mother tried to make their lives better. Watching the lines of worry deepen on her poor face was heartbreaking. Even so, Bridie vowed never to allow the same deep lines to mar her beauty.

'Power-mad he was,' she said to herself. 'In the end, he didn't care who he stepped on to get to the top, just so long as he got there.'

Mara's breath hitched in her throat, haunted by conflicting memories of her father. The man who sang her lullabies, and whose death plunged her and her mother into exile. This fascism was not the same cause for which her father fought – and was brutally killed. He believed that their land should be free. Owned by the men who worked the fields. Instead, she and her mother were turfed out of the only home she had ever known, while landlords like Karl and his family, who inhabited large, rambling mansions, set in parkland tended by gardeners, maintained by housemaids and cooks, could turf a mother and young child out of their home at a moment's notice. Mara was raised on the poetry of rebellion, believing her father had died for a noble cause.

But the older she got, the more she questioned whether his sacrifice had helped anybody or changed anything – or if it was a web of pride, betrayal and violence that left nothing but widows and orphans behind. Was her father's death truly martyrdom? Or was it all for nothing? Deeply proud of her roots, she had to find the truth.

'Here's to changing the world!' Bridie, deprived of answers about her future, raised her teacup and gave a rallying cry. Mara, laughing, did likewise, drawing the attention of a nearby onlooker. The two young women covered their mouths and gave a conspirative giggle. Bridie had an idea...

* * *

'Where are your lodgings?' Bridie asked. Gathering her vanity case and gloves, she noticed Mara's hesitation. 'I'm not being nosy, honest.'

'I... I thought I might stay in the nurses' home, at the hospital,' Mara answered.

'You don't need to do that.' Bridie's mind was working overtime. She knew her mother would never turn anybody away. 'You must come and stay with us in Beamer Street. It's near to the hospital, and Mam will love having you to stay, especially with you coming from the Emerald Isle.'

'Are you sure?' Mara looked doubtful, although if Bridie's family were as nice as she was, it would be better for her to stay in Beamer Street than at the hospital.

'Of course I'm sure,' Bridie said with all the certainty of a woman who was used to getting her own way. She also had an ulterior motive.

Bridie knew her mother would be busy with the engagement preparations, at the same time she would completely, under the guise of sociability, probe Mara's reasons for being in Liverpool. Therefore, thought Bridie without a shadow of remorse, her mam might not have the same urgent need to know why she had decided not to go back to London.

6

As Bridie suspected when the black cab pulled up outside her mother's soot-covered house, half the street had suddenly found a need to be at their front door. A black hackney cab in Beamer Street was a rare sight, and very soon every Tom, Jim and Bobby was being called in by their mother for one reason or another.

'If you drop a plate,' Bridie explained to Mara, 'most of the street would know about it before you had time to sweep up the broken pieces. I think that's one of the things I missed most when I was in London – everybody there kept to themselves.'

'I know what you mean,' said Mara as the taxi driver lifted their heavy suitcases from the front luggage platform and placed them onto the pavement. 'It's the same back home. You can't have a good old cough before someone calls the undertaker!' The two girls threw their head back and laughed aloud, giving neighbours cause to share curious glances.

'Hiya, Bridie, luv!' called Mrs Jones from across the road opposite. 'Nice to see you back. Are you home for good, or just for your Daisy's engagement party?'

'See what I mean?' said Bridie and the two girls looked at each other, setting forth a fresh peal of laughter.

The landscape never changed, thought Bridie. Children still played the same games she had played as a young one. Some were turning a thick rope in opposite directions and jumping in to skip, some were kicking tightly balled newspapers against the high wall of the railway lines known locally as the 'ralla' and losing sight of the paper ball momentarily when grey smoke belched from a passing overhead locomotive.

She watched in much the same way she often did, when sitting on the step or playing out with her siblings. But times and people changed, even if the scenery did not.

She let out a little squeal of delight at the sight of her mother. Molly hurried down the stone steps of the house with her brothers, twenty-four-year-old Freddy in the merchant navy like their twenty-six-year-old brother Davey, who was studying for his Master Mariner's Certificate, which would grant him the authority to command his own vessel. Bridie was ridiculously proud of both her brothers.

Hugs and questions about her journey postponed introductions until Molly realised there was someone else to greet.

'And who's this?' Molly asked, her eyes glistening with tears of joy at the sight of her youngest daughter, thrilled her family were all home now and complete once again.

'Mam, this is Mara, she's going to work at the hospital.' Bridie knew such a position would impress her mother and she deliberately left the next piece of news to the last, suspecting her mother would insist on Mara coming to stay in her friendly comfortable home. 'She's from County Mayo, Mam! And she's going to be staying at the nurses' home.'

As she suspected, her mother's eyes widened and she nodded to her sons by way of silent request to pick up Mara's luggage, which they did without question. Bridie smiled from ear to ear, knowing her mother would want to know everything about her new friend.

'Well then,' said Molly, who was well known for her open-handed friendliness, 'I would never see a poor girl go without a loving family roof over her head. She doesn't need to be staying in the nurses' home. We've got plenty of room right here.'

She linked her hands through Bridie and Mara's arms and led them towards the front door. 'We've got two good size rooms going spare, so you can take your pick, Mara, depending on whether you want to overlook the docks at the front or overlook the canal at the back.'

Bridie laughed, satisfied her assumption was realised.

'Tell me,' Molly said informally, hoping to get as much information as possible before they got indoors, where, no doubt, Ina King's nose would be twitching like a mad thing. 'What part of Ireland did our Bridie say you are from?' Molly knew a lot depended on Mara's answer. Was she from the North or the South? She hadn't heard Mara speak much yet, so it was hard to determine.

'County Mayo,' Mara repeated the news in her low sweet voice.

'My first husband came from Cashalree, it's on the border, is that anywhere near you? What did you say your surname is? Will I have met you?' The questions came thick and fast, making Mara's head spin. Which answer to the probing questions should she invent first?

'Mam, let her get in the house!' Daisy appeared and gently admonished her mother, the only one who would ever do so, and smiling as she gave her younger sister a welcoming hug. 'You'll frighten the life out of the poor girl with all your questions.'

'Oh, I'm fine.' Mara smiled. 'You all look very busy.' Compared to the quiet country lifestyle she was used to at her aunt's farm.

'It's a bit hectic, what with our Daisy's engagement party in the offing,' said Molly as Mara was led up the hallway, past the open front-room door, which showed a long table covered in a pristine white tablecloth.

'For later,' Daisy told Mara and rolled her eyes as they entered the back living room, which everybody called 'the kitchen.' The room was cosy, 'the heart of the home', thought Mara, surprised when Molly flicked a metal light switch with a bronze finish and suffused the kitchen with golden light from a vellum pendant lampshade dangling from an ornate plaster ceiling rose, and a matching chinoiserie-inspired standard lamp with tassels that showed off the glass-fronted cabinet in the alcove, next to the coke-burning boiler that heated the room perfectly.

'Here, come and sit by the fire,' said Molly, 'you look half frozen.'

'We never had the luxury of electricity at home,' Mara said, obviously fascinated as it produced a warm and friendly ambiance to the whole room as she took her seat on the sturdy moquette-covered chair that matched the three-piece suite she could only dream of.

'Our Freddy put it in when he was doing his apprenticeship, he's an electrical engineer, there's nothing my lad doesn't know about electrics,' Molly said, pride oozing from every pore. 'He says every house will have electricity one day. Imagine...' Molly didn't say what she imagined as she took the teapot off the hob and filled Mara and Bridie's cups, which rattled on the saucer as she handed over the tea. 'Sugar?' she asked Mara, who shook her head.

In no time at all, two other women came into the room from the back kitchen and proved just as inquisitive as Molly, who had introduced them all.

'Mara from Mayo,' said Molly and the other women nodded, taking all in from her beret to her brown polished lace-up shoes.

'Ahh,' said Ina King, 'didn't the Protestant missionaries travel to Mayo in an attempt to turn people's heads?'

'I do believe they did,' said Mara, who realised she was going to have to be careful what she said. The woman, Ina, whose Irish accent sounded more Northern than her own, seemed a little fierce. Mara was fully aware that religion was linked to their national identity. Her father had told her every day that their struggle was a fight for religious freedom as well as political independence. 'But their indoctrinating only went to make the Catholic faith much stronger.' She had said more than she intended and silently vowed not to be so quick to defend her beliefs.

'Indeed, it did,' said Ina.

Molly knew Ina's reluctance to welcome new people to Beamer Street. Hadn't she tried to give poor Mary Jane a hard time of it when she first came to the street with that eejit, Red, all those years ago. But – Molly gave a secret smile – Mary Jane was no fool and she soon gave Ina short shrift when she tried to intimidate her. Molly sometimes wondered what it was that drove Ina to castigate her own people so openly.

'Bridie, do you want to show Mara her room, while I make us all a fresh cup of tea, and we can have a little natter.'

Bridie nodded, then winked at Mara. Her job was done. She breathed a sigh of relief knowing there was no such thing as a 'little' natter where her mother was concerned.

'Come on, your room is next to mine. Isn't that right, Mam?'

'It is.' Molly threw the answer over her shoulder in her haste to follow her neighbours into the kitchen and inform them of what she had already gleaned, and, knowing Mam, even some she had imagined.

* * *

'So, you made it then,' Daisy said, knowing wherever Bridie was, there was sure to be a drama of some kind or another. 'That's a heavy suitcase you lugged up the stairs. Are you staying home for a while?'

Daisy watched as her sister shrugged her elegant shoulders and ignored her question, 'Mara's going to be working with the lady almoner at the hospital. Did Mam tell you?' Bridie tried to prevent any personal questions.

'What a coincidence, I had a call from the hospital only this morning,' Daisy told her sister, as Mara was included in the conversation, 'they want me to host a charity shindig to raise funds.'

'I doubt Mara will know anything about that,' said Bridie.

'I haven't been offered the job yet,' Mara remarked.

'Well, if it's any help, I can always put in a good word,' Daisy offered. 'Any friend of yours and all that.' She gave her sister a tight smile. Something in Bridie's demeanour was not as conversational as it usually was and she was dying to know why. 'Is everything all right, Bridie?'

'Of course!' Bridie almost snapped the words. 'Why wouldn't it be?'

'You seem a bit... distant.'

'Just tired after the train journey, that's all.' Bridie was in no mood to answer questions. 'But not too tired to fix your hair into looking fabulous. You don't want to be late for your own party.'

'If I had my way...' Daisy didn't finish what she was going to say. If Bridie got a whiff of her uncertainty, she would go straight to her mother under the guise of concern but would be out to cause trouble. Because the only person Bridie worried about was Bridie. She could cause war in an empty house.

'If you had your way...?' Bridie wondered what her sister meant by that.

'So, you're home for a while, then?' Daisy said quickly.

'I don't know yet, it depends,' Bridie deflected the question with a weak attempt at humour. 'So, if you had your way... What?'

'A slip of the tongue,' said Daisy, 'it was nothing.' All her family were here now to help her celebrate her engagement. She couldn't throw the cat amongst the pigeons at this late stage. This wasn't the right time to upset everybody, let alone her family, Harvey, and his mother. Her heart sank. *When will be the right time?*

'I'm sure Mara would like to come too, if that's all right?' asked Bridie, through the mirror.

'Of course, she's very welcome.' Daisy answered.

'I'll just go and see what I could wear,' said Mara, knowing her suitcase was under the bed and time would be tight if she was to see the lady almoner before the party.

* * *

The door creaked open with a soft moan, revealing the small back room at the top of the narrow stairs. The floral yellow wallpaper was faded, its pattern clinging to a past someone clearly tried to preserve. The narrow bed, neatly made, smelled faintly of lavender. A porcelain lamp sat on the bedside table, slightly chipped but still dignified.

Mara took a step down into the room, her handbag bumping against the doorframe as she entered and she stood there for a moment, letting the silence settle around her. The kind of stillness that pressed against the ribs – gentle, but insistent.

Kneeling beside the single bed, she pulled her suitcase from underneath, opening it with practised fingers. Beneath a toilet bag and the worn spine of a paperback, she reached into the lining and withdrew a small green velvet pouch her mother had given her when she was younger. The pouch came out at night along with tales of her heroic father and the ultimate price he had paid. A freedom fighter who gave his life for Ireland.

Her fingers tightened around the brass case still in its velvet sheath, remembering the hushed voices in candlelit kitchens, her family telling stories of brave men with rifles and causes worth dying for, when they thought she was asleep. Loyalty, not just emotional, but cultural, ancestral, was wrapped up in songs and sorrow.

She drew out the round object slowly, as the thing inside might flinch at the light. Her father's half of the pocket watch case gleamed dimly in her palm. Scuffed, its hinge broken clean through. She turned it over, tracing the lettering inside with her thumb, stopping where the jagged metal once connected to something whole.

He still had the other half – the man who'd been beside her father when the world had lost him – and Mara sat back against the bed, the velvet pouch empty beside her. She held the case piece against her chest, feeling its strange weight – a fragment of something lost, something unfinished. But that was a tale for another day. Today was about arriving. Unpacking. Pretending not to watch the door too closely. Outside, footsteps echoed down the hall.

* * *

'You won't be too tired to join us for our Daisy's big night?' asked Bridie when Mara came into the kitchen, knowing Daisy would not dare ask any more questions in front of a stranger.

'Tough as old boots, me.' Mara laughed, her pale freckled skin pinking. 'If you're sure?'

'Of course,' said Bridie, 'the more the merrier, isn't that right, Dais?' Bridie sounded over-bright. Excited, as she began expertly shaping Daisy's dark, bobbed hair around her head. Something she had not done for such a long time, glad she hadn't lost her artistic touch.

'I thought you were bringing Mr High and Mighty.' Daisy watched her sister flinch through the mirror. Blink, and she would have missed it. But it was there all the same.

'Karl isn't coming,' Bridie said in that off-hand way she had when she didn't want to discuss something, concentrating on styling Daisy's hair like it was the most important thing she had ever done.

'Didn't you get my letters?' Daisy asked. 'I wrote quite a few, but you never answered.'

'Busy, I'm afraid,' Bridie murmured. 'You know what it's like.'

'Yes, I do,' Daisy answered, 'but I still wrote.' She watched Bridie roll her eyes. There was something she wasn't telling. But Daisy always knew when her younger sister wanted to evade a subject, she ignored it completely, like it never happened. 'How is the salon going?' Daisy persisted. She knew their Bridie was hiding something. And she intended to find out what it was.

'Oh, you know, work's work.' Bridie spent an age making sure every hair was perfect. If there was one thing Daisy was certain, her sister's work was her pride and joy. Nothing came close. She had never heard Bridie call her chosen career 'work.'

'If you're too tired, you can finish my hair later. Why don't you go, and have a little nap before the fun begins?' Daisy saw the look of horror in Bridie's eyes.

'Most certainly not,' Bridie said. 'I'm enjoying myself.' She was also looking forward to the praise her work would glean. 'I'm going to make you look like Olivia de Havilland – pity Harvey looks nothing like Errol Flynn.'

'None taken...' said Daisy when her sister refused to apologise for her thoughtless retort.

'If you can't be outstandingly gorgeous at your own engagement party then when can you? Isn't that right, Mara?'

'Oh, it's not for me to say,' Mara answered, turning an even deeper shade of pink. 'I really must be off to go and see the lady almoner.' Putting her cup back on the saucer, Mara placed them both on the table and went to fetch her hat and coat.

'Good luck,' Bridie called, holding up crossed fingers, and the other women who moments before had been working in the back kitchen followed suit.

Mara smiled. She liked the Haywood family and was glad she had met Bridie at the railway station.

7

The lady almoner's office was just like Mara had imagined. A sturdy wooden desk stacked high with a mountain of heavy-looking files. Two straight-backed chairs, one either side of the desk. Miss Josephine Treadwell was conducting an interview with a would-be patient and Mara was 'observing' from a small desk in the alcove.

Miss Treadwell's face was all sharp angles, high cheekbones, pointed chin, small eyes that could be kindly one minute and scrutinising the next. Her salt-and-pepper coloured hair looked like it had been parted with a hatchet straight down the centre of her head and snatched back into a tight knot of thin hair at the nape of her neck, adding to the severity of her features.

Her office reflected her administrative role and the delicate position between charity and concern was evident. A typewriter sat on the small alcove desk, and Mara imagined herself clacking away doing clerical work, as well as helping the nurses on the ward when they were busy, as Miss Treadwell had informed her. A Jane-of-all-trades, as it were, she thought.

Although the notion did not faze her. Her aunt Bridget owned a typewriter, and Mara had taught herself to type to a passable standard. She'd also liked to help her father, the eminent village doctor, and organise his desk or call the patients into his consulting room from an early age. Putting case notes into pigeonholes, like those on the wall. Each folder, she surmised, was a story of hardship, illness and means testing.

A small window high on the wall was the only evidence of natural daylight. Sparse but functional, she thought, noting a heavy green curtain that offered only a semblance of privacy in the shared room near the outpatient department.

As Miss Treadwell finished writing up her notes, Mara was acutely aware of the ticking clock next to a copy of the hospital's rules, which she had been told she must learn and strictly obey. A charity handbook, placed on the small desk for Mara to read, highlighted the almoner's role in assessing whether a patient could contribute financially to their care. Miss Treadwell had to make sure those who were truly deprived received the help they so desperately needed.

'However, I do not flinch in my duty to combat those deemed able to pay,' said Miss Treadwell, who did not seem as old at close quarters as Mara had first thought. 'Those who need it most will receive the care and consideration they cannot afford.'

Then she showed Mara how to assess patients' financial means, which would determine whether they qualified for free or subsidised treatment at the Mersey Infirmary.

'You will be expected to interview and visit the homes to verify living conditions,' said Miss Treadwell. If they were deemed able to pay, some patients were kindly pointed in the direction of the nearest provident dispensary or to a general practitioner.

'Our precious funds can only go so far, Miss Foy,' said the older woman. 'We are the gatekeepers, who will refer patients to charitable organisations for additional help – be it food, housing or employment assistance.'

'There is much more to consider than I imagined,' said Mara and Miss Treadwell nodded.

'We keep meticulous case notes and reports, often reviewed by hospital boards.' She went on to explain that the records helped shape their concern about public health and poverty. 'Although not our primary role, I like to offer a listening ear and practical advice on the wards, especially to women and children who are already experiencing illness in perilous living conditions.'

'Mother would do the same thing,' said Mara, knowing her parents were the most considerate and caring people. Her father was not only a staunch supporter of Ireland's freedom but also the village doctor. Her mother, headmistress of the village school, raised funds for the village hospital to help those who could not help themselves.

'We shall see some of the people who need our help. It may be the best Christmas gift we can give.'

* * *

Mara had never considered herself well-off, but when Miss Treadwell took her to see some of the dockside hovels, the awful sight shocked her to the core. Children barely covered in rags, their bodies crusty with filth, and worse, their heads walking with lice. The poor mites were sleeping on bare earth floors, their bodies malnourished and wasted. Dying for the want of food. Surely there had to be some light in the deepest darkest winter for these families.

There was no turning away from the poverty-stricken depravation that these poor wretched people succumbed to, and Mara vowed to do all she could to ease their suffering.

When they returned to the hospital, Miss Treadwell's pale hands were stark against the dark polished oak of the desk as she leaned on it.

'The hospital fulfils several other functions,' she said. 'This establishment turns newly qualified men *and* women, fresh from medical school, into excellent doctors, which benefits rich and poor alike.' Her aquiline features were animated.

'They also gain the benefit of working under the best brains in the medical profession, which is also an incentive, is it not, Miss Treadwell?' Mara offered, allowing Miss Treadwell to see that she was not just a country yokel. 'The hospital also allows over-eager young doctors the ability to develop their bedside manner before they launch out by themselves.'

This might be her first position in a busy hospital, but it was not her first encounter with the principles of a voluntary hospital. Mara promised herself, she was not going to be just a meek and mild money-collector who swelled the hospital coffers.

'I will make every effort to ensure those in need get the professional care and attention they so desperately deserve.'

'You have a determination that does you proud,' said the lady almoner, not even trying to hide the admiration in her voice. 'New methods of treatments and equipment are tested here, pioneering experience is constantly gained. And all that costs.'

'I do not doubt it, Miss Treadwell, and I promise to uphold the duties expected of me.'

'The spirit of service has run through the hospital system for centuries.' Miss Treadwell stopped momentarily, drawing in a theatrical lungful of dusty particles, and Mara nodded. 'As the

Poor Law has been abolished,' said Miss Treadwell, 'all hospital duties have been transferred to the local county borough councils, leaving the Public Health Committee to do the necessary work.'

'I understand that the old Poor Law infirmaries have now become municipal hospitals.'

'That is correct,' Miss Treadwell said. 'You have certainly done your homework, Miss Foy. But we are not free hospitals, there is still much work that needs to be done to make sure the service we provide is not exploited.'

'Of course.' Mara understood there were always those who tried to get something for nothing if they could get away with doing so, even though they may be able to pay.

'One has to be alert to the tricks of those who can afford to pay for treatment,' Miss Treadwell said in hushed tones, looking directly in Mara's eyes, 'those who have the means but have no wish to do so.'

'I see,' Mara said on a sigh. For hadn't her mother told her that her father's practice was all but reduced to its last bandage because of his inability to turn away anybody who needed care. 'My mother took over the administrative duties of my father's practice and knocked it into shape.' She recalled her mother, rooting out those who could afford to pay and ensuring they did not take advantage of her kind-hearted father. 'You won't find me idle in my endeavours.'

'In your visits to the poorest dockside dwellings, you saw poverty you could never imagine.' Miss Treadwell lowered her chin and looked at Mara through sparse eyelashes. 'Are you prepared for such undertaking?'

Mara felt her spirits soar. She had not been so confident she would get the job. She nodded, hardly able to breathe, let alone speak.

'Well then.' Miss Treadwell stood up behind her desk and reached out her soft white hand to Mara. 'You will begin tomorrow.'

Mara did not feel it was her place to remind Miss Treadwell that tomorrow was Christmas Eve, especially when people got sick every day and were not inclined to wait until after Christmas. Some, she supposed, needed the help the hospital offered even more at this time of year. Just because it was Christmas didn't mean all people would be fine and dandy.

'I will be here bright and early,' said Mara, eager to begin work. Also, to see if she could discover the whereabouts of the man who was at her father's side when he drew his last breath. The years may have been long since he was taken from her and her mother, but she could not rest until she knew the truth.

8

The back room of the Tram Tavern was strung with Christmas bunting, some of it fraying at the corners, but no one seemed to mind. The piano player belted out a rousing singsong as the smell of best ham sandwiches and brown ale mingled in the cigarette-smoke air. Someone had strung fairy lights around the mirror, their bulbs flickering like they couldn't quite commit.

Mam looked very fetching in the navy-blue two-piece she had bought when she married Percy, who grinned like a Cheshire cat every time she looked at him. Uncle Jim had already knocked over his pint, and Ina King was singing 'Red Sails in the Sunset,' two verses early.

Amidst it all, Daisy, bride-to-be, clenched her hands tightly around a glass that had held pale ale, but had been empty for ages. She might as well be invisible for all the notice Harvey was taking of her.

This was supposed to be *their* celebration, yet he had hardly spoken to her, apart from asking her what she wanted to drink earlier. However, he didn't seem to have any intentions of buying her another drink when he nodded to the barmaid, simulating over the festive hubbub to pull him another pint, even though the glass he was holding was still half-full.

Daisy suddenly felt as if she shouldn't be here. She knew Harvey had some old-fashioned ideas, one of which was that women should not be allowed in public houses, where men swore and told lewd, music-hall jokes. He had too much respect for her, he'd once said when Daisy had asked why he never brought her here. He liked his drink, did Harvey, who was now laughing too loud at something her brother had said, his fingers resting possessively on the small of her back. He thought she might run away. The notion would be laughable if it were not so near the truth, she thought. Her mam was sitting next to Harvey's mother, singing another verse of something lively, whilst Harvey's mam looked like she'd been slapped with a wet kipper. She couldn't look more disapproving if she tried. Daisy sighed.

Harvey worked hard, and was good-hearted most of the time, but he was steady to the point of dull, if truth be told. Is that what she wanted for the rest of her days? His mother didn't seem to approve of the party if her dour expression was anything to go by. But she wasn't intending to marry his mother, a little voice in her head scolded.

Maybe not, she reasoned, but nor did she want to live in his mother's house. She wanted a place of her own that they both could share and be happy in. She couldn't imagine ever being happy living like a domestic servant looking after his mother, which was what Harvey had stated was going to happen.

Her mother said she'd be mad not to marry such a steady man. Daisy knew Molly wanted to see her settled with a home of her own, but Daisy doubted her mam thought it would be the front parlour of Harvey's mother's house. Nor did she know that underneath that amiable facade was a man who believed he would rule the roost. He had told her, more often as their approaching engagement grew closer, that he expected her to walk away from the business she had worked so hard to build.

Daisy had grown up surrounded by strong women who could hold their own in any given situation. They held the country together during the war. They were emancipated. They could vote and have their own bank account. They could buy their own home if they had the means and the inclination. So, she had no intention of being beholden to Harvey – or any man, for that matter.

She had worked since she was twelve years of age to help her widowed mother, first as a Saturday girl in the Pier Head teashop, then full-time when she left school at fourteen, before Mary Jane offered her a job and taught her everything she knew.

Looking around the room at all the cheerful faces, Daisy could not be less happy. She knew that as the engagement grew nearer, Harvey had taken it for granted she would leave her business, telling her how happy it would make him to know that his mother would have the company and the domestic help she needed. And as each day passed, the scales dropped from Daisy's eyes.

'A glass of pale ale please,' Daisy asked the barmaid for a drink and noted the horrified look on Harvey's face.

'What do you think you're doing, making a show of me like that!' Harvey spoke scathingly through his teeth, his eyes livid.

'You forgot to buy me a drink when you ordered your own,' Daisy answered, and the determination in her voice seemed to bring out a side of Harvey she had not seen before.

'You've got no right showing me up like that,' he said, looking over her head towards his mother.

And in that moment, Daisy knew that Harvey was not the man for her. Her thoughts turned to the long training she had perfected, which had allowed her to build a successful career. Daisy could not justify staying in his mother's house after she wed, to scrub, clean and cook for Harvey and his mother. While his life would barely change hers would be destroyed forever. She was being tricked into a marriage of convenience, and no matter who's feelings got hurt, she could not marry a man she did not love.

Hearing Max's voice on the wireless earlier had brought all kinds of half-forgotten feelings to the fore. Feelings she had never experienced with Harvey. And she knew, without a doubt, her heart lay elsewhere.

Letters came for a while. Then stopped. When she heard his voice again today, after so long, it stirred something she could not ignore. She knew then and there she could not marry Harvey.

'Speech!' someone shouted over the din, and a rousing cheer went up. Daisy moved away from the bar. The room spinning slightly with heat and nerves. The glass slipped from her fingers and shattered on the floor. A hush fell.

'Sorry. Just nerves,' Daisy whispered as she watched Harvey pick up the pieces with a laugh. But there was no mistaking the hard look in his narrowing eyes when he looked up at her.

She cleared her throat.

'Thank you... all of you. For being here. For... making this night special.' Her voice faltered. 'Harvey's been good to me, and I know he'll make a fine husband.' She paused.

Somewhere, there was a clearing of a throat thickened with dockside soot. Daisy heard a heavy sigh. Everybody was eager to get back to the singing and dancing. Her mouth now paper dry, she found it impossible to form the words her guests expected.

'But...' Her voice dropped, barely audible. She looked to Harvey. 'I can't do this... I'm sorry.'

She heard a gasp. An embarrassed cough. Then silence.

Harvey stared at her, his mouth tight.

'What are you saying, Daisy?' Harvey caught her arm in a vice-like grip and she saw a glint of steel in his eyes that had flashed once or twice before when she hadn't agreed with him.

'I'm saying I can't marry someone for the sake of being married,' she whispered. Unable to tell him she didn't love him in the way he deserved to be loved. Not here in front of all these people. That would be too humiliating.

She turned before she could see the disappointment in her mother's eyes, or the hurt in Harvey's. She grabbed her coat and headed for the door. Outside, the harsh wind blowing in off the Mersey was sharp, full of soot and salt. Daisy drew in a long breath and felt her shoulders ease. She'd done it. She'd done what she thought was right. And she was glad.

9

'Well! This is a fine how-do-you-do, I must say!' Molly could hold her tongue no longer when she got back to the house. The table, laden with enough food to feed an army, remained untouched as Percy uncorked a bottle of sherry and poured the ruby-coloured liquid into a gold-rimmed schooner, then passed it to his beloved wife. Molly drank it in one swig.

'I didn't know where to put my face! Everybody staring at me like I could offer an explanation after you ran out of the pub. I didn't have a clue!' Molly held out the fancy gold-rimmed glass for Percy to refill, which he dutifully did, knowing it would be a brave man who would do anything to upset his furious wife any more than she was already. 'You'd better have a good reason for showing this family up – that's all I can say.' Molly could not believe Daisy could do such a thing. 'In front of all the neighbours, too.'

'They'll get over it,' said Percy, 'especially when I told them they were welcome back here.'

'You did what?' Molly's eyes were like saucers.

'Well, we can't let all this good food go to waste, and we've no way of keeping it fresh.' Household refrigerators were unheard of in Beamer Street.

'Can anybody tell me why our Daisy didn't say something sooner?' Molly asked, as if Daisy wasn't even in the room. 'Well? Somebody say something before everyone turns up! What am I going to tell people?'

Even though her mother said she had little to say on the matter, Daisy soon realised she found plenty of words. Distractedly, separating herself from the brewing situation, Daisy watched the smoke from the crackling coal fire blazing in the grate, sail up the chimney. And wished she could follow it.

The newly papered front parlour – used only for special occasions or Christmas – seemed to close in on her as the smell of fresh paint on the doors and skirting boards filled her nostrils and gave her a headache. She could hear the distant singing from a throng of inebriated guests who were on their way back to the house. Then she heard a knock on the front door.

Freddy went to answer it as Percy, her peace-loving stepfather, did his best to console her mam. 'Hey, lass, you can't make the girl do summit she doesn't want to do, just to save face.'

Her mother, stridently stoic and quietly devout, who had held this family together through good times and bad, stared at Percy like he had just peed on the cat. Her eyes wide in disbelief.

'She's too independent, that's her trouble,' said Molly, who, although she was as proud of Daisy's success as any mother could be, still thought a woman's place was in the kitchen.

'I've come for a word,' Harvey said as he entered the front parlour, circling his best flat cap worn for Sunday mass between his fingers and thumbs.

Daisy felt a bit sorry for him. Harvey was *steady*, he enjoyed a pint in the Tram Tavern after work and was liked by all her family. But it wasn't her family who were going to have to marry him and live with him for the rest of their life. Nor would they be expected to look after his mother, as she was expected.

The room grew silent as the family waited for her to speak, but Daisy didn't have the words. How could she tell Harvey she didn't want to shrink her own life to accommodate his? Mam looked like she'd been hit in the stomach, and Freddy was leaning against the parlour door, while Harvey awkwardly shifted where he stood, not looking at anybody, yet Daisy knew he missed nothing, taking all in.

'I can't live my life to please others,' Daisy whispered.

'What's that supposed to mean?' Molly asked. 'Harvey's a good man. He's not a drunk. He has steady work. What more d'you want?'

'I want more than, *he's not a drunk*. I want to breathe, Mam. To be more than...' Daisy stopped herself from saying *someone's housemaid*. She couldn't bear them all looking at her, waiting for an explanation. Heading for the door, she made her way swiftly to the back kitchen. She had to think.

I should have called it off earlier. Even before she heard Max's voice on the wireless, she knew she could never make Harvey happy. Not in the way he wanted her to. She was not the subservient type of woman who fetched and carried for another woman who was quite able to look after herself but, with lashings of emotional blackmail, chose not to.

Daisy knew without a shadow of doubt that she would become bitter and resentful. And she never wanted to feel that way. Neighbours had already arrived and were balancing sandwiches and glasses of pale ale, which Bridie and Mara were passing around, while a popular jazz song played on the gramophone in the corner. Radiant in a sapphire-coloured dress that matched the pendant Max gave her when he left, Daisy moved through the crowd with the grace of a she-cat. Her smile fragile, practised. Excusing herself, she walked to the back kitchen and closed the door.

Out of the view of guests, Daisy leaned against the stone-cold sink, breathing deeply. A small noise behind her made her straighten and quickly turn. Harvey was standing behind her. He wanted answers and something in the cold stare of his grey eyes made her wary. 'We've got people here congratulating us. Couldn't you wait?'

Daisy supposed she owed him an explanation, but for the life of her she could not bring herself to tell him the truth. She didn't love him.

'I thought you wanted to be married,' Harvey said, 'I thought you wanted to marry me. What am I supposed to do now – you've humiliated me at our engagement party. What am I supposed to tell Mother? She was expecting—'

'Too much, Harvey. She was expecting more than I am prepared to give.'

'What's that supposed to mean?'

'Harvey, can I ask you something?' He nodded, and she continued. 'Do you love me?'

'What kind of a daft bloody question is that?' he asked, looking at her like she'd just asked him to dance naked on the table in the front room.

'I'm not your solution, Harvey,' Daisy explained as quietly as she could, even though she wanted to screech her brains out. 'This – whatever it is – doesn't feel like love.'

Harvey walked past her, peering through the kitchen door at the guests.

'I don't want to be like every other woman who wants marriage just so she'd not left on the shelf – that's not my way.'

Harvey gave a short, sharp scoffing laugh. 'No, you'd rather run a business, have folk at your beck and call. You've always got to be in control, that's your problem, Daisy. And I won't have it.'

She looked at him. Control was not something she was familiar with. She had no wish to influence or manipulate anybody. The people who worked with her did so because they enjoyed their work, not because she forced them to. 'You don't know me at all, Harvey. I'm not like other women.'

'Aye, you can say that again,' said Harvey. 'And while I think on it, you're right. I don't know you. Because if I did, I'd have stayed well clear.'

From the parlour, there was a burst of laughter, a livelier tune was being played and Harvey watched, as detached from her as it was possible to be.

'You never asked me what *I* wanted, you only ever asked what I could do to help your mother.'

'Talk sense, woman.' His voice was full of scorn and Daisy felt she was now seeing Harvey for the man he truly was. He looked her in the eye, there was no warmth, not a sliver of emotion in his gaze. All pretence at courtship was gone now. He had nothing to strive for, nothing to prove. Then, after a moment's pause, he thought better of it, and said, 'It's not too late for me to stay. All you have to do is smile. We'll get through the night without losing face.'

'I don't care about losing face.' Daisy felt she was talking to a brick wall. 'I'm sorry if I hurt your feelings, but I'm sure the right girl is out there for you – one your mother will approve of, but that girl isn't me.' Daisy swept past him, her posture proud, and headed out of the kitchen. She had no intention of going back to the party. She was going to bed.

* * *

'Mam,' said Bridie as people were preparing to leave later, 'Ina King said if nobody wants that trifle she will put it to good use on Christmas Day.'

'Of course she did,' said Molly.

10

An unusual hush still hung over the house. It was like someone had died. The party had proceeded like nothing untoward had occurred, and the neighbours accepted the lie that Harvey had to leave early because he had to take his mother home and didn't like to leave her on her own. But Daisy knew the pretence wouldn't last.

Her mother muttered prayers with a hint of accusation, recalling neighbours asking her outright if Daisy would be in church with Harvey on Christmas morning. 'When I walked down the street to go and pick up the Christmas capon from the butcher's,' Molly told Daisy, 'the neighbours spoke in whispers at their front door.' Nothing was kept secret for long in Beamer Street.

'They didn't say anything about scoffing best ham and drinking till all hours, then?' Daisy said drily when her mother told her she didn't know where to look. 'Well, Mam, I've made peace with the humiliation, and I refuse to be guilt-ridden.'

'We've waded through worse tides than this, my girl,' Molly said without a shred of irony, changing her mind about the situation when she saw how determined Daisy was to be a modern woman who did not need a man to depend on. 'You got that attitude from your mother,' she said proudly.

'As a matter of fact,' Daisy said, 'for the first time since me and Harvey were courting, I feel lighter, like a great weight's been lifted off my shoulders.' She could feel her old confidence rising again, knowing she would not be corrected or contradicted by Harvey any more. 'I didn't realise how much he undermined me,' she told her mother. 'Slowly but slyly, he somehow had a way of belittling me, especially in front of his beloved mother, who thought her son was right in everything he said and did.' Daisy sighed, never gladder that she had come to her senses before she was forced to give up everything she had worked so hard to accomplish.

'I never thought much of him, as it turned out,' said Bridie, who joined her mother and sister in the kitchen, 'he was a bit of a damp squid if you ask me.'

'Squib,' Daisy corrected, buttering a piece of toast, and smiling.

'What's a squib?' Bridie's perfectly pencilled eyebrows pleated in confusion.

'A damp firework. No spark,' answered Daisy, raising her hand in welcome as Mara came into the kitchen after her night's work. She looked tired and in need of a hot cup of sweet tea.

'No spark sounds right,' said Bridie, and Daisy rolled her eyes. Trust their Bridie to hit the nail on the head.

'Mind you, the next time I decide to put my heart and soul into marrying someone, it will be because it's what *I* want to do without persuasion – when the thought of living without the man I love is too unbearable.'

'Women proved they are as capable as any man, and have

done since the war,' said Bridie and Mara nodded in agreement. 'The opportunities are there if they wish to take them.'

'I know you're right,' said Daisy. Nevertheless, this knowledge did not comfort her for long. Giving rise to a yearning she had long since tried, and failed, to bury. And it went by the name of Max.

'Do you want to come Christmas shopping this afternoon?' Bridie asked. It was Christmas Eve, and she hadn't bought a thing for anybody. 'It'll take your mind off Harvey.' And also stop her worrying what Karl would do if he ever came here looking for her and his money.

11

The bar of the Tram Tavern was crowded with men who had given their wives the space they needed to complete the Christmas Eve traditions: peeling the vegetables for the following day's feast, making mince pies and trifles, boiling the ham, and wrapping the children's presents. Whatever they could afford: an apple, an orange, a wooden toy, a silk ribbon, or a mouth organ. A lot of the men had been out of work for most of the year, so gifts were few and far between. But this was not the time to dwell on such things. One of the biggest traditions around the dockside at this time of year was to prop up a local bar and leave the women to do what they liked to do best. Fuss.

'I can't be doing with it all,' said a toothless man in a flat cap whose wife had got his suit out of pawn that morning, knowing it would go back in again as soon as the pawnshop opened again the day after Boxing Day.

'Aye,' said Davey Haywood, who was still home on leave from sea in time for the big day and was looking forward to listening to his team on the wireless, Liverpool was playing Arsenal, and the match was being relayed live.

'Will you be going to the match tomorrow, Alf?' Davey asked the toothless man.

'Too right I am,' said Alf. 'Christmas is a time for the children, and when I get home from the match, half frozen, my missus will have my dinner waiting. Same on Boxing Day.'

Davey would have loved to go to the match on Christmas Day, and then again on Boxing Day. Liverpool were paying Arsenal on both days, but his mother would have a fit of conniptions if he even dared suggest it. Mam believed that Christmas was a family time. The more people she had around her table in the front room, the merrier.

'I'm saving myself for the Liverpool–Everton Derby in the New Year,' Davey said, raising his pint glass just as the pub door opened. He turned to see Max coming through the door, brushing snow off his overcoat.

'Hello, stranger, what brings you around here?' said Davey, hand outstretched his face was alight, at the sight of his long-time friend. 'I thought you were still abroad. What are you having?'

The two men shook hands and, after collecting their drinks, went and sat at one of the tables to catch up on their travels. But even though he didn't say so, Max longed to know how Daisy was after his sister, Nancy, told him she had met Molly in the market and had told her that Daisy had called off her engagement.

'How's Daisy?' Max asked, impatiently unable to hold his question back.

'She's bearing up,' said Davey, which told Max nothing at all. 'Harvey was a good enough fella, but our Daisy was too strong-minded to be anybody's doormat.'

'Doormat?' Max was intrigued and listened intently as Davey filled him in on the latest turn of events. 'Not a match made in heaven then?' Max was pleased. Not because Daisy had been through such a troubling experience, but because, according to her brother, she thought more of her business than she had done about this Harvey fellow. 'His loss,' said Max.

'That's what Mam says, but only after a bit of persuasion. She thinks every couple should be as happy as her and Percy.'

'I like Percy,' said Max, 'he has the patience of a saint.'

'You can say that again, my mother is in need of an easy-going man.' Both men laughed, enjoying catching up on old times, when the pub door opened again. 'Here's our Bridie with her friend Mara,' said Davey, 'let me introduce you to her.'

'Hello, Max, good to see you back again. Does our Daisy know you're home?'

'I don't think so,' said Max, knowing quite well she didn't. 'What are you two ladies drinking?' He got up from his seat, while Bridie and Mara sat at the other side of the table.

'I'll have a gin and lime,' said Bridie, and looked at Mara.

'I'll have a glass of stout, please.' Mara had never tasted the dark drink so popular with her countrymen, because she wasn't a drinker.

'Coming up,' said Max cheerfully, knowing Bridie would brighten the evening with a song and didn't even need a couple of gins. She didn't believe in hiding her talents.

When Mara took a sip of bitter stout, she tried hard not to grimace, but her face betrayed her.

'It's an acquired taste for some people,' said Bridie, who rarely saw anybody in London drink stout when she worked behind the bar.

As the night wore on, Bridie was asked to get up and give a

song, which she did without any show of false modesty. She loved singing and the locals clearly enjoyed her rousing songs.

'You've got a lovely voice,' said Henry Beamer, son of the owner of the local electrical works, obviously full of his own importance when he snapped his fingers to eighteen-year-old Connie Sharp helping out behind her parents' bar.

Connie raised a single eyebrow and glared at Beamer. There was a hush as the regulars waited for Connie's response. It wasn't unknown for her to bar hardened dockers from the Tram Tavern. And so, this tuppence ha'penny toff was no challenge whatsoever.

'Did you just snap your fingers at me?' Connie asked, her voice calm as Henry Beamer was jolted out of his usual chat-up line to Bridie. He never could resist a girl with film-star good looks, and this one was a scorcher. Definitely his kind of girl.

'I am so sorry, Connie,' said Beamer. 'I was so taken with this beautiful girl I completely forgot my manners. Here, let me buy you a drink.'

'Point taken,' Connie answered. She'd met many Henry Beamers, and this one didn't impress her at all. 'No need to over-egg the situation.'

'Mine's a gin and lime if you're in the chair,' said Bridie with a cheeky giggle, 'and my friend Mara will have a lemonade.' Bridie was impressed with this chap's blond good looks and swagger.

At closing time, Bridie had drunk enough gins to sink a battleship and was not as steady on her feet as she thought she was when the chill of the night air and the icy ground almost took her legs from under her.

'Oops!' she giggled and was promptly caught by the drink-induced chivalry of Henry Beamer, who insisted on walking her home.

'I'll take her home, seeing's I'm going that way,' said Davey. He had heard some unsavoury stories about Beamer and didn't want his sister having anything to do with him. Money or no money.

'Come for Christmas dinner!' Bridie called excitedly. 'Mam would love to have you.'

'I think she'd rather have the chicken,' Davey quipped, and Bridie looked bemused. Then, running the conversation through her head she suddenly got the joke and roared with laughter.

'Don't forget, Henry, number forty-three, Mam will be made up.'

'Let's get you home before you invite the whole street,' Davey laughed before turning to Max. 'Call in any time, Max. Our Daisy will be thrilled.'

'I'll do my best,' called Max as he made his way to the car he had borrowed from his sister. He had stopped drinking long ago and was more than capable of driving back home, knowing the roads could be treacherous in the snow, and if he got so much as a scratch on his sister's Ford Model T he would never hear the end of it.

Max was determined to drive as carefully as he could because he knew, even before he got behind the wheel, that he would be back again tomorrow. He wanted to see Daisy very much.

12

CHRISTMAS DAY 1935

Max opened the sitting-room door, got down on his haunches, and opened his arms wide. His heart sang with love for this four-year-old curly-haired angel, dressed in her best frilly frock and red buckskin shoes, which he bought her a couple of years ago on a trip to London. The shoes had obviously been far too big then, but he knew that one day they would fit. And now, as she ran into his arms, that day was finally here. Burying her round cheeks into his neck, he felt her happy tears trickle down his collar.

'Daddy,' she whispered.

That one word brought a tight knot of guilt to his throat, preventing him from saying or doing anything, except folding her in his arms and wishing this moment would last forever. She had been asleep when he arrived home last night, much to his disappointment. But here she was looking forward to seeing what Santa had brought, already growing faster than he ever thought possible.

The house smelled of furniture polish and something delicious cooking in the oven.

'I've missed you so much, little Poll,' he whispered when he regained control of his voice. Coming home was the best when he felt those pudgy little arms curling around his neck and the loud smack of her little lips on his cheek. 'Go and look what Santa left you under the tree,' Max said, pointing to the decorated tree beside the fireplace.

She drew back, her wide, pale blue eyes looking into his almost identical pale blue eyes, her mouth shaped in a little O of surprise. 'For me?' she gasped, pointing to herself, and Max nodded.

'Santa brought you something because you have been a very good little girl for Aunty.' An investigative journalist, his work took him away a lot. He'd had important news to relay to Downing Street from Berlin that could not be left until after New Year. News that, if it were to be made public would cause much panic, especially here on Merseyside.

His sources in the inner sanctum of Nazi headquarters had informed him that Herr Hitler spent his days studying London and Liverpool. The dockside being of particular interest.

Hurrying over to the tree, she lifted the beautifully wrapped gift box, which he had a store assistant at Hamleys wrap specially with bright, shiny paper and a big yellow bow. He watched Poll sit down on the floor, her eager fingers carefully pulling at the yellow silk ribbon, before her patience escaped her, and she tore at the perfectly wrapped paper.

'*Bebita*!' Poll squealed with delight, holding the baby doll close to her.

'That's right, Poll,' said Max, 'she is your baby girl.'

'Me, Mummy?' she said, holding her head to one side in that endearing way that melted his heart.

He nodded, amazed she still used the occasional Spanish word of her mother's native tongue, considering she had been so young when her mama was killed by a speeding car when she was covering the story of women being permitted to vote in the national elections for the first time in November 1933. Max remembered it like it was yesterday. That was the time he had brought his then two-year-old daughter home, to be brought up here in his home near the shore, overlooking the sea.

'Yes, my darling.' Max could feel the pressure of poignant tears welling behind his eyes. 'What are you going to call her?'

He watched her little mind working hard to think up a name for her new doll and, after hugging it close to her again, she said with all the magnitude she could muster, 'Her name is Max!'

'Well, what did you expect,' said Nancy, his older sister, bringing a tray in from the kitchen and placing it on the table. 'Of course she was going to call it Max; she talks about you all the time.'

'I don't intend to go away and leave her again,' he said, moving a curl from her cheek with a gentle finger. 'She is growing so fast. I fear she will forget me one of these days.'

'You're back for good, then?' Nancy asked, knowing her brother had more important commitments here, at home.

Max nodded. 'I've completed my last overseas assignment. From now on, I am going to be right here, where I belong, with my family.'

This was not the day to tell Nancy that if his investigations proved true, it was not a case of *if* there was another war, as much as *when*. And he wanted to make sure he was as close as he could be to his daughter.

'I'm glad to hear it,' said Nancy. 'She misses you so much.'

They both smiled as little coos and gasps filled the familiar sitting room as Poll played with her new doll.

Walking over to the large bay window, Max gazed out at the

shore of the vast Burbo Bank coastline, where the view changed with the tide to reveal immense expanses of sand at low tide and partially submerged at high tide. The panorama never more welcoming than it was right now.

'I've got to go out later, Nance, is that all right?' He looked to his beloved sister who had stepped into the breach when Margarita was killed, and who came from her home in the Lake District to look after his darling daughter every time he had to go away.

'Anywhere nice?' asked Nancy.

'I've been invited to see an old friend,' Max said, not wanting to divulge the fact that he longed to see Daisy again after such a long time. According to her brother, his good friend Davey, she had called off her engagement. And Max was eager to offer a shoulder to cry on. If that was what she wanted.

13

Daisy's dark eyes travelled the length of the long Christmas table, flanked on both sides by friends and family. Her mam liked to celebrate the festive season with as many people as she could muster, and Daisy knew this year was extra special as Freddy had introduced them to his girlfriend, Violet.

Mam was thrilled she had a house full of guests, and Daisy supposed it went back to the days when they had very little to celebrate. And even less money to do it with. But at least the family had each other.

Now, every chance she could, Molly would have a family get-together. Percy too loved to socialise, and there was never any shortage of goodwill in the house.

'Sorry to hear your news, Daisy?' said one of the guests and Daisy forced a smile, knowing there was nothing to be sorry about. Harvey had disappeared from her life without so much as a backward glance. 'Marriage isn't for everybody.'

'Where would I find the time?' She rolled her eyes and gave a negative shake of her head. 'If I ever did marry, and the chances are slim, any would-be husband would have to be very understanding.' As far as she could see, there weren't many understanding men about, at least not around here. Most men thought the same way as Harvey did, expecting the wife to give up every dream to wait on him hand and foot.

'In what way?' asked Freddy, who was still in the throes of romance.

'I would be looking for a man who doesn't mind coming home and cooking his own tea,' she piped up, amused at Mara's look of shock. 'I will be far too busy building my empire.'

'I hear you're hosting the fundraiser dinner for the hospital?' The warm motherly pride in Molly's eyes could have lit the Christmas candles.

'There's a lot of organising to do before then,' said Daisy, knowing that to make the fundraiser a success, she would need to have everything in place. She would need extra staff. She had been told there would be some very important people invited, even royalty. 'It's not something we can throw together in a couple of weeks.'

Making an event look effortless, even a small Christmas reception like this one in her mother's front parlour, took careful planning. Grander affairs for the charitable hospital fundraiser were something else altogether. Nevertheless, she was going to keep such delicate information quiet. Her mother would dance in the snow-covered street if she knew her daughter was going to be catering for the aristocracy – let alone royalty. They would never hear the end of it.

'Well, you wouldn't catch me allowing any wife of mine go out to work,' Henry Beamer said to Bridie. 'I have no intention of permitting my wife to slave over anything or anybody – except me.'

'*Allow!*' Daisy could hardly believe what she was hearing. '*Permitting! Slaving!* I've never heard such utter rot.' Daisy was more furious than was hospitable. She took a deep breath, knowing she ought to calm down before she caused a scene. However, she was not the only one who thought Henry Beamer's neanderthal belief so outrageous.

"S'cuse me, squire,' said Percy at the other end of the table. 'We don't go in for subordination in this house. Everyone is equal.'

'Surely not!' Henry seemed genuinely shocked. 'Women must know their place. There is a natural hierarchy.'

'You sound like one of those fascists, like Oswald Mosley,' Daisy countered.

'I tend to believe he has something worth saying,' said Henry, oblivious to the seething women sitting around the long table whom he was blatantly insulting. 'I hear he is very successful in his speeches. People have had enough of the wishy-washy ways of the government. They haven't got a clue about the working man.'

'Or woman,' Daisy piped up. 'If Mosley and his ilk marched into Liverpool and tried telling the locals how to live their lives, they'd be getting marched straight back out again!'

'I hardly think that,' said Henry, looking down his nose.

'You should go with him. We don't want fascist talk here,' Mara whispered.

'This is a Christmas tea, not a party-political broadcast.' Molly had no time for politics at the best of times and wanted to stop this kind of talk before it escalated.

'We're in no mood to listen to some toffee-nosed pipsqueak spouting government policies,' Percy whispered to Molly. Slow to anger usually, he didn't like talk of politics or religion at the table, or at social get-togethers. In his estimation, it brought out the worst in people. 'Bridie's new friend is getting right up my nose.' Then, in his usual cheery manner, he said loudly, 'We should be enjoying the compliments of the season – and Molly's excellent Christmas table.'

'Here, here!' Davey had never heard such utter claptrap as the stuff this Henry fellow was spouting.

'Well said...' Daisy muttered.

Murmurings went like a wave around the table, and Molly looked directly at Daisy, who suspected something like this would happen when Bridie had told her this morning she had invited Henry Beamer.

'I think Percy would like to say a few words,' said Daisy in her sweetest voice. She motioned for Percy to stand up and say something before a riot broke out.

She understood Bridie's reasons for inviting Henry. Freddy, who'd worked at Beamer's as an electrician, was thinking of giving up the sea and hoped to secure a position in the New Year. Daisy knew he had joined the navy because he'd been overlooked for promotion many times, even though he was as good an electrician as the best of them. But, in her usual cack-handed way, Bridie had almost ruined any chance Freddy had. And, if Freddy and Violet's lovey-dovey expressions were anything to go by, they would soon be saving every penny for their future.

Daisy watched Bridie batting her dark mascaraed eyes at the upstart, Henry to silently sooth his crushed ego. On days like today, caught up in the romance of the festive season, her younger sister would jump at the chance of a proper date with Henry Beamer. But Bridie was also fickle, changing boyfriends as many times as most girls changed their bloomers.

Daisy was not so inclined. When, and if, the right man came along, she would know immediately. And that hadn't been the case with Harvey... When and if, the realisation would be so sudden and so strong it would hit her between the eyes like a thundering boxing glove. And she would accept nothing less from now on.

She saw everybody having a good time, and that was good enough for her. Although Mary Jane didn't seem as happy as she should have been. As the afternoon wore on, the table was cleared away and one of the guests took his seat at the piano, and as the drink flowed, the singing began in earnest.

Henry began a deep conversation with Mary Jane's husband Cal, who, unbeknown to the residents, owned most of the properties in Beamer Street, including the land on which the Beamer Street factory stood.

'Bridie tells me young Hollie has left school and is working in the accounts department at Swanne and Swanne, the land agents.' Henry did not even try to hide his surprise when Cal told him she was just filling in for the Christmas holidays and had not yet left her education at a prestigious private school in Crosby.

'Mrs Everdine and I hope Hollie will go on to university,' said Cal, ignoring his young daughter's raised eyebrows, knowing she had no such ambitions.

'Don't you think university is wasted on such a beautiful young girl?' Henry asked. 'A good education would be wasted when she marries and takes care of her husband.' Henry's glib assumption gave Cal's eyebrows cause to shoot to the roots of his hair. Nonplussed, Henry continued, 'I find a woman's place is in the home, looking after her family.' He shared this nugget of misinformation with a pompous swagger, obviously expecting Cal to agree with him. However, given the disapproving glare from Mary Jane, Henry was forced to say, 'Not that homemaking suits all women.'

'Some women can manage more than one thing at a time, especially when she has a supportive family around her.' Cal reached for Mary Jane's hand, hoping his fiery red-haired wife didn't swipe this young upstart in the mush.

'I hear you,' said Henry, too dense to realise Cal had just slighted his narrow-minded views. 'But I would never allow any wife of mine to go out working.'

'I'd keep my voice down if I were you,' said Cal. 'My daughter shares her mother's ambition. She does not need a husband to rely on, and if truth be told, few women do these days.' Cal's forward-thinking gave him the opportunity to realise that one day women would do their own thing and not have to go cap in hand to ask their husbands permission for anything. Something this young fool would find hard to antici-pate. 'We are very proud of both our daughters,' Cal said in his deep Anglo-American drawl, 'we want them to be happy in whatever they choose to do with their lives.'

'I don't think those kinds of views will ever catch on,' said Henry. 'Men won't stand for it.'

Cal decided it wasn't worth his while arguing the point. Hollie and Neve, like Mary Jane, could be anything they chose to be and didn't need the permission of a boorish oaf to do so.

Henry Beamer couldn't see that some women had been earning their own money since the Great War. A time when they discovered they were just as good as men when it came to keeping the country going while the men were overseas, fighting the enemy. They now had a say in how this country was run, and by whom; they now voted and owned their own property, without a man's permission. Such a blessing, Cal thought, because if the country were in the hands of this boorish dunderhead, they would be in a fine old mess.

'When my father retires and I am chairman of Beamer's, there will be a big shake-up,' Henry said, stubbing out a Senior Service cigarette onto his plate, before Daisy could retrieve it, even though there were polished ashtrays on the table. 'I will be head of the firm. Ruler of all I survey.' He lowered his voice and leaned towards Cal, saying in a conspirative tone, 'And there will be no Jews or Catholics working at Beamer's, that's for sure.' Henry gave Bridie a suggestive wink, and tapped the sofa cushion beside him, a cocky smirk curling his thin lips. And Cal felt a tinge of dismay when her eyes lit up.

Daisy, too, heard the remark, and with the weight of foreboding pressing on her shoulders, she felt a cold chill cloak her, knowing, as everybody did these days, that there was a ranting little man in Germany who talked the same way as Henry, who also thought that the world was his for the taking, and to hell with the rest.

To these fanatics, certain people were not human. They were faceless nobodies. Not worth taking up the same air the fascist dictators who wanted everything for themselves. Some sections of society were treated as subhuman.

Daisy watched her sister return his flirtatious smile, knowing if it was the last thing she did, she must get Bridie away from Henry Beamer. Otherwise, her sister's life would never be her own again.

'Apparently,' Mary Jane told Daisy a short while later, when the guests had dispersed into other rooms, 'old Beamer's wife is much younger than old Willy. I heard a rumour she only married the ould fella for his money.'

'Well, I've seen the state of him,' Daisy whispered, 'he reminds me of a bald blancmange on two short fat wobbly legs.' The expelled eruption of schoolgirl guffaws attracted a caustic sneer from Henry, who made no secret of the fact he was bored stiff.

'Do you think he heard us?' Mary Jane, with tears of

laughter running down her cheeks, said from behind her napkin as she wiped the corner of her lips.

'I hope so,' answered Daisy, equally amused.

'Henry will make some unlucky girl a demon of a husband,' said Mary Jane, glancing in Bridie's direction at the top table, 'but hopefully not your sister.'

* * *

'I don't know what I'd do without you today, Dais,' said Molly as the afternoon turned to evening.

Daisy gave her mother a loving hug. She didn't know either but never mind.

Molly had done them all proud by being a good mother, who had raised a warm-hearted, loving family, so now, Daisy thought, it was time her mam slowed down and enjoyed herself a bit more. After all, her children were grown up and off her hands. 'And I don't know where that brother of yours has got to.'

'You know our Davey, Mam, here one minute, gone the next.' Daisy smiled. 'You just concentrate on having a nice time, you deserve it.' She took a tray of sausage rolls into the hallway, heading to the parlour, just as the front door opened. Davey came through the front door, shaking snow off his overcoat.

'Look who I met in the Tram Tavern last night, Dais!' Full of Christmas cheer, Davy watched his older sister for her reaction. He didn't have to wait long. 'I'll just go and pay a visit to the little boys' room.'

In that fragile sliver of time, Daisy's thoughts tumbled like scattered paper in a windstorm – disordered, raw, full of contradiction. Part of her brain didn't believe it – years of picturing his face. She wondered if she was dreaming.

'Hello, Daisy,' Max said. His eyes, still the same blue with the promise of charming laughter.

Part of her wanted to run to him, another part wanted to walk past like he was a stranger. But she knew she couldn't do that. She was measuring everything in heartbeats – the years apart, the tenderness of his eyes, the softness of his voice when he said her name. She was not the same girl he left behind, she wanted to say. But she couldn't speak.

Max stood by the front door, uncertain whether to step forward, and break whatever spell had brought them to this moment. His hair was shorter; his temples threaded with flecks of silver, even though he was just turned thirty. He wore a woollen overcoat and a guarded expression, which at one time she would have peeled away with laughter.

'Five years,' she breathed, her voice tight, barely louder than the tick of the grandfather clock. 'You said three months. And then nothing.'

Max swallowed. His throat bobbed once, twice.

'I thought if I came back sooner, I'd ruin your ambitions.'

'You ruined me.' Daisy stood now, her breathing shallow. 'I didn't stay ruined, though.' Their eyes met and held fast – his full of regret, hers full of everything else. Anger. Love. Yearning. Joy.

'You are more beautiful than I recall,' he whispered, and she stepped forward, stopping a few feet from him.

'I'm a lot stronger now.' Or at least she thought she was.

14

The guests moved into the sitting room, so the front room could be prepared for a less formal buffet, and Daisy noted the look of disdain, which Phoebe Beamer, Henry's stepmother who had not even been invited, bestowed upon her younger sister Bridie dancing with Henry. Daisy's hackles rose.

Bridie was enjoying the day immensely, throwing back her head and laughing uproariously at a tale Henry had just told. Daisy was glad her sister hadn't noticed Phoebe's withering expression. Bridie loved dancing and parties – what young girl didn't? If the rumours were to be believed, the youngsters of this country would need all the fun they could muster. Because if that fanatical little German got his way, entertainment in all its guises would be a thing of the past.

'A little bird tells me your sister worked in a private members club in Chelsea.' Mrs Beamer seemed a little tipsy, rolling her shoulders and giving the impression the ginger fox fur around her shoulders was having a leisurely stretch.

'She worked in a top-class lady's hair salon,' Daisy answered, careful not to be overheard by Bridie, who was

Lindy-Hopping across the dance floor, which had been made bigger by chairs being pushed back to the wall.

'Is that what she told you?' Mrs Beamer asked slyly.

'That's the thing about some little birds,' Mary Jane interjected, her smile intact as she watched young couples dancing cheek to cheek to a gramophone recording of Fred Astaire singing a song of the same name. 'Some have large beaks, far too big for their tiny heads, and even smaller-headed birds believe every word?' She had seen how this Jezebel had been trying to catch Cal's eye when she arrived, and she wasn't impressed, having heard how Mrs Beamer had a fondness for flirting with other women's husbands. 'Cal, will you be a darling and swap seats so I can fix Neve's ribbons.'

'My pleasure.' Cal was glad he no longer had to listen to the woman's wittering on about her wealthy husband and his new factory in the Lancashire countryside, before announcing she was bored and must be off home.

As Henry guided Phoebe into the hallway to fetch her hat and coat, he sounded livid when he was heard saying, 'That kind of information could prove extremely dangerous in the wrong hands.' He found Bridie and told her he would take Phoebe home and be back a little later.

'I've come across her type before,' Mary Jane told Daisy. 'Women like her are a penny a dozen.'

'I wish our Bridie – and our Freddy – could see Henry Beamer for what he really is,' Daisy said later, when Henry Beamer put in another appearance and was filling Bridie's gullible head with nonsense. 'I've heard stories, and they are not very flattering.'

'What kind of stories?' Mary Jane was not to be enlightened when Ina King appeared with a tray of sherry-filled schooners, earwigging everything that was being said.

'Sherry?' Ina made her way to the sofa and offered a drink to Bridie and Mr Beamer, who, in Ina's opinion, was as plain as a pikestaff and thought young Bridie could do better.

'There was quite enough in the trifle,' Henry Beamer answered, seeming quite put out when Ina offered no other choice of alcoholic beverage.

'That trifle is the best I've tasted,' Ina retorted, whipping away the sherry tray, 'you don't know what's good for you.' She could not look more insulted if she had made the dessert herself. If there is any left over at the end of the party, Ina thought, she was sure Molly would let her take some home. *All the more for my lot.*

'Everybody knows Daisy makes the best trifles this side of the Mersey.' Bridie's smile did not reach her eyes when she raised a slender hand, her red bullet nails dismissing Ina with a flick.

Daisy, watching the scene unravel, was disappointed that Mara was out helping those less fortunate. She would have enjoyed talking with Mary Jane and Ina. Daisy was reminded of the day Mary Jane came to Beamer Street back in 1921, with nothing except a pillowcase filled with her meagre belongings and a clock she inherited from her mother, which now stood proudly under the words, *Time for Tea*, in the window of her baker's and confectionery shop on the corner over the road.

'It's a marvellous spread.' Daisy, engrossed in her thoughts, jumped a little when Max sat next to her.

'I was up early preparing it,' she said. 'Do I look tired?'

'No, you look beautiful, your eyes are sparkling. Radiant, I'd say.'

'You make me sound like Blackler's Christmas tree,' Daisy laughed, pleased when Max moved his chair a little closer.

'You are much more dazzling,' he whispered in a tone that made Daisy's eyebrow twitch.

'Less of your flannel,' she said, not trusting his motives just yet. After all, he had been gone five years. A lot had happened in that time.

Max wondered if he should ask her to go out with him. To talk. Catch up on old times. This was not the time or the place.

'We could go out. Take the ferry over to New Brighton?' His throat was dry. He was nervous. She would say no.

'In this weather!' She immediately saw the look of disappointment on his face and realised she had been quick to dismiss his suggestion. But, flustered now, she couldn't take the words back. 'I'd better wash these dishes.'

Daisy got up from her chair and, collecting half-empty side plates, stacked them ready for the kitchen. She had felt much too relaxed talking to Max. She should have been interrogating him, not encouraging him. But she couldn't. He was here. And she still felt the same way now as she had always done.

* * *

Max smiled as he watched Daisy hurry out to the kitchen with the stack of plates. He enjoyed her unsophisticated charm as much now as he had done all those years ago. If only he could turn back the clock. If only things had been different. If only...

Even though he had travelled the world, gathering news of distant places, Max had never met anybody as beguiling as Daisy. Not even Margarita, if truth be told.

'Need a hand?' Max asked, removing his jacket, and rolling up his sleeves. Daisy turned quickly from the sink, so deep in thought she hadn't heard him coming out to the back kitchen.

Her eyes caught his and she could feel the heat that turned her cheeks a pink tinge, and once more Max held her gaze.

Daisy dropped a plate, flustered. Why did she feel so confused? When she'd heard Max on the radio, she was thrilled. Now he was here, all she could think about was washing dishes. It didn't make sense.

Breathing a deep sigh, she turned back to the sink, trying to slow her racing heart as Max picked up a tea towel like it was the most natural thing in the world to do. Harvey would never have done that, she thought.

Max took the soapy plate and wiped it thoroughly and put it onto the kitchen table. He wanted to be here. With Daisy. Alone. There was so much he wanted to say. So much he wanted to tell her. To try to make her understand. But how could he tell her she wasn't the only female in his life any more. He had responsibilities now.

The time wasn't right.

15

'Here, Dais, listen to this.' Davey, a bit tipsy as he came into the kitchen, caught her attention and, laughing, he put his half-empty beer glass on to the table and said, 'This'll have you in tucks. Tell her, Max... About that day you fell overboard and nearly got eaten by a shark!'

'A shark!?' Daisy turned from the sink, up to her elbows in soapsuds, her dark eyes as wide as side plates. 'Really?'

'The shark might be a bit of an exaggeration,' Max laughed. 'More like a jellyfish.' He shook his head and gave his friend a little shove. 'But I did fall overboard.'

'What happened was...' Davey interrupted, before Max took up the story again.

'We were waiting for the ship to drop anchor...'

Daisy couldn't help but smile, they were like a double act.

'He was taking pictures for his editor and moving back, back, back, then he did a backflip – like one of those Olympic gymnasts,' interrupted Davey, throwing his hands in the air and howling with laughter.

'I kid you not,' Max chuckled, getting into his stride,

enjoying her merriment. It had been a long time since he'd enjoyed this woman's laughter. 'I could see this huge jellyfish coming towards me and I scrambled into the lifebelt that was thrown to me, but the bugger still filled my leg with barbed stings...'

The sound of laughter grew with each part of the story, and before she knew it, Daisy had tears running down her cheeks, holding on to her aching sides.

'The crew were ready to drop their pants and...'

'Stop,' she cried through her laughter, holding up her hand, recalling the days when Max, a junior reporter back then, would come into Mary Jane's bakery and have everybody in stitches. 'I can't breathe!'

She watched Davey, still chuckling, drain his glass before handing it to her to wash.

'That's a myth by the way,' said Max. 'There was no chance I was letting a ship-full of hairy seafarers evacuate their bladder on my leg! The doctor removed the stings with tweezers.'

Davey was now crying with laughter. Moments later, wiping his eyes with the pad of his hand, he took a deep breath. 'D'you fancy a proper pint in the Tram?' he asked Max. 'This bottled stuff bloats me. I could do with a real pint.'

'Aye, go on. If you insist, Squire,' Max said, looking to Daisy. He would rather have stayed here with her. However, as was customary in the house parties, the men sloped off to the pub while the women tidied up. 'Is the lovely Daisy going to join us?' Max asked hopefully. He enjoyed her company, and it did his heart good to share stories with her. Especially now.

Daisy felt a little deflated, she had been enjoying Max's company. 'I've got things to do.' Daisy didn't want to see the inside of the Tram Tavern ever again. She didn't want to chance seeing Harvey, knowing he was a regular in the pub. But, watching Max follow Davey out of the back kitchen, she felt as if she'd lost ten bob and found a penny.

Mary Jane, coming into the kitchen, was rolling up her sleeves, talking about how drunk Henry was. 'I can't watch another minute.'

'You look like you're ready for a bout of fisticuffs,' Daisy said.

'Don't tempt me,' said Mary Jane, 'he's drunk as a lord, and narky with it. I feel sorry for your Bridie having to listen to his drivel.'

'Mara's due back from the hospital soon,' said Daisy, 'so our Bridie won't put up with him much longer.'

Max popped his head around the door looking in to say cheerio, but Daisy was already in conversation with Mary Jane, so he left without saying anything. He wanted to get back home to Little Poll, to read her a bedtime story and tuck her in before coming back to the party later.

'Do you think there's anything going on with Pretty Beamer and Daft Henry?' asked Mary Jane, her face mock serious, and Daisy gasped at the thought, before they both burst out laughing.

'That's a terrible thing to say,' Daisy answered, 'she is his stepmother.'

'She's his father's much younger wife. There's a difference.' Mary Jane cocked her head to one side. 'I don't trust either of them, Phoebe looked far too friendly with Henry if you ask me. More cosy than was respectable if you get my drift.'

'Well, you know how fickle our Bridie is. Anyway, she's got that chap Karl in London. She'll soon get fed up with Henry Beamer.'

'Did she say how long she was home for?' Mary Jane asked, adding another dried plate to the column on the table.

'You never can tell with Bridie,' said Daisy, 'here today, gone tomorrow.'

'Anyway, forget about them. Tell me all about Max.' Mary Jane, fluttering her eyelashes like a silent movie star, was curious. 'He couldn't keep his eyes off you.'

'Oh, behave yourself, Mary Jane,' Daisy retorted. 'You know Max, he's worse than our Bridie. Here today...' *Gone tomorrow*. 'No girl will hold him down.'

'I heard him tell Cal he was staying closer to home from now on. He was offered a job with the BBC. But he decided to work on the *Liverpool Post* instead.'

Daisy couldn't help but smile. She felt there were a thousand butterflies fluttering inside her, and try as she might, she could not hide the fact she was more excited than ever that Max was back home where he belonged.

'Does he still live in the big house in Blundellsands?' asked Mary Jane. 'The one he inherited when his father passed away?'

'Yes, I think so.' Daisy had never been to his home and Mary Jane had that look in her eyes that spelled mischief.

'Those houses are beautiful out that way. Big enough for a family, I believe.' There was a definite twinkle in Mary Jane's eyes. 'Cal tells me the area was created as a suburb for wealthy businessmen back in the middle of the last century.'

'Really.' Daisy tried not to show much interest, but she was dying to know all. 'I believe his grandfather was a shipbuilder and his father a journalist, like Max.'

'Not that you took much notice of his past.'

'Of course not.' Daisy smiled. Mary Jane knew how she felt about Max. 'You're right, though. He probably has a wife and a dozen kids by now.'

'Fat chance of that, he's been abroad for the last five years and he didn't have any children when he went overseas.'

In no time at all they had tidied, ready for the revellers return.

'What are you two nattering about out here?' Bridie asked as she came into the back kitchen. Daisy could feel her face flush a bright warm pink and quickly denied any *jangling*.

'Oh, that's a shame,' said Bridie. 'I love a bit of salacious gossip. Daisy, be a love and put the kettle on. I'm dying for a cup of tea.'

'Of course, madam,' Daisy answered with mock servitude. 'Would madam like me to peel her a grape too?' Just then, Mara came out to the small gathering.

'Been busy, Mara? I bet there's no rest at the hospital just because it's Christmas.'

'You are so right, Daisy,' said Mara. 'Ill health stops for no man, woman or child.'

'I bet you're dying for a cuppa?' Daisy offered and Mara nodded. She didn't dare go into the horrors of some of the dreadful sights she had seen today.

16

Daisy knew the instant her brother Davey came back from the pub, singing off-key and swinging a bottle of rum. He was certainly worse for wear. Stumbling into her back, she almost toppled into the arms of Percy who was in deep conversation with her mother.

'I am so sorry.' Davey slurred his words and, putting his finger to his lips, made a shushing noise. 'We had a couple of jars, just a couple, and I opened up the piano and that was it!' Davey shrugged. 'And then all these drinks were lined up on top of the old Joanna, and everyone was dancing and singing...'

'You look like you drank them all,' Daisy said, 'which is why you're having trouble standing still.' She watched her brother's feet make a diamond pattern on the kitchen floor, more disappointed than she expected to be when Max was not with him. 'Maybe you should sleep them off.'

'You're right, as always, dear sister. I think I need a little bobo.' Davey gave a conspiratorial tap to the side of his nose.

'Yes, Davey,' answered Daisy in the same tone she used when he was younger, 'a little sleep will do you the world of good. But I wouldn't like to be inside your head when you wake up.' Max had gone home. It had been a long day.

Then the parlour door opened, and Daisy's spirits soared when she saw Max coming into the room filled with friends and family enjoying the party. Everybody was having a fine old time.

'Max isn't in the same state as you, how come?' she asked her brother.

'Ahh—' Davey waggled his forefinger '—thereby goes a tale... You see, being a bit of a late white... No, that's not right...' He looked puzzled and tried again. 'Being a bit of a light-weight... Yes, that's it... He went home.' Davey hiccupped, and Max offered to make his friend a cup of black coffee.

'We've only got chicory essence,' Daisy answered, knowing there was a bottle of Camp coffee in the kitchen cupboard, 'but I doubt he'll be awake long enough to drink anything more tonight.'

'I can help you get him to his room, if you like?' Max said, perfectly sober.

'Lead on, Macduff,' Davey quipped, while Max took one arm, and Daisy took the other. 'Shall I sing you a song?'

'Maybe later,' Daisy answered, 'after you've had a little lie-down.'

Staggering up the single flight of stairs was the easy bit, but trying to turn him at the top onto the landing was a bit trickier as Davey put one foot on the step and slipped off again, laughing like it was the funniest thing he had ever experienced. Eventually, with Max's help, Daisy managed to put her sozzled brother to bed, covering him, still fully dressed, with a heavy eiderdown before going to fetch the bowl from one of the few bathrooms in Beamer Street.

'Is he all right?' asked Molly, coming up the stairs. She had seen her eldest son's performance. 'He never could hold his drink,' she told Max, who was rolling Davey onto his side and putting a couple of pillows behind his back. 'Two shandies and he's away with the mixer.' She didn't know why the mixer had anything to do with anything, but it was one of her favourite sayings and suited most occasions.

Daisy came back into the room with the white tin bowl, a glass of water and a Beechams powder for when her brother woke up. 'I'll leave the lamp on in case he gets up and loses his bearings,' she told her mother.

'I don't know how he manages to get around the world under his own steam,' Molly told Max, shaking her head. 'It's a good job I've got our Daisy, I don't know what I'd do without her.'

Daisy rolled her eyes, knowing her mother always looked to her when there was anything to be sorted. 'He'll be fine now,' Molly said, looking at Davey, peacefully snoring in his bed, before heading out of the bedroom.

'You're a regular mother hen,' Max told Daisy, his voice full of admiration. 'Does nothing ever faze you?'

'Not really,' Daisy answered, heading for the door. 'When you've spent most of your life trying to fix everybody's troubles, it becomes second nature.'

Max's comment kept going around in her head as they descended the stairs. What did he mean when he said she was a regular mother hen? she wondered. Did he think she was a busybody?

'And where have you two been hiding?' Henry, his eyes half closed, stumbled out of the parlour, heading towards the kitchen as they both reached the bottom of the stairs. 'You both look like you've been up to something you shouldn't.' His intoxicated tone was one of sly insinuation, and Daisy felt her hackles rise. How dare he imply there had been something improper going on between her and Max!

'I beg your...' Daisy's words were halted when Max shook his head and spoke in a forthright manner she had not heard before.

'That's for us to know. You need not worry yourself with matters that do not concern you.'

'I'll let you know what concerns me, shall I?' Henry answered, leaning forward, glaring, eye to eye in Max's face. His drunken manner had become suddenly hostile, and Daisy's heart began to pound. She could see Henry was spoiling for a fight. He had been goading various people, including Cal, who was the most peaceful man she knew, for much of the afternoon. 'I've seen you sniffing around her...'

'Here, we'll have less of that kind of talk, if you don't mind.' Daisy's tone was firm, mirroring the days when her siblings were young, when she had cause to discipline them about some misdeed or other. But her strong voice belied the anxiety she felt. She didn't want any trouble to spoil their Christmas Day. Mam would be mortified if the day were marred by this upstart who had more money than sense. 'If you don't mind your manners in my mother's house, Henry Beamer, I can always show you through the door.'

Henry, it appeared, was showing his true colours now all right. He seemed quite affable, if overbearing, when sober but highly belligerent in drink. He was a troublemaker who liked nothing better than a bout of fisticuffs. Daisy ignored the sneer on his face as he zigzagged towards the buffet table.

'Remind me never to get on the wrong side of you,' Max laughed, and Daisy's shoulders relaxed, knowing an unruly commotion had been averted. She would be so disappointed if the day was remembered only for a fight near the end.

'Would you like something to eat?' Daisy asked, knowing Henry had been put in his place. But would the humiliation she had heaped upon him spoil Freddy's chance of a job at Beamers Electricals? She hoped not.

'The buffet is exceptionally good, and I am tempted, but maybe later,' Max said, eyeing the food Daisy had expertly prepared.

'Henry turns my stomach. I don't know what our Bridie sees in him,' Daisy said, trying to cover her embarrassment over Beamer's remark about her and Max up to no good upstairs. Fancy him saying a thing like that. She didn't know where to put her face!

Daisy made up her mind there and then, she was going to have a word with Bridie and warn her what a sneak her new boyfriend turned out to be.

'Care to dance?' Max asked and Daisy felt that familiar little flip in her stomach, once again. There was something about him, something had changed, he seemed more grown-up than she remembered, so very much... something she couldn't put her finger on. He enjoyed a laugh and a joke, but there was something else, something deeper. Something that had nothing whatsoever to do with her any more.

Max took her elbow and led her into the parlour, where guests gathered around the piano, listening to Molly strangling her version of 'It's a long way to Tipperary,' a favourite song of her dearly departed husband.

'Do you know what I would like to do, most of all,' Max, standing behind Daisy, whispered in her hair, 'I would like to hold you in my arms and kiss you.'

'Oh!' Daisy exclaimed, quickly glancing around in case anybody heard what he just said. 'I didn't... I don't...' She hadn't reckoned on any kissing lark, leaving all that caper to Bridie and the rest of the young ones. The invitation took her by surprise, but if that crinkled skin around his sparkling eyes was anything to go by, Max was amused. Just like the old days.

'Don't worry,' he whispered, 'I won't turn you into a scarlet woman. Well, not in front of your friends and family.'

'I should think not,' Daisy replied, not knowing whether to be vexed or pleased. Yes, she found him one of the most handsome, kind, and thoughtful men she had ever met, and she always would. But that did not give him permission to toy with her reputation. 'You won't be turning me into anything at all.' Daisy raised herself to her full five feet four inches, trying not to imagine what it would be like to be kissed by Max again. But she could not put the thought from her mind and now it was all she longed for.

A furnace burned in her cheeks and Daisy was filled with mortification. What would he think of her if he knew what was going on inside her head? She must lock such thoughts in the compartment of her mind that had long since been closed off.

'I don't dance much,' Daisy admitted, pushing her rampaging thoughts to the back of her mind. Then, to cover her embarrassment, she laughed, 'I don't want to break one of your toes.'

'In that case,' he whispered, 'I will take you in my arms and we will shuffle around the floor.'

'Oh well, if you're brave enough,' she replied with a giggle, 'shuffle on.'

Daisy could not deny the thrilling darts of delight that ricocheted through her body when he took her hand and led her onto the dance floor.

Relaxing into Max's arms, they began swaying to the sound, once more, of Fred Astaire's 'Dancing Cheek to Cheek,' which Davey had brought home from America. This was the most natural place she had ever been. She knew every time she heard that tune, she would immediately think of being taken into Max's arms.

The evening passed quickly as they danced to the big band tunes of Duke Ellington and Benny Goodman also brought back from America. It was rounded off by a record of Frances Langford, singing 'I'm in the Mood for Love' from the film *Every Night at Eight*.

'I could take you to see the film,' said Max as led her back to her seat. 'That is, unless you've already seen it.'

'No, I haven't. I'd like to see it with you.' Daisy knew all good things must come to an end when he said he had to go. Most of the guests, tired, happy, well fed, and tiddly made their way to their own homes.

As the last reveller, he said goodnight. When Daisy helped him on with his overcoat, Max pointed to the ceiling. She looked up to see a sprig of mistletoe hanging from the lamp-shade in the hallway and giggled like a light-headed schoolgirl in anticipation of her first kiss.

Cocooned in a bubble of euphoria she never knew existed, all thoughts of her family, her work or her duty disappeared into the night air as his lips met hers, and she melted into his arms, imagining herself sliding onto the floor in a puddle of liquid desire, her heart racing as it had done years before.

A blissful eternity later, their lips parted, and Daisy felt she was hovering somewhere above her own body, never wanting the moment to end. Whatever had just happened to her could only be described as an awakening, a longing she had felt only once before. And Daisy felt her life would never be quite the same again.

'I have to go.' Max sounded hesitant, as reluctant to break this spell as she.

'You don't have to.' Daisy's words were low and sounded more intimate than she intended, but as the pleasant hum warmed her in the draughty hallway, she didn't care. She felt reckless and knew it had been Max's kiss that caused this feeling of abandonment. 'You could bunk in our Davey's room. Our Freddy's bed is empty,' she said quickly to cover her embarrassment. What would her mam think if she heard her talking like this?

'Believe me, I'd love to stay.' Max's words were low, his eyes bright. 'I must go home. I have commitments, it's just that...' Max didn't finish his comment and the sparkle in his eyes dimmed.

Suddenly, Daisy's mind was asking all sorts of questions. She recalled Mary Jane's remark earlier. What if Max *was* married? She should have listened to her head and not her heart. She should not have allowed herself to be swept along on a wave of elation, caught up in the romance of the Christmas Day. Her head was in a spin. Kissing the man who had walked out on her five years ago. What was she thinking? Had she lost her mind? This kind of behaviour would make her the type of person who got themselves a bad name. 'I don't think the buses are still running.'

'I have a car,' Max answered apologetically, 'I have to go to London tomorrow.'

Daisy knew when she was being fobbed off, and this was one of those times. She had been a pleasant pastime, nothing more. 'Well, goodnight then,' she said, opening the front door and letting in a cold blast of snowy air. 'Mind how you go.'

As soon as Max stepped out of the door, she closed it behind him. No lingering goodbye. No watching him walk out of her life once more.

Mary Jane had been right, she thought. The night was

treacherous with a blizzard hurling about outside. What man in his right mind would want to drive in such conditions? One who considered it necessary to drive back to a wife perhaps? Leaning her back against the door, the elation Daisy had felt dissipated, and in its wake left her feeling empty.

Dragging herself from the door, she switched off the lights and decided to leave the washing up for the morning. She couldn't face it right now. All she wanted to do was bury her head under the covers and try to forget what an idiotic fool she had been to let her guard down. *You should have ignored him.* However, the words of caution were too late. She did not want to ignore him. She did not have the strength to do such a thing. The voice in her head was defiant.

17

JANUARY 1936

When Daisy came downstairs, she found her mother in tears.

'He's dead,' Molly sobbed into her black-edged hand-kerchief.

'Who's dead, Mam?' Daisy felt her mouth dry, and her heartbeat thundered like a runaway train against her ribs. Percy? Where was Percy. Daisy was too afraid to ask. 'Mam...?'

'The King is dead. It was on the early news this morning,' Molly wailed. 'While we were sleeping soundly in our beds, poor Queen Mary was distraught at the news she had lost her beloved husband,' Molly informed her daughter. 'The country has lost a devoted monarch.'

'Oh Mam, that's terrible news,' Daisy said, giving her mother's shoulders a loving squeeze.

As a mark of respect, Molly left the curtains closed when Daisy went to the office to pick up her post and received a telephone call from the lady almoner of the Mersey Infirmary, Miss Treadwell.

'Good morning, Miss Haywood,' the lady almoner said,

'owing to the King's demise, I feel it necessary to postpone the charity fundraiser until a later date.'

'I understand,' said Daisy.

Although she was surprised to learn a few days later the new King had broken royal protocol by watching the proclamation of his own accession to the throne from the window of St James's Palace. And he was in the company of a married woman.

* * *

'Would you look at that.' Molly poked the *Liverpool Post* with her index finger. 'Page four! Page four! – mind the advertisers aren't put out even when our beloved king dies!' Molly's outrage was palpable, and the family agreed that the news should have been reported on the front page, edged in black, no less. Everybody knew how patriotic Molly was. 'It's poor Queen Mary, I feel sorry for,' said Molly, sitting at the table in the kitchen surrounded by Percy and her girls, Daisy, Bridie, and Mara who had quickly become part of the family. 'I know exactly how that poor woman feels about losing a beloved husband.'

'The picture houses and the dance halls will be closed as a mark of respect,' said Bridie, who, although sorry the poor king had died, felt miserable at the thought of staying in listening to the news repeatedly on the wireless.

'No Henry tonight?' Daisy wondered why her sister never once mentioned the boyfriend she left back in London any more.

'No Max?' Bridie retaliated in a heartbeat. 'Or, has he flitted off overseas – again?'

'I'm not his keeper,' Daisy answered irritably. She had hoped to see Max after Christmas. But New Year came and went with no sign of him. An unusual dark cloud hung over her and meant she was fast asleep when the new year had showed its face. And now the whole country was feeling as desolate as she had felt then, but for very different reasons.

'And to think,' said Molly interrupting Daisy's thoughts, 'when we saw His Majesty opening the new Mersey Tunnel that would be the last we saw of him.'

'That was a lovely day out,' said Percy, reminiscing. 'The sun shone for the opening. I don't care what anyone says, you can buy anything these days, but you can't buy nice weather.'

'It was glorious.' Molly sniffed into a black-edged handker-chief. 'I'll never forget it as long as I live.'

'Then we were allowed to walk through the tunnel, following the royal car,' said Percy.

Bridie squirmed in her chair, recalling the times she had told customers at the London club she had made the walk too, when in reality she did no such thing.

'Queen Mary actually waved to me,' said Molly, 'like she knew me personally. A lovely woman she was...'

'She's not dead, Mam,' said Bridie.

'You have some respect, our Bridie,' said Molly, 'that's our King's wife. *She's* the cat's mother.'

'Sorry, Mam,' said Bridie, 'I didn't mean to sound disre-spectful.' Knowing how much her mother revered the royal family, Bridie didn't want to upset her. 'Don't you think Henry looks like King Edward?'

'Not really,' said Daisy, who thought Henry was so conceited and haughty she couldn't bear to look at him.

'It said in this morning's paper, King Edward is the first bachelor king since George III who was crowned in 1761,' Mara said, knowing there was a world of difference between the new king and the poor people she saw every day at the Mersey Infirmary. If all the money being spent on the Coronation was spent building better homes and jobs, then this country would be a better place. However, she dare not voice those kind of thoughts. Molly would be outraged, and Mara doubted she would have such comfortable lodgings for long.

'I'm sure the King won't be a bachelor for long,' said Molly, 'he's a very handsome chap.'

He looks a bit shifty to me, thought Percy. But he too kept his thoughts to himself.

* * *

From the twentieth to the twenty-eighth of January, Molly refused to open the curtains in homage to the late King. On the day of his funeral, the whole family listened in silence to the service, broadcast live on the BBC wireless service, which was relayed across the empire. And, when Pathé newsreel film of the funeral procession was later shown at the local picture house, Molly and Percy were at the front of the queue, whilst Max covered the funereal story in London, forbidden to report on rumours that King George had voiced a premonition that within twelve months of his death his son, King Edward would 'ruin himself'.

Only time would tell, thought Max, on the train back to Liverpool, after being informed by a reliable female journalist that for the last two years, the new king had taken a divorced American mistress. There was nothing new in that, he thought, Kings had been taking mistresses for centuries. Daisy's mother, Molly would be scandalised.

Thoughts of Daisy were never far from his mind, and he wanted nothing more than to tell her his true situation, but he dare not. Daisy was ambitious. A free agent, as he had been when she said she would not be tied to domestic drudgery. She had seen enough of that when she was growing up.

She told him all about Harvey and his dependent mother on Christmas night, and how she could not see herself giving up her career to become a housemaid to them both. Max hadn't recognised the 'new' Daisy then. She had always struck him as the most caring woman he knew. But people changed, he supposed, as he had. So how could he expect Daisy to take on a young child? Max didn't expect Daisy to raise his adorable daughter. Of course not.

But he couldn't bear it if she never wanted anything to do with him again when she found out he had a young daughter. That was why he hadn't contacted Daisy since Christmas, believing she would want nothing to do with him when she realised he was not the free man she thought him to be.

18

Mara could not believe her own ears when Miss Treadwell told her she had to go out to visit an elderly couple, informing her that the husband, Seamus O'Flanagan, needed their help and the lady almoner was to make a visit to assess their circumstances.

'Please allow me to go instead, Miss Treadwell,' Mara tried to keep her voice steady. After all these years, could this man be the same Seamus O'Flanagan who had been with her father on the day he died? 'The weather is atrocious, and you have been suffering with that dreadful cold.'

'You have a heart of gold, Mara, I appreciate your kindness.'

'It is nothing,' said Mara knowing Miss Treadwell was a good twenty years older than herself and not as robust, but she would never voice such thoughts. 'You don't want to risk a bout of pneumonia.'

'Certainly not,' said the lady almoner, grateful the younger woman was so eager.

* * *

Dripping wet in a sleety gale blowing in off the River Mersey, Mara shivered as her wet clothes clung to her slender frame. The proof of poverty and desperation showed in the grim-faced huddles of men gathered along the dock wall, waiting to be allowed into the Pen – the hiring shed where they silently prayed to be chosen for a morning or a whole day's work.

The shiny collars of worn jackets were turned up against the icy blast. Their flat-capped peaks pulled down low as rough, hard-working hands dug deep into empty pockets. She watched them moving from one foot to the other in a futile attempt to keep warm. The sad news of the King's passing last month would mean little to men who could not put food on the table or coal in the grate, and Mara knew only too well the shadow of despair would grow longer, not for the repose of the sovereign's soul, but for the want of a job and a bite to eat. The proof was right there in front of her.

When she reached the address of Seamus O'Flanagan, she was disappointed not to get an answer to her determined knock and decided to call back later. She went on to pay a visit to a family whose main breadwinner was in the last throes of consumption. There was no doubt the family were poverty-stricken; there was no evidence of any comfort. Not even a mantle clock to pawn. Just one big black empty cauldron pot hanging over the unlit fire.

Mara promised to make arrangements for the master of the house to be transferred to the TB hospital but doubted he would live long enough to reap the benefit. She enquired about Mr O'Flanagan, but the family shook their head, as she expected them to. In the face of what they considered *authorities*; these people kept their cards very close to their chest and did not give information easily to strangers.

'Does anybody know a man called Seamus O'Flanagan?'

Mara called out to the men trying to shelter from the bitter wind and driving snow beside the thick walls of the dock.

Most shook their heads and said nothing, and Mara knew her attempt to find the man who had once been her father's comrade was futile. These man gave nothing away either. Especially information that could hinder a fellow worker.

She was a woman. An Irish woman at that. No man could tell if she wore a gold band under her thick woollen gloves. They were never going to tattle on one of their own, even if they did know who and where he was.

A working man trying to keep body and soul together with a morning's work deserved privacy. Not some interfering busybody asking questions. Mara could have been anybody. They didn't know her. She could be his wife. His money lender. A woman scorned. They would never take that chance.

'If you do happen to see him, would you ask him to call into the lady almoner's office at Mersey Infirmary, please.'

'You'll find him soon enough, if he wants to be found,' a lone voice in the crowd of waiting men told her.

* * *

Seamus O'Flanagan watched Mara's straight-backed advance along the dock road and remembered the day he thought he was the luckiest man in the world. Straight off the boat from his homeland, he was greeted by a landlord's agent who assured him and his beloved Freda that he had a decent place for them to live. A place surrounded by his own people.

But arriving back to the damp, flag-stoned cellar, eight steps down from court level, he knew immediately that the unsanitary conditions would either make or break them both. He suspected the latter. But what choice did they have? He'd been

told by the parish priest, Father O'Hanlon, that better conditions were almost impossible to come by. The mortality rate of
children under a year old was 299 in every 1,000. So it was just
as well he and Freda were never blessed with any children.
God's will, he supposed, for running away when he should have
stayed in his own country.

'I'm sure I will find something soon, sweetheart,' Seamus
told Freda later as he hung his soaking wet jacket on the fireguard. Not sure at all. Jobs had been scarce for the first half of
the thirties, and he prayed this year would bring some kind of
hope.

His permanent limp was a constant reminder of his loyalty
to a country who never asked if he had a mouth, or a bite of
food to put in it. The pain he still endured in the freezing
temperatures, whose draughts permeated their inside space
just as much as the outside when coal was scarce. The crude
surgery to remove the bullet in his leg had severed nerve
endings, which made the leg almost useless. The colour of
candlewax, it was painful even on the warmest of days.

On the rare days he had been lucky enough to get a sniff of
work, his obvious affliction gave the impression he would not
be able to cope, let alone hump, and load cargo into ships
holds, or the vast warehouses that lined the docks. He would
hold up the job he was told more times than he cared to recall.
He proved a good worker in his younger, stronger days but now,
in his fiftieth year, the jobs were few and far between.

'I ask the chargehands time and again just to give me a
chance. Prove what I can do. But it's like talking to the wall.
They just shake their heads,' he told his wife. Heaving a lungful
of sooty smoke from the belching chimney, Seamus knew his
breathing was getting worse and doubted he would see another
summer. He wondered if he should tell his wife about the

young girl asking about him this morning but thought better of it. Freda was a worrier.

'You can work as well as any man.' Freda's voice hitched in her throat. Always supportive, she knew Seamus did his best, going out day after day in all weathers, but most days it was useless. If it weren't for her job cleaning the dock offices they would have starved long ago. 'Even young men find it hard to get work these days, me darlin',' she said, trying to ease the guilt she knew ate him up inside.

'So, what chance do I have?' Seamus answered, trying hard not to sound bitter, blaming himself for their predicament. 'If we had stayed in Mayo... If we had had just...'

'If ifs and buts were apples and nuts, we'd be greengrocers,' Freda, always one to look on the bright side, chuckled as she bustled around the cramped room, where cooking was done on an iron-barred grate, burning any fuel they could find, including old boots, which he'd brought home this morning. The acrid smell of burning rubber soles made their eyes sting, but what choice did they have? Freda had filled a bucket with water from the outside tap and placed it on the oven attached to the black range, warming water for when it was needed, while the ever-present blackened iron pot hung over the meagre fire.

She took two cups down from the shelf and placed them on the oilcloth table cover, scarred by hot teapots and knife cuts, the inevitable tin of condensed milk sitting in the centre of the table, a wooden trestle on one side so they could eat together. Their situation may have declined, but they still had standards.

A smelly paraffin oil lamp provided the light they needed, and the sleeping quarters were separated from the kitchen by a faded curtain. Seamus had tried so hard to work for his Freda. It was a crying shame.

'I'm not long for this world, old girl.'

'Hush your carping, old man,' Freda said, holding a piece of bread to the iron fender She would not allow him to sink into low spirits. 'Something will turn up soon. I'll have this bread toasted any minute now.' Freda was, trying to spread a little cheer into the dismal day. 'Then you'll be right as rain.' Her husband had been one of the hardest-working men she had ever met. He could put his hand to anything before that terrible day when...

No, don't dwell on that now. A deep breath made her thin shoulders rise as she tried to find something to raise her own spirits.

'I managed to get some scrap-ends of bacon from the butcher,' she said as cheerfully as she could muster, knowing Seamus felt powerless. The *accident* had robbed him, not only of his work, but of his sense of worth. Providing for her had been his goal. If he couldn't do that, he often asked, what good was he?

'Scraps?' he muttered bleakly, holding Freda's gaze for a moment, before looking into the pitiful fire, knowing he was not getting any younger. Every day, his back hunched a little more, his head hung a little lower. *This is what we've come to, and it's all my own fault.*

'Now, now,' Freda gave her beloved husband a warning glance, 'none of that. Going down self-pity road will only lead to a dead end. And that's no good to any of us.'

'You're right, me darlin', I'm sorry.' Seamus despised himself, even more than the man who had shot him, knowing when he was in this black mood his mind was a torment to him.

'Look on the bright side,' Freda said with forced cheer, 'when I get back, I'll bring potherbs and some neck-ends of lamb, then we'll have a good feed. Things always look better on a full stomach.'

'I know.' Seamus nodded, his mind drifting back to this morning. He wondered what the young woman wanted. When Freda went to her cleaning job, he would take a walk down to the infirmary. Just to quieten his curiosity. 'Something will turn up,' he told his Freda before she left for work, knowing she was fighting a losing battle, trying to keep their meagre dwelling clean and warm, but fight it she did, never stopping in her endeavours to make a home for them both, no matter how difficult. Seamus marvelled at her resilience. No matter what life threw at her, Freda saw it through with a smile for everybody. And he knew he too must remain positive for her sake.

The least he could do was give the impression he could see a better tomorrow. He may not be able to provide the comfortable lifestyle they had once enjoyed back home, but, like his beloved wife, he must never give up hope.

Five minutes after Freda left for work, he picked his steaming jacket from the fireguard, put it on, and went back out to the morning squall.

* * *

Mara's loyalty to her father had been unquestioned. But her work in the hospital forced her to face the truth. Suffering was not political. Protestant or Catholic, loyalist or republican, bleeding was bleeding. And everybody on God's earth bled the same colour.

The lean years had taken their toll on the docklands and its people, and there seemed to be no let-up in their poverty-stricken circumstances as far as she could see. The only balm to today's raw feelings of inadequacy was knowing she was doing something – not much, but something to ease the suffering she saw.

There were times when she felt betrayed by the cause, the violence and, yes, even by her own beloved father. His death had left her mother heartbroken and bitter, while she was shuffled like a secret across family lines.

Part of her still clung to loyalty out of love. But another part of her resented how that loyalty had cost her everything. Her safety, her identity, and her peace of mind.

She gave an almost imperceptible sigh as she took another set of handwritten notes from Miss Treadwell to type up. Thinking like this ate her up inside. She didn't like the person she had become. Questioning her father's belief felt like a betrayal.

She spoke his name to nobody, gave nothing away regarding her past, worked silently and diligently, upholding her duties with a dignity that calmed her and suppressed her doubts. But the secret rippled through every connection she made, coloured her trust, her ability to be vulnerable and even what she let others know about her. She wrote letters to her mother. But she never posted them. What could she say to a woman who had lost everything she held sacred. Mara wanted to ask if her mother still believed in the cause. Tell her that the ideals she had been raised on didn't match the pain and suffering she now saw. Emotionally adrift, Mara felt spiritually tethered to a home that no longer existed.

When Miss Treadwell closed the almoner's office for the night, Mara would help out on the wards. In the quiet moments, dressing wounds, spooning broth, reading aloud to patients on the charity ward, she let her heart speak.

Her kindness was instinctive, not political. Here she had a sense of purpose beyond beliefs and ideals. In the eyes of the

infirm and forgotten, she saw echoes of a fractured nation –
worn down but still worth caring for.

When she looked up from feeding a patient, too sick and
weak to manage, she saw a familiar face. His eyes were closed,
but still she recognised the man she saw in the line for a job on
the docks. He had collapsed outside the hospital, one of the
young nurses told her, his breathing was unable to sustain him,
and he was brought onto the ward on a stretcher.

Seamus O'Flanagan. Mara's heart almost stopped when she
read the name on his admission form. After all this time, he
was here in front of her. When he was settled, she approached
his bed with quiet efficiency, but he didn't stir. His wife was
called in and listened more than she spoke, while Mara offered
a gentle hand and steady presence. She treated each patient the
same, with kindness. But her emotions she kept to herself.

As she spent more time among the familiar faces of injured
dockworkers, malnourished children, widowed mothers, Mara
saw a reflection of her own grief in theirs. Unintentionally, she
sometimes offered glimpses of herself: a soft Irish lullaby for a
feverish child, a joke shared with a man who was missing an
arm in a dockside accident. A memory of Mayo when a patient
mentioned sheep in the mist. These moments weren't planned,
and they surprised her. But she built trust and something even
more rare, affection.

Before long, some patients came to her not just for
bandages but for her steadfast reliability, knowing they could
tell her things that would never go any further. Her silence was
like a shelter in life's torment.

As the patients confided in her, something shifted. Something Mara had not known before, and she realised that
offering a quiet dignity spoke volumes. This was surely what

her father might have missed. This was the democracy she could believe in – one of mercy, not martyrdom.

'Don't I know you?' Seamus O'Flanagan asked one morning when she was bringing cups of tea to the patients.

'Do you?' asked Mara, her heartbeat accelerating like a runaway horse. 'I saw you in the line at the docks.'

'No,' said Seamus, 'I never forget a face, and you are the living image of your mother – but, the name is wrong...' His white bushy eyebrows joined in the middle of his forehead. He looked puzzled, racking his brains for an answer.

'I must get on,' said Mara and hurried silently down the middle of the ward. Now the time had come to face the truth, she didn't know if she could bear it.

19

Every act of kindness Mara performed at the hospital built her new identity, yet part of her feared that forgetting who she was dishonoured who her family once were. Her days were filled with listening, comforting the sick, helping the poor, saying little. But inside, her silence was not just saintly patience, it was fear. Fear of speaking the truth about her past. She could lose everything. And yet, the truth clawed at her ribs.

Whispers on the dockside hinted that the man who may have collaborated closely with her father lived here in Liverpool. She didn't know what she would do if she found him.

Confront him? Expose him? Forgive him? That uncertainty shook her tenacity to find the truth. She helped others find peace yet could not find it herself.

Mara's conflict between loyalty and disillusionment was like a thread pulling too tightly – it bound her, but it was fraying at the edges. As a child, she was taught that her father was a hero – a freedom fighter who gave his life for Ireland. This man Seamus O'Flanagan was a recognisable ghost from her past.

Older, more wizened, there was something behind his rheumy eyes that wanted to be set free. She recalled hushed voices in candlelit kitchens that told of her family history, stories of brave men with rifles and causes worth dying for all wrapped up in songs and sorrow.

Trying desperately to understand the beliefs she once held, she was confused. Here in Liverpool, she met men who had lost limbs in Belfast riots, women who fled burned-out villages. Their stories were not poetic. They spoke of chaos, betrayal, and comrades turning on each other.

If the republic her father died for led to this kind of suffering, what was the point? Mara's loyalty to her father, once faithfully unquestioned, began to waver. Her work in the hospital showed her another way of thinking.

She began to feel uncomfortable with the glorification of sacrifice, realising that true courage might lie not in dying for a cause, but in living respectfully for others. The shift in recognition didn't erase her father's memory, nothing could do that. But the insight confused the thoughts in her head and the pain in her heart. If he had lived longer, would Papa have changed too?

There were days when she felt deceived by the cause, the violence, and yes, even by her own beloved father. His departure had left her mother broken and bitter, while she had been shuffled like some enigmatic spirit from one part of the family to another. Never still. Always keeping her eyes and ears open for strangers. Especially strangers.

Part of her clung to loyalty out of love. But another part resented the fact that loyalty cost her everything: safety, identity, and peace.

But even when her faith faltered, she punished herself for

it. To question her father's cause felt like betrayal. She spoke his name rarely, upheld her duties quietly, and suppressed her doubts and fears. But they still surfaced, in her writing, in her prayers, in the haunted way she looked at boys carrying sacks, and shifting crates on the docks, already angry and much too young.

The cause rippled through every connection she made, colouring her trust, her ability to be vulnerable, and even how she refused to let others care for her, get close. She didn't confide in Bridie, or anybody else, apart from the scant information she offered in the station tearoom before Christmas. She said nothing new. Her conversation included work details, nothing personal.

Mara was afraid that if the lady almoner knew the truth about her background, her father's politics, her shadowed identity, then everything might change. More than likely, she would be banished.

Suspicion, especially now with all this talk of unrest in Europe, was rife. Miss Treadwell was keen to keep political matters out of the workplace, and Mara was only too glad to oblige, knowing her family's political views would be a raw cause of conflict in some quarters. She overcompensated by working long hours, avoiding mistakes, always being deferential. Her loyalty to the hospital was never in question, but she never truly let anybody *see* the real her.

There was an older man, Jake, who had joined the staff as a porter. He was once a firebrand union speaker, who so reminded her of the man her father once was. A man who spoke out for what he thought was right, who believed in a fair day's pay for a fair day's labour. But that was not all Mara suspected he was.

She had witnessed his kind before, also his compassion to those less fortunate. She saw him take his last penny out of his pocket and give it to a hungry child. With strong hands and sharp eyes, he had a way of looking at her with a sort of haunted calm, like he could see right inside her soul.

He gently teased her for being 'stuck-up,' unreachable, and she would smile, but say nothing, knowing he was challenging her. Not goading, exactly, but trying to get her to relax enough to trust him.

'You're far too young and beautiful to be stuck in a place like this,' he whispered one day when they were alone in the staffroom. 'This place is for old maids who can do no better,' he said in his usual forthright manner, and for the first time, she laughed out loud.

'You can't say things like that,' she exclaimed, her eyes wide with disbelief that Jake could utter such a bold thing. Sometimes, his outspokenness against the establishment gave her cause to believe she could tell him anything, yet she dared not.

Each time she inched closer to opening her heart, a distant memory held her back. A rebel song, the soft echo of her father's voice saying, *'Some secrets protect more than they destroy.'* She refused to tether anyone to her past... or risk losing the friendship she and Jake had built if he found out the truth. Mara never asked which side he supported, in power, religion or even football. It was none of her business.

'Do you fancy going to the pictures with me?' Jake asked one afternoon and for a moment she was like a rabbit caught in the headlights of an oncoming omnibus. He was a good deal older than she was.

'I have to write to my mother,' Mara said, knowing she never posted the letters she wrote. In them, she asked questions about her father, about why they changed their names, about whether her mother still believed in the cause that separated them. She could not tell Jake what she truly believed. Instead, she told him she was tired. Her work from early morning until late at night left her no time to socialise.

20

Henry Beamer opened the office door to check the corridor was empty. He didn't want any nosy parkers ferreting around the office and telling tales. Seeing the corridor was empty, the only sound he could hear was the blood rushing through his head. Quietly closing the door, his jaw clenched.

'You are doing the right thing, Henry,' his stepmother, Phoebe Beamer, told him from the other side of his desk, upon which he had brought her to the point of ecstasy only moments earlier. The apprehension of being caught had added to her already heightened frisson of desire and the kind of abandonment her pompous blob of a husband, Henry's father, never could. 'All of this will be ours one day.'

Having satisfied his lust, Phoebe was now surplus to Henry's requirements, and he didn't want her hanging around any longer. He had work to do. Work to which she had originally introduced him, but he no longer needed her. He had his own contacts; Karl, who had persuaded Bridie to join him in London, and another in Berlin. Henry walked his own path.

'Won't Father be wondering where you are?' he asked,

noting the flutter of her eyelashes, which usually held a promise, but now looked pathetic. He wanted her gone. However, he knew it would not do to upset her. Phoebe had a destructive temper and, sometimes, she came in very handy. She was the one who had introduced him to the operative in Berlin.

'I should be going,' she said, rising from the chair in one sinuous movement, approaching him, and leaning in for a kiss. Prematurely breaking from her embrace, he quickly headed to the door and unlocked it again, peering along the corridor before turning back to her, putting his finger to his lips.

'The cleaners,' he hissed, 'you must hurry.'

'I will see you later, my darling,' Phoebe whispered before slipping out of the door and along the corridor. 'I will give your father his nightcap and will listen out for your return.'

Henry suspected the nightcap must contain a sleeping draught, because his father was usually unconscious within twenty minutes of drinking it.

'Don't forget you are taking me to the hospital charity fundraiser, seeing as your father isn't well enough to go,' said Phoebe, 'there will be some very important contacts there.'

Henry nodded. How could he forget when she reminded him constantly.

When she left, he locked the office door and looked at his watch. A quick bath and a change of clothes would take him up to the time he was to meet Bridie.

Opening the filing cabinet, he removed a wad of classified documents and slipped them into his briefcase before he left, knowing he would pass them on to officials later.

He descended the wooden steps two at a time down the side of Beamer's factory and headed to his car, almost bumping into Daisy, who had been going over the seating plans with Miss Treadwell in her office at the hospital.

If she hadn't been so deep in conversation with the Irish girl, Mara, Daisy would have seen Phoebe and him leaving the office, and that would have let the cat out of the bag after he had told Bridie he was going to be late, because he had a meeting in Manchester.

* * *

'Off out with Mister Smarm again?' Daisy made no secret of her dislike for Bridie's boyfriend as she watched her sister apply another coat of pillar-box red lipstick to her generous lips.

'What if I am?' Bridie asked, her pencilled eyebrows pleating. 'I don't know what you've got against Henry, he thinks the world of this family.'

'Does he now?' Daisy asked. She didn't believe a word of it. 'That man doesn't think of anybody but himself.'

'He's not like that!' Bridie's face grew red as she dragged the ladder-backed chair from under the dressing table and sat down with a thump. Henry could not live without her. He had told her so before they made love in his car down a country lane. 'You have to admit though, Daisy, he is a bit of a dreamboat, don't you think?'

'A bit of a drip more like,' Daisy said, stretching her arms above her head to take off the white blouse she wore under her business jacket.

'At least I can keep a man,' Bridie whispered, half hoping Daisy heard her. But if she did, her sister didn't take the bait.

'You want to watch him.' Daisy had heard Bridie but decided not to pursue the matter as they went downstairs. 'He's a bit too full of his own importance if you ask me.' And if he saw Phoebe as a mother figure, she would eat her hat. There was something odd going on there. But she would keep the doubt to herself until she had proof. She didn't want to go upsetting Bridie, who seemed a bit on edge lately.

'You will never guess what Mary Jane told me earlier,' said Molly when the girls settled at the table with a nice cup of tea, ready to catch up on all the day's news. She paused just long enough to make sure she had her daughters' undivided attention.

'Come on, Mam, spit it out, it might be a gold watch,' Bridie said, leaving a crimson imprint of her bottom lip on her teacup. She knew her mother liked nothing more than passing on a juicy bit of news.

'She and Cal have only been invited to the hospital charity do!' Molly's voice ended on a squeak, she was so excited, her nostrils flaring in triumph, like she had been the one to set up the invitation in person.

'That would be a dream come true,' Bridie breathed, her eyes wide as Daisy leaned forward. Of course, she knew Mary Jane and her husband Cal had been invited to the charity fundraiser. All successful business people had been invited, and they didn't come much more successful than Mary Jane, who now owned a string of bakery shops across the north-west, and her lovely husband Cal, a prosperous engineer who had been involved in the building of the new Mersey Tunnel, considered to be the eighth wonder of the world when it was opened in July1934 by poor old King George himself, and was now working on the new Anglican cathedral.

'Told me herself, she did. When she got the invitation.' Molly loved to be the first in the know. She had a nose for gossip and was never happier than when she was passing it on, to Ina in particular. 'I think she told me before anybody else.'

Daisy smiled, she would not burst her mother's happy

bubble by telling her that she was the one who sent out the invitations.

'I would love to go,' Bridie sighed, imagining herself walking down the sweeping staircase of The North-Western, while everybody gazed up in admiration from below, like those gorgeous film stars on the pictures.

A heavy-handed knock on the front door stopped the conversation as Molly went to answer.

'Sounds like the rent man,' said Daisy.

'Hello, Mrs Haywood, I like your hair.' Henry's compliments were sickly sweet as Molly led him into the front room.

Molly patted her Marcel waves, which Bridie had styled. 'Very nice of you to say so, I'm sure.' Molly accepted the tribute, knowing Bridie had been going out with Henry much longer than any of her other boyfriends. It would be lovely if they got engaged, or even... dare she think it? Imagining her Bridie being the wife of a managing director of Beamer's. Their Freddy would certainly get his promotion then. She could have a word, on the quiet, like.

'My mother wore her hair that way, too – when she was alive, of course,' said Henry, and Molly gave him a look of compassion that words could not better. But that didn't mean she was not going to say them anyway.

'I understand suffering,' she said, her voice full of regret. 'When my Albert died, I thought my life was over...'

'Don't dwell on it now, Mam,' said Bridie quickly. She had heard this story a million times and she was in no mood to let her mother put a damper on her evening. Bridie didn't even know her father. He passed over before she was even born. 'Henry has just paid you a lovely compliment.'

'Our Bridie does the best Marcel waves in Liverpool,' Molly

said, changing her voice to a more cheerful tone in the blink of an eye. 'Nice and deep.'

'Don't you think Henry looks like King Edward?' Bridie repeated her observation as she gazed fondly.

'I can't see it myself,' said Daisy, wishing her sister didn't think Henry was the be-all and end-all of manhood. He still hadn't told her he was invited to the fundraiser. Nor that his partner for the evening was Phoebe! Daisy was desperate to tell her sister everything. But decided to wait a little longer, determined to get to the bottom of Henry's devious intentions.

21

Next morning, Davey wandered into the kitchen and flopped down onto the brown leather sofa to read the *Daily Express*.

'Hiya, Dais, you look nice. New hat?' Daisy wore a fetching pale blue pudding bowl style with a matching velvet bow on the side.

'I'm going into town,' she said. 'I've ordered new uniforms for the fundraiser dinner and I'm going to pay for them. They are being delivered tomorrow.' Daisy wanted the staff to look pristine for this function, where anyone who was anybody would be in attendance. She had ordered the plain black dresses, white frilled aprons, white caps, and black stockings a couple of weeks ago.

'Well, isn't that just the ticket, my much obliging sister,' said Davey from behind his newspaper. He was home on weekend leave and was making the most of it by doing nothing except lounging around and reading the newspaper.

'What are you after?' She smiled, suspicious when one of her brothers decided to pay a compliment.

'I'm not after anything,' he said, feigning interest in the

news, 'but I was just thinking... seeing as you are going into town, anyway.'

'I'm going to George Henry Lee in Basnett Street,' Daisy answered.

'In that case, would you be a sweetheart,' Davey used his most persuasive tone, 'and pick up a couple of books I ordered...'

'I don't suppose you want me to read them for you too?'

'That would be a great help, and if you could take my exam that would be wonderful.' Davey was studying for his Master Mariner's licence, which would allow him to serve as the master of any merchant ship operating anywhere in the world – the highest level of professional qualification – but most important of all, making Molly the proudest mother in Beamer Street. 'I want to earn enough money to buy my own house somewhere nice, with a garden big enough to grow my own food.'

'Well, I don't think Mam will be digging in the soil while you're careering around the world. Mind you, I think Percy would take to the idea.'

'Put it this way,' said Davey, and he lowered his voice in case his mother was within hearing distance, 'one day, we may have to grow our own food.'

'What makes you say that?' asked Daisy.

With rumblings of unrest in Europe, notably Spain, Italy, and Germany, with the slew of fascist dictators at the helm, Davey had enough worldly knowledge to know that the first line of attack in case of hostilities towards this country would be to disrupt food supplies and stop them getting through. But he wasn't going to start scaremongering.

'You'd be amazed at how much of our food comes from overseas,' Davey answered grimly, 'most of the things we use every day come from abroad. I want to grow my own. Eat it fresh from the soil in my own garden.'

'Is that the only reason?' Daisy asked, remembering how her mother had to scrimp and scrape by, years ago, when their father was at war in Flanders.

Davey said nothing. He couldn't. Not even to warn his own family. But he knew Daisy wasn't daft.

'Surely the powers that be in this country wouldn't be so foolish as to go to war again – not after the last time.' The country had nearly lost a whole generation of young men on land, at sea and in the air. 'Memories are not that short, surely?'

'It's the quickest way to win a war. Starve us into submission. I know Liverpool docks are gearing up for every eventuality. They are already taking on more men. And you mark my words, the powers that be don't give a damn, especially that German despot whose bully boys are killing their own Jewish countrymen,' he rested his newspaper on his lap. 'The men at the top want ultimate power. They want a superior Aryan race of Germans. The leaders are unhinged – believe me, I know. We have to be prepared,' Davey said, and by the sombre look in his eyes, Daisy could see he was not joking. There had been war rumours since the last one. But nothing ever happened. It was all hot air and nonsense.

'I don't give it much thought,' said Daisy, knowing there were going to be some high-profile Germans at the charity fundraiser. 'I'm sure it won't come to that,' she said, changing the subject. She didn't know enough about the situation, but she did read the papers. 'So, about those books?'

Davey was glad the subject was closed, knowing, as Max did, that given the preparations going on behind the scenes, war could be nearer than people contemplated.

'Have a penny for going,' Davy laughed, using the phrase his mother would use when she sent them on an errand.

'Don't skint yourself now,' Daisy laughed too, knowing he was trying to take her mind off their earlier conversation.

'It's good of you to collect the books,' Davey said, 'I'll pay your overhead rail fare.'

'There's really no need; I'm going into town anyway. So, it's no hardship.' Also, it would be nice to do a bit of window shopping. And, hopefully, her trip would take her mind off Max and why he always blew hot and cold.

Not that she expected to see him when he was working, anyway. Nor was he under any obligation to call her. But why was he so devoted when he visited, yet so remote when he left?

* * *

Daisy collected Davey's books from the library in William Brown Street and put them in her basket before heading towards the German Consulate to deliver the invitations, which had been added to the list yesterday, when she saw a large crowd of demonstrators moving in the same direction, protesting about the Nazis' dreadful treatment of Jews in Germany and Austria since that awful Hitler had come to power.

The demonstration was slowing her down, and she didn't want to be late, so Daisy cut through the shops around Church Street and headed on towards the south end of Liverpool. When she reached the Rodney Street address, she was not surprised to see the flag of Nazi Germany flying over the door of the building. The flag, with its red background showing a black swastika on a white disc, had been adopted as one of Germany's duel national flags following the appointment of

Adolf Hitler. It flew on every organisation operated by Germans, even here in Liverpool. But for some unknown reason, the sight made Daisy shudder.

'Good afternoon, madam,' said a polite young German whose blond hair was immaculately brushed, his blue eyes shining as he held open the door for her to enter. 'This way,' he said, dressed in a black *Allgemeine* SS uniform, and led her across the highly polished parquet floor to a double door.

As she entered, a man of indeterminate age stood up and held out his hand. Behind him, above the fireplace, was a huge picture of the German chancellor, Herr Hitler, and something about his staring eyes made Daisy feel uncomfortable, like he was watching her every move. She quickly delivered the invitations, said her goodbyes and left the embassy.

22

A bitter wind blew in off the Mersey, even though the sun was shining. Daisy was glad she had worn her warm woollen coat with its wide lapels and turn-back sleeves. Although her feet, clad in two-tone Cuban-heeled Oxford brogues, were soaking wet and she needed a reviving cup of hot tea.

Crossing the busy road from Church Street to Reece's cafe on the corner of Parker and Leigh Street, Daisy was glad of the warmth that cocooned her as she entered the cafe. Soft jazz music playing in the background, the smell of toasted teacakes and the low buzz of conversation all brought back memories of the night Max had brought her here. They had gone upstairs to the top floor ballroom where he folded her in his arms. She had never felt so loved, so wanted. The following day he was gone.

Daisy found a secluded booth, took off her damp rain-spattered coat, and settled when the waitress went to fetch her order, her eyes slowly scanning the room. She looked forward to relaxing with a warming cup of tea and rereading the list of things Miss Treadwell had requested for the charity fundraiser when she caught sight of him.

Max had his back to her. But she would recognise him anywhere. He was unmistakable in a navy-blue Crombie overcoat. And even though he was seated, with his back to her, there was no mistaking the deep, educated timbre of his voice. That self-assured presence she was immediately and so emotionally drawn to.

Daisy held herself rigid, taking deep steadying breaths that did nothing to slow the rapid thundering of her heart. She should run. What if he turned and saw her? Daisy slid down in her seat. As this powerful feeling overtook her, she was unable to stand or even move when her senses took in the bigger picture.

Max was engaged in animated conversation with a little girl of about four or five, dressed in a pale blue woollen coat and matching hat. The woman sitting opposite Max was smiling fondly at both him and the little girl. The group looked so happy, content, and Daisy felt she was intruding just by watching them. But she could not drag her gaze from this happy snapshot of family harmony.

She was here. On her own. While Max was with his family. She didn't belong here. The realisation created not only raw hurt, but also something else. She felt ashamed. Because from Boxing Day until a few moments ago, Daisy had been swept up in some kind of romantic haze, believing Max had really felt something for her. She imagined he was away on business, which was why he hadn't been to see her.

That had not been the case. Obviously, given the scene being played out before her very eyes, Max saw their bond only as a casual friendship, whereas she had put her heart on the line. She had left herself wide open and vulnerable. When the day and the night, especially the night, was over, when his kiss meant everything to her and she sailed to her bed on a cloud of bliss, savouring the imprint of his kiss on her lips. When she refused to feel guilty for breaking off her engagement to Harvey and letting the whispers of disdain go unanswered, she knew she had done the right thing. After five long years Max had returned to her.

But she had expected too much, and the kiss meant nothing to him. And now she knew why. Max was a married man. Daisy suspected he hadn't given her a second thought once he left Beamer Street. She imagined he was satisfied by the day, which had been pleasant enough, then blithely trundled off to wifey. And his real life.

The saliva in Daisy's mouth turned to glue. She would never have believed Max could lead her on like that if she hadn't seen the proof with her own eyes. He had been so attentive, so... Dare she even think it? So, loving. But now Daisy thought about it, Christmas was the perfect atmosphere for romantic thoughts.

How could she have been so stupid. Daisy knew she had to get out of here before she was spotted. If Max saw her, she would never be able to hold her head up again. She had to leave.

The curly-haired child giggled softly as her mother bent to wipe something from her face leading Max to reach over and touch her hand. It was a small and simple gesture, but to Daisy it felt like a slap in the face.

Blindly reaching to grab her belongings, Daisy knocked the basket, and the books fell to the floor with a loud clatter. Annoyed she was drawing attention to herself, she pushed back a chair, making a loud scraping noise as the legs protested along the floor, alerting the few people who may have missed the books clattering episode, and were now all too aware of the madwoman scrambling across the floor as the waitress approached her table. Quickly depositing the tray onto the table, she bent to help Daisy.

'No, it's fine, I've got it,' Daisy's rapid-fire words were tense. She did not want to draw attention to herself, but she was doing just the opposite. *Calm down, Daisy.*

Every person in the cafe was staring, she was sure. Then, she suddenly noticed a pair of buckskin shoes next to the hard-backed book on the black and white chequered floor.

Raising her eyes, she saw the little girl bend down and pick up the book. As Daisy stood up, the child held out her hand and offered it to her. Her blue grey eyes, so like her father's, were twinkling with delight.

'Thank you,' Daisy whispered.

Max had said he was on a working trip in London when he'd telephoned her just two days ago. Yet, here he was, large as life with his wife and daughter! He'd lied to her. And the innocent smile from the friendly little girl made her heart lurch.

How could he do this? To her. To them.

What did you expect? The voice inside her head was mocking. Of course, he was going to be married. *Men like him don't wait around, until the dried-up old spinsters earn their fortune. Fool!*

Daisy had desperately tried to keep romantic thoughts at bay, but it was impossible. Longing for him. Yearning to hear his voice. She had spent every night, dreaming of nobody and nothing, but Max. Imagining the feel of his gentle caress on her love-starved body. But now she knew that was never going to happen.

Hindsight is a wonderful thing.

Max stood up now, helping his wife into her coat and kissing her on the cheek.

'Daisy, fancy seeing you here!' Max's voice, deep and mellow, sailed across the floor as moved towards her table after telling his wife he would see her back at the house. The attractive woman smiled as she passed by and then she was gone. 'I tried to call you this morning, but...'

'Don't give it another thought.' Daisy's words were sharp, abrupt. She did not need his excuses. 'Obviously you are busy.' *And you forgot to mention a wife last time we talked.*

'Please, come over and have a cup of tea,' he said, nodding in the direction of his little girl. 'I'd love you to meet Poll.'

'I'm in a bit of a hurry,' Daisy insisted.

Max picked up Daisy's basket, pretending not to hear the frantic pleading in her voice. He had wanted their reunion to be perfect, not like this. However, if this was the way it was meant to be, so be it. They would have to make the most of it. He knew, by the time they reached the table where Poll was now seated, he wanted to ask her something very important, if she would be prepared to take him on.

'Poll, this is my very good friend Daisy. She bakes cakes,' said Max, who did not even try to hide the absolute adoration he had for this little girl, whose sparkling eyes were smiling up at them. 'And Daisy this is my daughter, Miss Marguerite Galant, or to give her a proper title, little Poll.'

'Oh Daddy, you are the only one who calls me little Poll,' she said. 'Everybody else calls me by my real name,' said the child, who turned to Daisy and said, 'I have a loose tooth.'

Daisy didn't expect to smile, nor did she intend to smile. But given this little girl's openly friendly, assured nature, it was impossible not to.

'Daisy has come to have tea with us, Poll, isn't that wonderful?' Max seemed genuinely pleased, while Daisy wondered what he was up to.

'Yes, Daddy, that's wonderful.' Poll gave a wide smile and pushed out her bottom tooth with her little pink tongue. 'Daddy promised me cake; did you make it?'

'Not this one,' Daisy answered, dubiously taking the seat Max had pulled out for her.

'You will have some too,' said Poll, and Daisy felt the child had included her in some kind of innocent collusion.

'That's very kind of you,' Daisy answered, 'but I'm sure your daddy didn't mean for me to have some.'

'Of course, he did,' answered the little girl, whose unassuming straightforward manner made Daisy feel a closeness she didn't expect to feel, 'he is the kindest daddy in the whole world, and when I grow up, I'm going to marry him.'

'Won't your mummy have something to say about that?' Daisy asked while Max ordered a pot of tea and a selection of cream cakes.

'No,' said Poll, her little forehead wrinkling, 'she doesn't say anything.'

How could Max be so relaxed about this, thought Daisy, her shame replaced with confusion. He was acting like this meeting was the most natural thing in the world and for her to be sitting here with him and his young daughter, sharing a pot of tea and cakes – after what he had done! He seemed eager for her to engage with his daughter initially, but now, watching them both with unreadable interest, he seemed a little nervous, which was understandable, she supposed.

Daisy imagined the raw betrayal his daughter would experience, if she were ever to find out Daddy had kissed a woman who was not her mother. Even though, when she kissed Max, Daisy didn't know he was married or even that Poll existed.

Her cup of tea remained untouched, knowing she could not swallow a thing, not even her pride. 'I'm so sorry, I have to rush off,' she told Poll, trying desperately not to look at Max. 'I have an appointment. But it has been lovely to meet you.'

'It's been lovely to meet you too,' said Poll, and held out her hand. Daisy took it in hers, it felt so small, and she gently shook it. 'Maybe Daddy will let us have afternoon tea again one day, when you don't have to rush off.'

'That would be nice.' *But unlikely*, Daisy thought. She was going to be no man's mistress. Not even Max.

Standing up to leave, he leaned forward, kissing her cheek and Daisy felt the heat rise from her neck to her face. The gall of the man! In front of his daughter too!

'Will you tell Davey I'll call in to see him with the negatives in the next day or so.'

'Negatives?' She felt dazed, as if walking through her own nightmare.

'He may want to get another set of photographs developed – of Christmas,' Max said, and then the penny dropped.

'You could post them.' Daisy's words were blunt, her shock still palpable. She wanted nothing more to do with a man who could introduce his own daughter to... To whom? Who was she to Max? A friend? A recruit into his bed. The thought shocked her.

Daisy could not be sure if she ran out of the cafe, but she reached the street in double quick time, heading towards the tram stop, inhaling the smoky air of the cold, wet street, and reached the stop just as her tram pulled up.

Sitting down, she wiped the condensation from the window and looked out. Seeing nothing. Her mind full of questions she could not answer. Her heart full to bursting with regret and shame, at the yearning thoughts she found so difficult to erase from her memory.

What had she done? If her mother found out she had kissed a married man, she would never be the same again. If there was one thing Mam could not abide, it was a woman who played fast and loose with another woman's husband. She could hear Molly now.

Trollops the lot of them.

23

'How would you like to go to a posh do in town one weekend?' Henry whispered to Bridie. He could find a use for this dazzler of a girl he'd met at Christmas. She was a ray of sunshine on a gloomy day, and although she would not allow him to explore her slim curves as often as Phoebe did, he could see she would fit into his plans very well. Especially now.

'Where were you thinking of taking me?' Bridie whispered, ignoring the shushing of her immediate neighbours in the picture house.

'To paradise,' Henry whispered intimately into her ear.

'Henry, you are shocking!' Bridie answered with a throaty giggle. He did say the most outrageous things, sometimes. But she wasn't satisfied with his vague answer. She wanted his guarantee she would be the girl on his arm at the charity fundraiser. And he wasn't going to have the pleasure of her delights if she wasn't going to accompany him.

'I know you're not that kind of girl,' he assured her, pulling her closer, 'and you know I would never disrespect you if...'

'Ignore them,' Bridie said hearing the shushing audience,

snuggling into his shoulder, knowing already what his body felt like on top of hers. She loved being brought to the point of ecstasy, just like the girls in work said she would... but she had held out lately, driving him to distraction until he promised to take her to the biggest charity fundraiser of the year.

'If you give me the date of the charity fundraiser you mentioned,' Bridie said in her most seductive tone, knowing he intended to take that jezebel Phoebe on his father's behalf. But she would soon see about that. 'I'll check I'm not working that weekend.'

'It's Easter Saturday, a busy day for you at the salon, I imagine. By invitation only.' His mind was racing, not wanting to lose the chance of a tangle in the back seat of his car. 'But I'll see what I can do to get you an invite.' Henry did not want to tell her where the dance was being held, hoping she didn't ask questions. 'It's all very hush-hush at the moment.'

'I can't think why,' said Bridie, not easily impressed.

'I heard there are some very important people attending – and I mean *very* important people.'

'I'm booked to work on Easter Saturday, but I'll make some excuse and get the time off work.' She liked the sound of very important people and did not intend to miss out. She noticed the muscles in his jaw tighten and suspected he wasn't happy about the situation. But Bridie was determined. Henry would get what he wanted when she got what she wanted. 'All's fair in exclusive invitations, Henry, it cuts both ways.'

'What if you couldn't get time off?' Henry said realising Bridie, with her perfect locks and voluptuous figure, would have his friends from the German embassy, eating out of his hand. 'If you can't come, Phoebe will be only too happy.'

'Don't you worry about that. I'll get the time off,' Bridie said quickly, 'we will have such fun that night – but not before.' She playfully tapped the tip of his nose and saw his expression change to that hard stare he displayed when things weren't going his way.

'Not before?' he said and she shook her head. He could see how his plan to pass on important documents would be much easier if Bridie were the woman to accompany him, she would dazzle any man rather than Phoebe, who, he was certain, would understand.

'I *really* want to go with you, Henry.' Bridie said, her eyes holding a seductive invitation.

'Well, you know what they say about one good turn deserving another, Bridie.' *Game, set and match!* His loins were on fire.

* * *

When the lights went up in the picture house, Bridie blinked rapidly. She had been so lost in Henry's urgent kisses. She didn't even know what the film was about. On the way home, she hoped her mother wasn't up to ask about the film.

When she pushed her key into the polished brass Yale lock, letting them both into the darkened house, Henry could not keep his hands off her, but she had not counted on Daisy being still up.

'Bridie Haywood! What do you think you are doing? Coming in at this hour!' Daisy, still smarting from seeing Max and his daughter during her sojourn into town, was not best pleased when she saw her younger sister sneaking Henry into the house.

He looked like the cat who got the cream, a bit too sure of himself for Daisy's liking. She heard Bridie's small gasp of surprise, and in the firelight a quick sweep of her dark eyes told

Daisy that Beamer was more worldly-wise than her lively, trusting sister, who always seemed to fall for a scoundrel.

Henry gave Daisy a challenging look, daring her to throw him out when he had been invited in by her younger sister. But that meant nothing to Daisy, who knew he was out to snare her beautiful sister any way he could. And she could think of nothing worse than Bridie being tied to a man like him for the rest of her days.

Caught red-handed, Bridie's pretty face become a blushing flood in every shade of pink. 'Oh Daisy, we've been to see *The Little Rascals*,' Bridie said, quickly covering her guilty shenanigans, knowing her mother would never allow Henry, or anybody else for that matter, into the house once it had been locked up for the night. 'Henry has invited me to that posh charity fundraiser on Easter Saturday.'

Daisy could understand why his father would be invited, being a local rich businessman, but she could not see any reason why Henry would attend a charity fundraiser? He had nothing to do with the charity as far as she knew. But Beamer's business was none of hers, Daisy knew.

However, her sister was very much her business, and, against all her natural feelings of fair play, Daisy hoped that Bridie would see sense and dump him.

The angry retort earlier, when Daisy had tried to offer a little sisterly advice, still stung. Bride accused her of being jealous because she didn't have a man of her own. Daisy had longed to snipe back but knew it would be useless to do so. When Bridie was in this stubborn mood, it would take a ten-ton truck to move her to change her mind.

Bridie obviously had a blind spot for his shortcomings, and Daisy itched to enlighten her sister, who was much too good for the likes of him. Money or no money.

But she would be wasting her breath. Loyal to her family or not, Bridie's head had been turned by this slimy toad of a man. Although Daisy would never do anything to embarrass Bridie in front of an outsider. And Henry was most certainly one of those.

'Well, it was good of you to bring Bridie home safely,' Daisy said briskly, having seen enough of him already and longing to slide into her bed and sleep, knowing she would not be able to rest until Bridie was tucked up in her own bed, safe and sound. 'I must be up early to start work on the charity fundraiser, I hope you have deep pockets. The hospital needs all the help it can get,' Daisy said, ushering Henry towards the door. 'So, we will bid you goodnight, Henry.'

'I'll see Henry out.' Bridie sounded vexed. 'You go on up to bed.' Her remark made Henry smirk, and Daisy gave a tight smile. She did not want to undermine her sister. But she would if he did not stop grinning like a Cheshire cat.

'No. You go on up to bed, Bridie,' Daisy said in that no-nonsense tone that was rarely challenged. 'I'll lock up...' She walked behind Henry, her hand on his back, urging him towards the front door. 'As I said before, it's late, so goodnight, Henry. Bridie will see you tomorrow.'

When he was out of the door, she closed it firmly behind him.

'I'll make myself a cup of cocoa,' said Bridie, 'do you want one?'

'There's no need,' Daisy answered, resuming the role she knew her sister would not argue with. 'I've made you a hot drink, it's on your bedside table. Goodnight, Bridie.'

'Goodnight.' Bridie sounded peeved, but she agreed, much to Daisy's relief.

'I'll just check everywhere is locked up, and I'll be away to my bed,' Daisy said, making sure her sister had no last-minute deeds of defiance, like calling Henry back after she had gone to bed for the night. Bridie had become even more of a rebel since she'd met Henry.

Daisy dragged her tired legs up the stairs. She knew how to handle Bridie's rebellious moods. But what about the alternative, like an engagement or, God forbid, a wedding? It was too terrible to contemplate. The thought of her sister marrying such a man weighed heavily on her shoulders, and she was sure that it would all end in tears. Henry reminded her of Karl, with his smarmy ways in her mother's presence. A wolf in sheep's clothing if ever there was one.

'But what will be will be,' she whispered, resigning herself to not being able to change Bridie's mind once it was made up. She knew that her mother would never be able to manage Bridie on her own.

As she made her way along the landing, to the bedroom she had slept in all her life, Daisy passed her mother's bedroom, glad her mam had got a second chance at matrimonial happiness with Percy. She pondered on the improbable thought that it would have been nice if she had found one good man, let alone two. But she didn't begrudge Mam her happiness after what she had been through, widowed young with four children to raise on her own. That was tragic. She deserved the happiness Percy showered her with. Refusing to feel sorry for herself, Daisy wondered why life had to be so complicated where some men were concerned.

But she must not think those kinds of thoughts now. Max was a married man with a child, maybe more, and she was not part of that. Any dreams of romance she may have secretly nurtured well and truly squashed. Never to be revisited.

What you've never had, you'll never miss. Molly's words were as clear as if she were standing next to her. But Daisy knew her mam was wrong on that score. Not having a man of her own was the one thing she did miss. But not just any man. She desperately missed having Max in her life.

In the night's darkness, she could not stop thinking about him. The way he had been so attentive to her. And as she wearily climbed into her lonely single bed, Daisy's exhausted thoughts were not capable of dwelling on what could have been.

Her feet edged towards the hot water bottle that had taken the chill from her bed, but not from her heart, and she knew that was the only comfort she would be allowed tonight, not the loving arms of a good man. So, like a whole generation of women, she was bound to be single for the rest of her life.

In the blink of an eye, her alarm clock was jangling into her muddled thoughts and secret dreams, and Daisy knew it was time to drag herself from her warm bed to face another day, to prepare the food for the charity fundraiser.

24

Davey Haywood glanced in the hall mirror, he'd just returned from the barber's shop, not trusting Bridie to cut his hair before he returned to his ship. But, with hindsight, Davey knew he should have had more faith in his younger sister's talents.

'Would you look at this, Mam, I said short back and sides, not short back and whip it all off.' Davey spat on his hand, trying to flatten the crown of hair, which was sticking up like a cock's comb, and he grimaced at his reflection. 'It's going to take more than a drop of liquid paraffin to get that to sit down.'

'You're worse than our Bridie,' said Molly, 'always looking at yourself in the mirror.' She thought her son's new haircut looked very smart, though, and was visibly proud of her good-looking offspring, who all had a look of their handsome father, her first husband, Bert. He also had a swarthy Mediterranean look about him, while Percy, her second husband, was grey now, in a very distinguished looking way, and the best husband any woman could wish for. 'Have you seen what that cheeky Bridie has done?' Molly asked, standing in the hallway as her husband came through the front door, home for his midday meal.

Percy shook his head. 'Nothing Bridie does surprises me,' he chuckled, lighting his pipe. Easy-going and friendly to everybody, Percy was his usual affable self.

'She's only gone and had her hair lightened even more with powder bleach and peroxide, like that film star, Jean Harlow.' Molly knew Bridie was starstruck when she had her hennaed hair lightened by her new employer, Madam Fontane, the eponymous owner of a high-class salon in Bold Street. However, unbeknown to Molly, her daughter had an ulterior motive for dyeing her hair.

A sudden knock on the vestibule door stopped any further conversation.

'Hello, Max,' Molly beamed. She knew her daughter Daisy and Max had been close a few years ago, but his job as a reporter took him away, and she wasn't sure Daisy had ever got over Max. She hadn't been her usual chirpy self since Christmas, and Molly was getting worried. Nothing fazed Daisy, usually. But even her work wasn't bringing her the enthusiasm she usually showed.

'I've been working in London, Mrs Pierce,' said Max. 'I got home a few days ago and saw Daisy in Reece's cafe.' He needed to explain. Daisy deserved that much. 'She dropped her books. This one was hiding under the chair, so I've come to return it.'

'I was gonna ask her about that,' said Davey, realising one of his books was missing.

'You say *going to*, Davey, not *gonna*!' Turning to her son, Molly admonished him. 'You are not in America now. I won't have common talk in this house.' Then, turning back to Max, she saw the light of amusement in his eyes. 'He might be master of his own ship one day, but our Davey is still not too old to be scolded by his mother.'

'So, I see.' Max grinned. His good friend managed a crew of burly, tough-talking men who sailed turbulent, sometimes dangerous oceans with the assurance of a reliable second officer in the merchant navy. But he would never cheek his mother.

'Do you enjoy working at the post office, Max?' asked Molly, naturally inquisitive. Her inclination to ask as many questions as she could get into a few minutes of conversation was legendary in Beamer Street. Not that she was nosy, she told anybody who cared to listen; she just liked people.

'He doesn't work at the post office, Ma—' Davey grinned and shook his head '—he reports on current affairs, makes documentaries. Public information programmes you see at the pictures. That kind of thing.'

'Have you met anybody famous?' Molly asked, her voice rising with excitement.

'I've met a few famous people,' Max said, and Davey gave him a silent thank-you for changing the subject so quickly, 'and yes, you will have seen them on the pictures, Mrs P.' Max answered Molly's question with a happy-go-lucky smile that belied his strong belief there was trouble brewing in Europe. 'But, if I may say so, none were as lovely as you.' Max then adopted a broad Cockney accent when he said, 'Ain't you a picture in your flowered 'at.' His jovial banter disguised his usual clipped, middle-class articulation. 'D'you know something—' Max dropped the accent '—in this light, you could be a dead ringer for Elizabeth, the Duchess of York.'

Molly's face glowed at the tribute, and Max realised by the pink tinge on her cheeks he could not have paid her a higher compliment. Molly loved the royal family and talked about them like they were a loving, but distant part of her own family.

If only she knew what King Edward the eighth was getting up to, thought Max, who knew a gentleman's agreement between British reporters kept news of his relationship with a divorced American woman out of the newspapers. Nevertheless, the American and Canadian broadcasters had agreed no such thing and were having a field day about the new king's relationship with the twice-married woman, who, it was rumoured, was also having a relationship that put her in the position of serving as a German spy, to the point, ministers had begun to edit and withhold some information shared with the King.

'The Duchess is the epitome of style and dignity, don't you think?' Molly said, taking a sideways glance in the oval mirror. 'It's a shame King Edward couldn't find himself a nice wife to share his new position with.'

Max decided to keep the news under his hat that King Edward had threatened to abdicate if he was not allowed to marry a twice-divorced American. But for how long could the news be suppressed. He really didn't know.

'You are such a flatterer,' said Molly. 'I can see now why our Daisy likes you so much,' she laughed, giving Max a playful nudge with her elbow.

'Does she really?' Max was delighted.

The door opened and Max saw Daisy coming out into the hallway, her dark Mediterranean eyes skewering him with steely regard.

'Here she is now,' Molly said, proudly, but a little surprised Daisy didn't look thrilled.

Daisy hadn't realised Max was in the house. She hadn't seen him since their awkward meeting in the cafe. The meeting that smashed her dreams to a thousand pieces. Flitting off to foreign countries to marry was just one of his many talents. Failing to reveal it was another.

'Here, Dais,' said Davey, 'Max brought back the book you dropped.'

'How kind.' Daisy's words were dull and flat as she looked Max in the eyes.

'It was under your seat,' Max said, his eyes pleading for a chance to explain.

'That was good of him.' Daisy could hear the brittle tone in her own voice, but she couldn't help it. She had desperately hoped he would contact her, but that was before she discovered he was married and had a daughter.

She had never told anybody that Max was the only man she had truly loved. But she was sure her family noticed at the Christmas party, which was why she felt so humiliated now.

'Have you seen what our Bridie's done to her hair?' Molly cut in, noticing an atmosphere developing. 'If you think our Davey's always admiring himself, he's got nothing on our Bridie.'

'You could put her in a cage with a bell and a mirror. She'd be in her element.' Daisy gave the same practised smile she reserved for her clients.

'She offered to colour Mara's hair too,' said Molly, 'the poor girl nearly fainted with horror.'

25

The ward smelled of strong disinfectant, toast and woodsmoke from the nearby timber yards as Mara moved silently between the narrow iron beds, checking dressings, plumping pillows, and offering sips of water with the same diligence in everything she did.

At the far end of the ward, near the long sash window, a draught crept in unnoticed by all except Seamus O'Flanagan's arthritic bones. He sat upright, unable to lie down for the coughing fits that wracked his body again since his last visit. Seamus had been admitted twice in just a few months, and the prognosis didn't look good this time, thought Mara. Late fifties, wiry, he was a former ship's stoker with a chest like an oil drum, and lungs ruined by years of dock work.

'I'm back again, Miss Mara,' he said, his voice rasping like cold cinders caught under a door. He didn't smile, but there was a gentle betrayal of fondness in his rheumy eyes.

Mara pressed the back of her hand against his forehead, checking for fever.

'Nurse will bring your cough syrup,' said Mara, 'the one you call liquid nails.'

'Foul stuff.' Seamus gave a theatrical shudder and Mara smiled. There was something about Seamus that touched her heart, making her more caring and observant towards him. Not just because he came from the same place she did and was said to be the man who was with her father the day he died. She had yearned to know the truth for such a long time. Now there was a chance to find out, Mara felt too afraid to face it.

'Try to rest,' she said, adjusting his pillows into a more comfortable position, so he could breathe easier. His wife had not long left the ward, causing Seamus to become a bit quieter. 'Nurse will be around with your cocoa soon,' Mara said.

'Do you like working here, tending the would-be ghosts in God's waiting room?'

'That's not how I see the patients,' said Mara. 'The medical staff do their best to make people better.'

'For what?' Seamus asked, and Mara could hear the hint of bitterness in his tone. He wanted to talk tonight. He had been at death's door when they had brought him in, gasping for every breath.

'Now, now, Mr O'Flanagan,' said Mara who would never be so bold as to address him by his Christian name, 'you mustn't give up hope.' How she longed to ask him if he was the same Seamus O'Flanagan who knew her father all those years ago. But she feared a resurgence of the past might undo the good work of the medics to make him stronger.

'What's your name, Nurse?' he asked, and Mara froze. She wanted to distract him by telling him she wasn't a nurse, but assistant to the lady almoner who helped the other nurses before doctor's rounds, but she knew Seamus would never fall for the distraction.

'My name's Mara,' she said as the air seemed to still.

'Not that one. Your surname?' Seamus insisted and she took a deep silent breath.

'Foy – Mara Foy.'

'You remind me of a girl I once knew back in County Mayo, married to a young doctor, not long out of medical school.'

Mara was silent. Not a breath, not a blink, but the kind of pause only someone truly watching would notice. She knew who he was talking about, but dare she ask. The revelation she was from Mayo stayed hidden behind her closed lips. She could not say anything.

'I bet you say that to all the Irish nurses.' Mara's smile was tight, her touch efficient, before moving to the end of the bed when the glint of something caught her eye. She turned but whatever Seamus had in his hand was now put safely in the locker beside his bed.

* * *

The following evening, after visiting time, while writing down daily observations in her large ledger, Mara noticed the polished brass watch fob, or at least half of one, sitting on the locker. Her fingers stilled and she couldn't drag her gaze from the sight of the identical other half of the fob hidden under her bed.

'You recognise it, don't you?' Seamus said, his gravelled voice barely a whisper. Mara nodded but said nothing. He tilted his head to one side. 'You know the name O'Murchu.' It wasn't a question.

Mara's world suddenly got smaller.

She stood so still, yet the jug of water in her hand trembled.

She shook her head and softly whispered, 'No.' He didn't press her.

Seamus asked her to sit for a while. He had something he wanted to tell her. He spoke in fragments – *ambush at Athenry, a man with a laugh like thunder, calling out orders in Irish. Grinning like he'd already died and come back proud.*

Seamus didn't mention the man's name, but Mara knew. *After being released following his arrest, he led hundreds of local men in occupying Moyode Castle. Within days a local priest informed us that the rising had failed. A young lad of seventeen. Terrified. Pulled from the line of fire.*

'"*You're not dying for this. Not today,*" said your pa, as he dragged young Jake out of harm's way.' The memory cracked his voice. 'He pushed my young brother under the haycart. Saved his life... I thought your pa had made it,' Seamus whispered. 'We scattered when more shots came. But they said... they said your pa had been taken. I never saw him again.'

Mara said nothing, clutching the hem of her jacket like a lifeline. Her chest ached with a strange, painful gratitude. This man had actually seen her father alive, witnessed his last unselfish act. The stories of his bravery were not a myth after all. They were true.

'This is yours,' Seamus said, holding the remaining half of the round brass fob 'your da dropped it when he made that last run for freedom. The bullet broke the clasp and well... you know the rest.' Seamus handed her the other half of the identical one under her bed. 'I kept it in the hope it might mean something to somebody.' He looked at her with tenderness in his pale blue eyes.

'He was a good man, a kind man who helped so many of his countrymen.' Mara's voice cracked.

'His name will live on in the hearts of those who knew him,' said Seamus, 'and even some who didn't. I understand why you changed your name. The change will keep you safe. Because there are still people who believe your father passed on names and places, and that knowledge would prove dangerous.'

When Mara looked up again there were tears in his eyes.

'I am relieved, it has finally found its home,' Seamus said, nodding to the polished brass casing of her father's fob watch, 'back where it belongs.'

'You get a good night's rest, your Freda will be in bright and early tomorrow, as she always is,' she whispered, tucking the precious casing into her pocket, and watched as Seamus closed his eyes.

The following morning, Mara was given the news that Seamus had died in the night. She had no need to pray he had gone to a better place because she knew he had, but she prayed for the repose of his soul, nonetheless.

26

'You will never guess who's coming to the hospital fundraiser dinner,' said Daisy, knife and fork in hand ready to tuck into her evening meal, 'and, keep this under your hat, Mam, because it's not set in concrete yet, but the rumour is, the King will be in attendance.'

Molly gasped as Daisy's fork delivered steak and kidney pudding to her taste buds.

'Oh.' Molly was fighting for breath, as she sat on the opposite chair with a thud. 'I'll have to sit down.' She fanned her face with a tea towel. 'Wait till I tell Ina.'

'Don't tell her just yet, Ma,' said Daisy, 'it's supposed to be a secret. I shouldn't have said anything.'

'Ooo. Ooo. Ooo.' Molly could not sit still; she was so excited. 'Did you hear that Percy? The King is coming to our Daisy's charity fundraiser.'

'It's not *my* charity fundraiser, Mam,' said Daisy, hardly lifting her head from her meal, 'it's the annual charity fundraiser for the Mersey Infirmary. The King just happens to be in Liverpool that night and said he *may* attend if he has time. He knows Miss Treadwell.'

'I could come and wash the dishes, if you want me to, or even wait-on?' Molly would love to see the King, in person.

'It's all in hand, Mam,' said Daisy, 'and the King may not attend, it all depends. But Mam,' Daisy raised a warning fork, 'the news must be kept as secret as possible, so you mustn't tell anybody just yet.' Lifting her eyes when the room descended into silence, Daisy could not help smiling when she saw her mother's crestfallen expression. 'Not a word, Mam...' Daisy said, waving her fork to make her point. 'Not one.'

Molly slumped on the straight-backed chair, struck dumb with disappointment. Her best piece of news – ever! And she wasn't allowed to utter a word about it.

'I'll have to go to mass and take a vow of silence,' Molly said eventually, not amused when her eldest daughter burst into peals of laughter, which subsided when there was a knock at the front door. 'Who can that be?' asked Molly, getting up from the table to answer it. And as she opened the vestibule door, she saw Max standing on the step, while at the same time there was a bit of a rumpus in the kitchen. 'Come in Max,' Molly said, eager to get back to the kitchen and find out what all the fuss was about. Max followed her quickening footsteps to see Mary Jane surrounded by Daisy and Bridie who were both talking at once.

'The actual King will be at the fundraiser!' Mary Jane's eyes were wide in surprise.

'You told her!' Molly exclaimed to Bridie, who had told Mary Jane about the King's possible attendance at the fundraiser. 'You had no right, our Bridie.' Molly was incensed her daughter had beaten her to divulging this tasty morsel of news. 'Daisy said...' She turned to her eldest daughter, 'Didn't you say, Daisy. Nobody was allowed to say a word! And now look what she's gone and done.'

'Don't worry, Moll,' said Mary Jane, who had come in through the back door, 'I won't breathe a word.'

'That's not the point,' said Molly, 'our Daisy said we hadn't to mention it to a soul...'

Daisy gave a wry smile, suspecting it was not the actual news her mother was upset about, but missing out on passing it on. Then, realising Max was standing in the doorway, she turned.

'Daisy, may I speak with you?' Max's words were low, intimate. 'Alone.'

Daisy went out and closed the kitchen door behind her. 'I'm with *my* family.' She stressed the word, wanting to let him know... what? What did she want him to know? That his secret had left her feeling emotionally exposed? Max would never know how much his cover-up had shocked and hurt her. The realisation had blown her unusually feeble heart wide open. He knew everything about her. Although it was plain to her now that she only knew what he wanted her to know about him.

'Can we go out somewhere?' Max asked. 'I need to explain. But not here.' He watched as she plucked at the skin on the back of her hand and could tell she wanted to say something, yet was doing her best to hold it in. Daisy's stiff reaction made her a completely different person to the one he held closely in his arms and danced the night away with. 'I should have told you about Poll,' he offered limply, knowing he should have told her a lot of things. But he didn't. 'I wouldn't blame you for not wanting to see me again,' he said. 'It was wrong of me not to tell you the truth straight away, but I can explain...'

'I don't think that's a good idea, do you?' Daisy spoke to him as she would a stranger. She needed to put some distance between them. He had been so plausible, and she had been so ridiculously gullible.

Daisy's insides tightened, wrung out like a washed-up rag. All thoughts of the delight of Christmas now filling her with shame. Lowering her head, she was unable to meet his gaze. She wanted him to leave; his betrayal had exposed her heart to nothing but anguish. A feeling she had tried to avoid.

'I want to explain...' Max pleaded. 'I need to explain.'

'Oh, you do,' she retorted, 'well, that's very good of you, but it's a bit late for explanations, Max.' His name sounded hard and bitter coming from her beautiful lips.

'I don't blame you for being annoyed at me,' he said. 'I only have a couple of weeks before...'

'You don't need to explain you have a family to consider – although why you didn't think to tell me about them before now is beyond me.' She wanted to hurt him as much as he had hurt her.

'When I saw you again in the cafe...'

'You had a stab of conscience? Or was it the shame of being caught out?'

'None of those things,' Max said, enraging Daisy with his flippant remark. 'I thought Davey might have told you.'

'How pompous can you be?' Daisy could not help herself. 'Do you think my brother has nothing better to do when he is on leave than to talk about his pals?'

'No, I didn't mean that.' Max was in danger of getting himself tied up in granny knots. He understood her annoyance, proving she was just the kind of girl he hoped she was. Moral and upstanding. Her mother's strength. Helping to raise her brothers and sister without any thought for her own happiness, to which she was surely entitled.

'I think you'd better leave before I say something I might later regret,' Daisy said, opening the front door.

'All right,' Max answered, defeated, 'if you won't listen to what I've got to say then I can't force you. It's all been a big misunderstanding,' he said, longing to take her in his arms, but he knew by the stern expression on her beautiful face she would not allow him to do so.

However, having been back and forth to London, he still had one more chance to straighten things out with Daisy. An investigative reporter, Max had been having meetings with working colleagues in the capital and was privy to things the public would never believe. Nor could he tell Daisy. She would never believe it anyway. Especially when it concerned the new King.

As the front door opened, Bridie, who had been listening to every word from behind the kitchen door, managed to slope quietly into the parlour. So, Daisy had been seeing a married man? What would Mam have to say about her saintly daughter if she found that out?

* * *

'You're home late, Bridie,' said her mother, the following evening. 'Your tea has been sitting on a pan of boiling water for hours; it's bound to have dried up by now.'

'It's my half-day off, so I went to the pictures with Henry, Mam,' Bridie, removing her hat and gloves, had been back in Liverpool for three months and had settled back into her usual routine of working in a first-rate salon and going dancing with Henry. It was as if she had never been away in London.

'Well, take your coat off and sit yourself down, while I go and fetch your tea.' Molly bustled out towards the back kitchen and, taking a clean tea towel from the hook by the back door, she lifted the plate from the pan on the stove. As she carried the food along the narrow passageway, she could hear her daughters talking, but the words weren't clear enough for her to hear.

'Daisy, I need to tell you something...' Bridie looked unusually worried, and Daisy stilled her knife and fork to listen. Bridie wasn't one for wearing her heart on her sleeve. She liked to go dancing and have a good time. But something in her quiet manner told Daisy whatever Bridie was about to say was serious.

'You remember Karl, my boyfriend back in London?'

Another Mister Smarm, Daisy thought, nodding. Bridie had a way of attracting men who thought they were God's gift to the female population. With her film-star good looks, her sister could have any man she wanted. It was a pity she wanted the wrong sort, though.

'Well, I didn't know this, but Karl and Henry are some kind of business colleagues...'

'What a coincidence.' Daisy raised a finely shaped eyebrow and waited for her sister to continue.

'As I said—' Bridie ignored her sister's cynical remark '—Karl and Henry move in the same business circles, and I wondered, seeing as you sent out the invitations, I wondered if you had sent one to Karl, too.'

'Would that be a problem?' asked Daisy, but there was no time to get an answer as their mother bustled into the room with Bridie's evening meal.

Seeing the girls had obviously finished their conversation, Molly took the tea towel and spare plate out to the back kitchen.

'If Karl's going, I'm not,' Bridie whispered, knowing if he

were coming to Liverpool he would certainly come looking for her – and his money.

Daisy was confused, why did Bridie want to avoid her ex so much that she would avoid a lavish fundraiser that included the cream of high society. 'Are you in trouble?' Daisy asked, her heart racing.

'I can't say,' Bridie answered, deliberately concentrating on anything except her sister's worried expression. 'Henry says he loves me, but he's going to Berlin on business immediately after the fundraiser.'

'What's wrong with that?' asked Daisy.

'I think he's trying to let me down gently, but you mustn't breathe a word.' Bridie wondered if she was doing the right thing, telling Daisy. The news that her sister was in love with a married man just went to show that Daisy was as susceptible as any woman.

'Is he willing to stand by you?' Daisy asked in a hurried whisper. 'He's more worldly-wise than...' Daisy hesitated to say he was more sophisticated than her sister, even if Bridie did think she knew it all.

'Of course,' Bridie answered, 'he's thirty-two and first in line to inherit Beamer's. We haven't spoken about it properly yet, but I know he will marry me, and we will move to a nice house out in the Netherford countryside.' She paused, then said craftily, 'After all, he doesn't have a wife to consider.' There was no mistaking the insinuation in Bridie's voice.

'What's that supposed to mean?' Daisy's voice was not as steady as she hoped it would be. Neither of them were as white as their mother expected. They were a respectable family, and their mother would be mortified if she knew the truth. 'It was obvious what Henry was after, trying to worm his way into

Mam's good books.' Daisy decided to face this problem full-on. 'Oh Bridie, you really must start to value yourself more.'

'Like Max values you?' said Bridie and saw the flinch in her older sister's demeanour.

Covering a yawn with the back of her hand, Daisy decided to have an early night. She had a lot to think about. Not least her sister's revelation. She didn't want to think of the hurt and pain Bridie may suffer in future. Because there was something about Henry. Something she could not put her finger on that unsettled her.

Max knew the hospital charity fundraiser was to be held in the great North-Western Hotel, the grande dame of Liverpool. The 330-room hotel, just steps from Lime Street Station, served as the perfect base for visiting dignitaries and was large enough for a formal fundraising event that included dinner, entertainment and, most importantly, the opportunity to donate to auctions and raffles. All to support the maintenance of the hospital, medication, and staff.

Posing as a silver service waiter, Max was going undercover to collect intelligence for a story on a fascist leader who would be in attendance. Supported by black-shirt followers, he was rising through the higher echelons of society, spreading right-wing principles that could pose a real threat to the country. All he had to do was try to convince Daisy he wasn't stalking her but was actually working on a story. Without going into detail.

* * *

'To observe silver service procedures,' Daisy told the trainees, eager to learn everything there was to know, 'you must follow the correct etiquette. Politeness and good manners go top of the list, and I am sure I don't need to tell you how important this function is to a friendly and efficient business.'

The younger girls nodded.

'Why is it called silver service?' asked a trainee, knowing Daisy had worked in some of the best hotels as part of her training years ago.

'The service has been around for hundreds of years,' said Daisy, picking up a spoon and a fork she was going to use to demonstrate with. 'Unless you've eaten at high-end restaurants, stayed in the best hotels, or worked in wealthy homes, you probably will not have experienced silver service dining.'

'Is that what we working classes call *having a scoff*,' the young girl laughed, knowing Daisy was easy-going as a rule and liked a laugh and joke. Such light-heartedness made the working day much easier, but not today, it seemed.

'In this instance, we never use the word "*scoff*".' Daisy sounded impatient, and Ina King's daughter, Betsy, the young trainee, regretted her flippant remark, knowing the business would rise or fall on the reputation of its staff. Something Daisy had instilled from the first day. 'The upper classes and those in command, admire and respect silver service, which has become the bar set for fine dining all over the world,' said Daisy as Betsy lowered her eyes to her highly polished shoes. 'Originating from the seventeenth century, Sunday was when the usual staff were given the day off,' the trainees were told, 'and the butler of the house would serve the food to the aristocratic family.' Daisy solemnly walked around the long table, usually used for rolling out pastry or pummelling bread. 'The butler would circle the table, serving the family and guests from the silver platter, directly onto their plates, which is why this ceremony is called silver service.'

'I can't get the meat to come off the platter as easily as you can, Daisy,' said Lucy, another trainee who could not get her fork and spoon to coordinate, and had dropped more food than she had served.

Daisy, usually so sweet-tempered, rolled her eyes. She was becoming unusually nervous as the function drew near, but she would never allow herself to show it. Training new girls for such an important function was a test of her reputation, and as two young girls bumped into each other they dissolved into a fit of giggles.

'We always serve from the left—' Daisy was in no mood for slapdash today '—and if you two wish to play silly buggers, you can go somewhere else. Do I make myself clear?'

Nobody had heard Daisy speak in such a way before and immediately regretted their error of judgement.

'In France, this service is known as "*service à l'Anglais*", or English service,' Daisy continued in a gentler tone. 'The guest to the host is served first. As they are typically the most prominent person. Service continues clockwise, so staff don't bump into other servers.' She gave the two girls a meaningful look. 'Plates and glasses are cleared from the right. Glasses are stacked in a diagonal line to the right. With wine served in order, by course, and water glasses in front.'

'It's all a bit of a faff,' whispered Betsy, who could not see the point in having five or six glasses when the guests only had one mouth.

'This is fine dining, Betsy.' Daisy heard her clearly. 'And discipline will be observed at all times.'

When she looked towards the door, she saw Max witnessing the activities and quickly went to find out what he wanted.

After explaining that he would be working as a waiter on the night of the fundraiser, Daisy was a little suspicious of his motives. Was he doing his best to talk to her privately, or chasing a confidential story of importance, given the amount of powerful and influential guests, she suspected the latter, which made her more nervous than ever.

* * *

The morning of the charity fundraiser was cold but bright, and Daisy had just finished putting the finishing touches to the food. She was too busy working and did not take any notice of the van driver who came to collect the trays, ready to stow them in the back of the delivery van.

'There's just one more tray to fill, and then we are ready to go,' said Daisy before calling the trainees into the back room to check their uniform.

'I feel ever so grown-up,' said Betsy, her eyes shining with pride, 'I won't let you down, Daisy, I promise.' She had thought the rules and regulations were a bit daft at first, but now, she suddenly felt very proud to be part of the special day, and her attire showed an eye for detail when her hair ribbon was an exact match for her uniform. She had not worn anything new since her father had stopped working on the dock back in 1929.

'You look a treat,' Daisy told her encouragingly, knowing Ina King's daughter had grown not only in stature but in confidence since she began working for her. 'What did your mam say?'

'You'll never believe it,' said Betsy in her direct manner, 'she burst into tears, she was that proud.'

'We'll make her even prouder when you are mixing with the aristocrats.'

'If I'm half as good as you, that would be a blessing.' Betsy's voice was full of wonder one minute, then the next she let out an almighty bellow that filled the room. 'Lucy!' Betsy yelled in a most un-lady-like fashion, making Daisy jump with a start. 'We're nearly ready to go.'

'All right, keep your pinny on,' called Lucy, 'I'm just fixing my cap.' When Lucy came into the room, she stood by Betsy's side and the sight made Daisy smile. Lucy, head and shoulders taller than Betsy, both the same age, reminded Daisy of a penny farthing.

'Come on, you two,' Daisy said, 'let's go and knock their socks off.'

Betsy and Lucy climbed into the seat behind the driver and Daisy climbed in afterwards, sitting in the passenger seat.

'Right,' said the driver, 'is everybody ready?'

It was only then that Daisy lifted her eyes to have a proper look at the driver. 'Max! What are you doing here?'

* * *

Daisy, with the help of Betsy and Lucy, began decorating the table that ran the centre of the vast hall before it was time for the guests to arrive. No expense had been spared. The long line of tables were graced with crystal vases of beautifully arranged flowers. There were delicacies that she had to order in specially. Glacé fruit compotes and bowls of sweets and chocolates added to the table decor, so if there was a lapse between courses, guests could enjoy helping themselves. Daisy made sure nothing was left to chance.

When she saw him a little later, Max looked like a typical English butler, dapper in his black tailcoat, grey pinstriped trousers, crisp white shirt with winged collar beneath a black waistcoat and black bow tie.

The sight took her by surprise, and Daisy secretly admitted just how dashing he really was. Max did not have to feign an air of authority; he stood out from the rest with natural composure and assurance. Trying to tame the flutter in her tummy, Daisy busied herself making sure everything was just as it should be.

When the guests began to arrive, Max and Daisy were there to escort them to their seats, while Betsy's and Lucy's eyes were nearly knocked out by the diamonds and gold on show.

'Some of those necklaces could feed a small country,' said Betsy. 'I'm sure I was a magpie in a former life,' she told Lucy with a grin. 'I'm a bugger for shiny things. If it glistens, I'm on it in a flash.'

'Not in here, you're not!' Daisy scolded, taking Betsy by surprise.

'There isn't a cat in hell's chance of owning something so beautiful,' said Betsy. 'Mam would have it in and out of pawn like a fiddler's elbow.' There were obviously no sides to Betsy, thought Daisy, unlike her mother, who kept her family's privacy very close to her chest even though she somehow got to know everybody else's business.

'Keep your voice down,' said Daisy, 'your words may carry beyond the kitchen walls.'

'I was born chattering, me mam says,' Betsy whispered.

'These charity affairs can go on for four or five hours, depending on how many courses and what speeches will be made, so pace yourselves, girls.'

The main course of roast beef and lamb served from a silver platter was presented for inspection to the lady almoner, host of the fundraiser, Miss Treadwell. Only when she nodded her approval would Daisy be allowed to proceed to serve the food to the esteemed guests, determined to get nothing wrong.

A society function like this, especially for charity, was sure to cause headlines. Miss Treadwell, after making a short speech, introduced King Edward, himself.

Daisy didn't realise she had been holding her breath until the lady almoner offered His Majesty the first taste of food, as was the custom. Daisy let out a long silent stream of air when he lifted his hand to show his approval, and she gave a discreet nod to the staff waiting in readiness in the wings.

'I see the German hierarchy are having no problems polishing this food off,' Max said to Daisy, while she was busy organising the next course.

'What do you mean?' Daisy's kitchen was running like clockwork. Nothing was left to chance.

'According to my sources,' said Max, 'Germany, like many European countries, is reliant on imported food, fodder, and fertiliser, making it vulnerable to supply disruptions. There-fore, Herr Hitler's goal is for food self-sufficiency, and relying on Germany's own resources, which has put a huge strain on the agricultural sector, making already expensive food in short supply.'

'It doesn't seem to be bothering those Germans out there,' said Betsy.

'I bet none of them have ever seen a hungry day,' Daisy said, noticing Henry and Phoebe, who were obviously having a good time, stuffing their faces with the finest food. She could not believe her eyes. Bridie had told Henry she had decided not to attend the fundraiser, for what reason Daisy could not fathom. It wasn't like Bridie to miss the chance to get dolled up and enjoy a night out – especially one as important as this. And here was Henry, large as life and twice as arrogant, laughing ad smarming with his stepmother and another man she recognised! 'That's never our Bridie's ex, Karl, sitting next to Henry?'

'I do believe you are right, Miss Hayward,' said Max, who had met Karl on assignment at a rally in London. 'Except he wasn't in a formal dinner suit then, he was one of Mosley's blackshirts!'

'I can't understand Henry having connections with black-shirts,' said Daisy, 'but he seems to be getting on very well with Karl and the rest of them.'

'I'll find out what he's saying when I go over to the table,' Max informed her. 'I'll try to find out what Henry's up to.'

* * *

Max had asked Daisy to let him know if she saw Henry involved in any covert business.

Daisy gave Max the nod, when she saw Henry take a package from the inside pocket of his jacket and pass it to Karl.

'You know who is expecting this,' said Henry to Karl. Max, expertly unassuming, refilled their glasses and then heard Henry say, 'I can have maps of the dockside sent any time. They must not fall into the wrong hands. If there is any possibility of intelligence getting hold of them, my name must be kept out of this?'

'That goes without saying,' Karl said.

Keeping the contents of the envelope secret had been easier than Henry expected it to be, knowing he could not ask Phoebe to keep them safe until he passed them onto the German High Command at the charity fundraiser. She had a mouth bigger than the Mersey Tunnel when she'd had enough gin down her throat.

* * *

'I've got something you need to hear,' Max whispered guiding Daisy into the large pantry and closing the door behind them.

'Here!' Daisy gasped. 'You'd better not be trying it on with me.'

Max put his finger to his lips in an effort to persuade Daisy to listen. What she heard chilled her to the bone.

'I heard Henry tell Karl...' Max whispered.

Daisy was horrified to learn that her sister Bridie had been eager to do as Henry asked, stashing the documents for him. 'I'm sorry to say he's been using her,' Max told Daisy, 'After he collected the documents today, he said poor Bridie is now surplus to requirements.'

'I knew he wasn't to be trusted,' Daisy said, eager to go into the lavish gala and tell Henry Beamer exactly what she thought of him.

'No need,' said Henry, looking through the kitchen serving hatch to see Bridie, as gorgeous and as dazzling as any of the rich ladies attending.

'What is she doing here?' asked Daisy watching her sister walk towards the King's table and open the large vanity case she was carrying.

'Your Majesty, my Lords, Ladies and Gentlemen, I would like to make this donation to the hospital fund on behalf of Mister Karl Cranford, sitting over there.' Bridie pointed to Karl and Henry's table before lifting the crocodile skin lid and emptying a colossal amount of white five-pound notes onto the lady almoner's table. She knew Karl would come looking for her and he would want his money. But, she had no intentions of giving it back to swell the bank account of that sleazy creep.

For a moment there was not a sound in the room.

Daisy was hardly able to believe what she had just witnessed. Where did her sister get all that money? And what did it have to do with her ex-boyfriend? 'What has she done?'

'Caused a sensation by the look of surprise on the King and Miss Treadwell's face,' Max whispered back.

A moment later, there was the sound of laughter and applause initiated by King Edward, who had stood up to congratulate Karl. The flash of anger in his eyes dissipating when he realised there was nothing he could do about Bridie's bold move except nod and smile. Watching, with the sound of applause ringing in his ears, he saw Bridie stride out of the room with her head held high, but not before she whispered something in Henry's ear. The colour drained from his inebriated face when she informed him she was having his baby.

A short time later, as the fundraiser began to wind down, Daisy saw Karl in the foyer. He passed an envelope to Henry, who put it in his pocket as Karl disappeared upstairs. Obviously thinking the coast was clear, Henry took out a thick sheaf of white five-pound notes from the envelope. There must have been over a hundred pounds at least. But that wasn't what shocked Daisy to the core of her being when Phoebe, dressed to the nines in furs and diamonds, came out into the foyer. Daisy's throat turned to tinder when she caught sight of Henry grabbing Phoebe around the waist, passionately kissing her in the most un-stepson-like manner. There was no mistaking the kind of relationship the two of them shared.

Outraged on her sister's behalf, Daisy could see Henry Beamer for what he was – a double-crossing backstabber. But that wasn't the most shocking thing. He was obviously selling secrets to the Germans.

'Leave it with me,' said Max, 'don't tell Bridie about Phoebe. The less she knows, the better.'

'Are you out of your mind?' Daisy could not believe what she was hearing, but Max assured her that everything would be made clear very soon.

'You'd better hope so,' warned Daisy, 'because if Bridie finds out I knew anything about this and didn't tell her, there will be hell to pay.' Hurrying back to the kitchen, she still had things to do before the long day and night was over.

'I've never seen so much food in my life.' Betsy's eyes were truly opened by this lavish occasion.

'I'll sort out some for you to take home,' said Daisy, recalling the excitement she felt when she took home her first batch of cakes when she had been training under Mary Jane's guidance.

When the fundraiser was finally over the youngsters, fuelled by excitement, were busy chatting ten to the dozen about the dazzling diamonds, the fur coats they helped the lady guests into and the tips they had earned.

'Sometimes I was spoken to, and sometimes I felt invisible,' said Lucy.

'I was actually slipped a ten-bob note with a pat on the backside.' Betsy was outraged. 'When it happened, I found it hard not to offer one of those non-verbal signals that Daisy warned me about.'

Later, when surplus food was packed up ready to go into the hospital kitchen for patients to enjoy, and the equipment was washed and put away, Daisy and the girls enjoyed their first cup of tea.

'My feet are singing,' said Betsy. 'I don't think I can walk another step.'

'That'll be the new shoes,' said Daisy. 'I said you should have worn them before today, to break them in.'

'That's what Mam said, but I wanted them to be brand new for the function. I think I've got blisters on me blisters.'

'Don't take the shoes off yet, then,' Daisy warned when Betsy bent to untie the laces, 'you won't get them back on again, they'll swell like Yorkshire puddings.'

'I don't suppose you want to give me a piggyback, Lucy?'

'No, I don't,' answered Lucy on a giggle.

'Here,' said Max, 'jump up on my back, I'll help you to the van.'

'I'll do no such thing,' Betsy cried, her face the colour of a post-box. 'My mam would skin me alive if she caught me climbing onto a man's back. I'll hobble along as best I can but thank you all the same.'

'You'll get used to it,' said Daisy as they made their way to the van to drop the two girls at their houses in Beamer Street, to make sure they got home safe and sound.

'I think they found it more challenging than they expected,' Daisy, tired but happy, informed Mary Jane, who, arm in arm with her beloved Cal, was about to enter her own house after enjoying the function. 'They did a grand job,' said Daisy. 'I'm sure I won't have any complaints.' The conversation with her neighbour took her mind off what she was going to say to Bridie when she got indoors.

'That's good to know,' Mary Jane answered. 'The good name of Silver Service Events will be known all across Lancashire. I'm away to my bed,' Mary Jane said as she went to her front door. 'Goodnight, Daisy. Goodnight, Max.'

'I'll lock the van in the stable yard for the night,' said Max, 'I have something to tell you.'

'Not now,' said Daisy, not sure she was in the mood for any more surprises. She had a lot to think about. Nevertheless, his explanation had to wait when they heard the excited cry of a young lad, who came skidding around the corner, and proceeded to shout through the Everdines' letterbox.

'Mister Everdine, come quick! There's been an accident,' the young lad shouted up the lobby of Cal Everdine's house.

'What kind of accident?' Mary Jane asked opening the front door. 'Who's been hurt?'

'Old man Spence,' said the boy, his patched jacket had obviously seen better days. 'He's fallen down a grid and ripped his kecks, there's blood everywhere.'

In no time, Cal was halfway up the street.

'Call into the doctor,' called Max to the young lad. 'Old Spence will need medical attention. Hurry!'

The boy raced towards the top of the street and the doctor's house. Cal and Max managed to pull old Spence from the grid, situated in the centre of the pathway leading down into the coal cellar.

'I stepped on the coal-hole lid. It hadn't been put back properly when the coal man delivered this morning, by the look of it. I don't think it's broken,' said old Spence, referring to his leg. Cal knew the old fella should have retired years ago, but he did not have the heart to take the job keeping the houses in good order, which he had done so diligently for years, from him.

'I remember when I was a boy, and you worked for my father,' Cal said as they waited for the doctor to arrive, hoping to keep the old man from inspecting the damage. These old soldiers were a stoic lot, and he would try to walk on it even though it was so obviously broken. Cal could see by the angle of the old man's foot that he had most certainly broken his ankle at least, which was not good at his age.

I don't think he'll be able to work for a while. If ever again, Cal thought, but he said nothing, knowing how proud the men around here were when they had a job to do.

'I think the job's given me up,' said the old man, 'it's a younger man's game is that.'

'You've done a sterling job,' said Cal, 'but don't you worry, I will give you a good pension, you won't have anything to worry about.'

'I wish I'd known that a few years back.' The old man tried to laugh, but the slightest movement caused screaming pain to rip through his leg and foot. 'You've been a good boss, Cal, as good as your old fella.'

'And you've been a good worker, Spence, that's why I'm asking you to finally retire and live the rest of your life in peace.'

'That's very good of you, sir,' said Spence as the doctor turned up and ordered the old man to the Mersey Infirmary, where he would be looked after.

'What are you going to do now?' asked Mary Jane. 'You're going to need a maintenance man.'

'And I know just the fellow,' said Cal.

28

'What's for you won't pass you by,' Ina King said, trying to stay positive for her family's sake. 'Our lives won't always be like this, Sid.'

'The gaffers don't want to know when there's young men looking for work.' Sid held up his hard-working hands that still bore the legacy of the effort of his labour.

'I am sure something will turn up.'

'Always the optimist, hey, Ina.' He gave a tired smile. 'Betsy's late,' he said, looking at the clock, which Ina had retrieved from the pawnshop earlier.

Having Betsy in full-time work was a gift from the gods, and even though her earnings were only that of a trainee, at least the money came in regularly and, along with the fresh bread and little treats she was given, they were managing a bit better than they once did.

'Hiya, Mam. Hiya, Dad,' Betsy called out as she always did when she pressed the latch and entered the kitchen carrying the heavy bag. She couldn't wait to tell the family of her tiring but exciting day.

Ina's eyes popped when she saw the contents of the bag. It was almost full to the top with food they could never afford, and the family gathered around the wooden table to see what she had brought. It was unusual to see this much food. There were beef sandwiches, and chicken drumsticks, jellies, and some kind of stuff Betsy had never heard of, called pâté foie gras.

'I haven't seen this kind of food since I worked up at the big house,' said Ina, who had once been in service to the Earl of Sefton.

Betsy nodded, pleased the whole family were so obviously thrilled with her bag of luxuries. She watched as her mam took a small spoon and scooped a little pâté from the dish.

'Oh Sid, you want to have a taste of this, it's delicious.' Ina took a bigger scoop and offered it to her husband.

Betsy watched on, thrilled when Daisy had said they could all choose which food they wanted and there was to be no skimping.

'How the other half live, hey, Ina.' Sid cheered when he caught sight of the goodies. 'Those toffs are thoroughly spoiled if you ask me,' he laughed. 'We're going to live like them tomorrow.'

'You wouldn't believe the amount of food that went to waste, Mam. Some people were so greedy, stuffing themselves with food and drink, and to think, the whole thing was supposed to be in aid of the poor, who scrimp and go without.' Betsy never saw herself as poor. 'Who brought you home, Betsy?' asked her father. 'The last tram stopped long ago.'

'Max brought us all home in the bakery van, he's a friend of Daisy's,' Betsy told them, 'Which was a bit strange because she tried ignoring him most of the time, but nobody can ignore Max, he doesn't half make us laugh.' Her mother listened with interest, knowing she and Molly would have a lot to talk about tomorrow. 'Apart from pouring drinks at the banquet, I don't really know what Max does, and I couldn't really ask, it's none of my business.'

'Fair enough,' said Sid placidly, satisfied with his daughter's answer.

'There you go, Ma,' Betsy said, placing a fresh loaf, which she had asked Daisy to cut on the new slicer, on the table.

'This sliced bread goes further than the uncut bread ever did,' said her mother, 'and there's plenty here for tomorrow.'

'Everybody's getting their bread sliced these days.' Betsy was pleased her parents were so impressed, this food was a perk of the job, she told them.

* * *

'How are you feeling today, Sid?' Ina had asked the same question every day for over five years. She knew he had been feeling under par lately, having no job to go to, but now the weather was beginning to warm up a bit, and there was plenty of food to eat, he looked quite happy.

'Aye,' he said, 'I'm chipper. All I have to do now is find some work.'

'You will, Da.' Betsy, so like her mother, was always hopeful, and she said it with all the conviction she could muster. 'Something will turn up, and it won't be Mam's toes.' They all laughed at the family line, which Betsy and her pallid, hollow-cheeked siblings had heard since the day they were born. 'We've got to look on the bright side.'

'I've been telling him that,' said Ina with a twinkle in her eye, nodding to her husband, who rarely won a dispute when both females joined forces.

'Well, seeing as you put it like that,' Sid mused. At fifty years old, he still had plenty to offer should the right opportunity come along. 'I don't suppose any of us know what the day will bring.' The future looked a little brighter when his family's bellies were full. Sat near the fire, he finished his bowl of porridge.

Staring into the dancing flames, Sid wondered what the world was coming to, when the higher-ups could eat as much as they pleased, and the poor people were half-starved. Not only that, but he feared for his family if the distant murmurings of war should ever become a reality. What would become of them all. His sons, his daughter. Living on top of the docks, he knew they would be far from safe. However, he did not have time to dwell when there was a heavy rap on the cellar door.

Ina rose to answer the knock, and Sid was surprised to see Cal Everdine, red-faced, removing his flat cap as he came into the room. Sid stood up to greet him, wondering what he was doing here.

'Would you like a cup of tea, Mr Everdine?' Ina asked, already pouring the tea from the pot, and Cal nodded.

'Is there somewhere we can talk, Sid?' Cal said, pushing splayed fingers through his thick hair. Looking around, he saw the family eating breakfast, not paying any attention to the adults' conversation once their welcoming greetings were respectfully adhered to.

'We can talk over here. What is said in this room stays in this room.'

As both men sat near the fire, and their cups of tea were delivered, Ina asked if Cal would like something to eat? They may not have much, but what they did have they shared willingly.

'I'd better not,' said Cal. His American lilt had never left him. 'It does smell good, but Mary Jane will have my breakfast ready when I get home.'

'I understand.' Ina, willing to share, was a little glad that Cal refused. 'If you need anything, just let me know.'

'Thank you,' said Cal, as Ina, too thin to be healthy, picked up Sid's empty bowl and went back to her own meal. 'How are you bearing up, jobwise?' Cal asked with a jovial lilt in his voice.

'Well, it's been a long time,' Sid answered, 'but given the chance, I can still work very well.'

'That sounds just the ticket,' said Cal, 'because I might just have what you are looking for. You are most certainly up to the job.' Cal knew Sid, like thousands of other men who could not get work, would take anything he could. 'You remember old Spence, don't you?'

Sid nodded.

'He's not getting any younger,' Cal told him. 'You see, his old legs are not as sprightly as they once were, and he had a fall.' Cal paused when he saw Sid's look of concern. 'You were the first person I thought of...'

'That's very good of you.' Sid's heart hammered in his chest.

'Do you think you could oversee the job?'

'You mean managing your properties, a caretaker, like?' asked Sid, hardly daring to believe what he was hearing.

Cal nodded, the ghost of a smile crossing his face when he saw the look of elation in Sid's eyes. 'I want you to take over the repairs. Rent collections will be done by the agency, so you won't have to worry about that.'

'I'm fine with figures, sir—' Sid grinned '—not that I've had many numbers to work on of late.'

'I knew you could do it, but there is already an agent who collects the rents,' said Cal. 'The properties must be kept up to scratch, and I know Spence was beginning to find the work demanding. Even though he never complained, the rheumatism made his joints weak. If you think you might have a problem, just let me know.'

'Don't even think it.' Sid's beaming smile stretched across his face, making him look ten years younger.

'Oh, this is the best news.' Unable to contain her elation, Ina crossed the floor and hugged Cal. 'You don't know how much this means to us.' Her voice trembled with emotion. The three adults gave each other a brief glance before the kitchen was filled with the rumble of laughter. Betsy knew it was the most beautiful sound she had heard since they had moved here.

'Oh yes, I almost forgot,' said Cal as he slipped his cap back on his thatch of dark hair. 'The job comes with accommodation, and as you already live here, it's rent free.' He had to put his hands over his ears to try to drown out the squeals of Ina's excitement.

29

'You're looking very serious,' Mary Jane said when Daisy called in on half-day closing. 'Penny for them.' She didn't like to see her friend down in the dumps.

'Oh, it's nothing,' Daisy answered, not really wanting to go into detail about her worries.

'Are you sure about that?' Mary Jane asked, pouring freshly made tea into two cups. 'Is it about Max?'

Daisy nodded.

'He's married,' Daisy blurted, unable to hold the news in any longer. 'He's got a wife and daughter, and I know you warned me it was a possibility last Christmas, but I thought you were joking, I didn't imagine I would feel this way about him, but I can't stop thinking about him, and I know I shouldn't, but you see—'

'Hold the bus!' Mary Jane interrupted Daisy's avalanche of words that tumbled out like rolling stones down a mountain, gathering momentum with each syllable. Daisy stopped suddenly, and Mary Jane took her by the shoulders and sat her on one of the four straight-backed chairs around the teashop table covered in a bright chequered blue cloth. 'You say he's married?' Mary Jane asked, and Daisy nodded.

She hadn't wanted to blurt everything out like that. The admission left her feeling vulnerable. Mary Jane was going to think she was being silly. Like a lovesick schoolgirl.

'I saw Max in town, he was with a woman and a little girl, pretty as a picture she was.' Daisy wanted to try to reduce the importance of what she was telling her friend, she wanted to make light of it, not give Max's tender words the importance she had clung so strongly to over the past months. Because when she voiced his words aloud, Daisy felt she would cheapen them, make them ordinary – and they were anything but ordinary. 'He told me he loved me, I was so confused, not knowing how to feel.' Daisy knew she must change the subject; the admission was too painful. 'Max told me he witnessed Henry passing documents to Karl, and later, I saw Karl giving Henry an envelope full of cash – I saw Henry pocket the money – and to put the top hat on the whole situation, I saw him kissing Phoebe, bold as brass, right there in the foyer. They didn't seem to care who was watching.' The words tumbled unremittingly from Daisy's lips.

The colour drained from Mary Jane's face. She had heard about this type of thing being carried out. 'Cal told me there are people sympathetic to a country's enemy, some even working for them, giving away state secrets, called fifth columnists. Nazi sympathisers.'

'I've heard about these people,' said Daisy, 'a hidden group working to sabotage a country from within, spreading misinformation, inciting panic.'

'Some fear Nazi infiltration and subversion.' According to what Cal told her, Mary Jane knew Liverpool, a great seaport with its world shipping anchored in the bustling docks, was second only to London in importance, and would be a main target in time of war.

'That's not all you are thinking about though, is it, Daisy?' Mary Jane knew her friend could not hide her true feelings for long.

Daisy shook her head. 'I know it's wrong of me to have feelings for a married man.' Daisy's voice was low, subdued. 'Mam would die of shame if she knew. My name would be mud. I wish I didn't have these feelings for Max, but I can't help it. Sometimes, when he comes into my dreams I don't want to wake up. I just want to stay in that ethereal world with him, and the feeling stays with me all day.' Tears formed in Daisy's eyes. She had never felt this way about anybody except Max. The attraction had been instant when they were younger, and he would come into the bakery café for his usual bacon on toast and she, a young trainee, would delight in making it for him. Even though she tried her best to fight it.

'Daisy, I have something to tell you,' Mary Jane said, putting her serviceable white cup back onto the matching saucer. 'Max is not married.' Only when she heard Daisy's audible gasp did she look up. 'He was married, but it's a long story and he may want to tell you about it himself.'

'I could never ask!' Daisy sounded horrified. 'I couldn't.'

'Then I suggest you stop being so pig-headed and the next time he asks to speak to you, speak you must. Even if it is only to clear the air and you can get a good night's sleep,' Mary Jane had not slept well either and was not her usual patient self, 'because I am not carrying you, Daisy – I haven't got the energy.'

'You're not...?' Daisy looked pointedly at Mary Jane's stomach. She had heard about older women being caught out when they least expected it.

'No, don't be silly.' Mary Jane shook her head, 'I'm fine. Although, if we are sharing secrets... Hollie said she doesn't want to go to university.'

'Oh no, what a waste of a good brain!' Daisy replied, knowing it had seemed to be a foregone conclusion that Hollie would make her parents proud when she was accepted into one of England's finest seats of learning. 'What does she want to do?'

'She wants to join the bloody Women's Royal Navy Service, according to some news reports it may be reformed. Can you believe it!'

'To be honest, I can,' said Daisy after a moment's thought. 'Hollie has always had a mind of her own and, and if you ask me, a fine mind it is too. She never was going to be the one to conform to what was expected of her – after all, she is her mother's daughter.' Both women laughed, Mary Jane was not one to follow the herd, she was usually at the vanguard, leading the parade. 'I suppose the apple didn't fall very far from that tree.'

* * *

The news that Max was not married lightened the heaviness in Daisy's heart, but she still could not discuss her new findings because he was away on an assignment. The shop telephone rang, and Daisy went to answer. She really wasn't in the mood to go back upstairs to her office. The voice sounded far away, and Daisy had to strain to listen. Then she caught Max's voice, and her heart soared.

'Daisy, don't refuse, please,' he was saying, 'I must tell you something.'

'I know,' Daisy called down the black Bakelite receiver. 'I have to tell you something too.'

'I'll be back this evening. Will you meet me in that teashop on the Landing Stage?'

'Yes,' Daisy called. She knew the teashop well. She worked there many years ago. It would be nice to see the old place again.

30

Daisy looked out of the teashop window at the flat-capped men in gabardine macs leaning on the iron rail, observing the boats and ferries coming into and leaving the harbour. Giggling girls whose hats were robustly pinned and perched on the side of their curled hair blowing in the wind as they bent their heads, trying to avoid the squall along the pier.

Nevertheless, she didn't have long to dwell when she heard the teashop doorbell give its familiar tinkle, and looking towards the door, she saw the welcome sight of Max.

Looking suave in a Harris tweed two-piece suit, his turn-up trousers were sitting perfectly on highly polished oxblood-coloured brogues. As he entered the teashop, he removed the fedora that had dipped low on his forehead and looked around, his eyes lighting up when he caught sight of her.

'I didn't think you'd come,' he said. 'Will you have tea or coffee?'

'Tea please,' Daisy said politely. She didn't fancy the chicory essence they served in here. The few minutes it took for Max to share some friendly banter with the waitress gave Daisy time to compose herself.

Keep calm, she thought, *let him say what he has to say without interruption*. She realised now she had been a little high-handed with Max the last time she saw him. He turned from the counter with the two teas. Daisy watched him. He had a daughter. What if he was divorced? There seemed to be a lot of that kind of thing these days, but not in Beamer Street. A lot of women put up and shut up in Beamer Street, which was almost as bad as having an affair with a married man, thought Daisy. Girls who did things like that got themselves a bad name.

'Sugar?' Max asked, sitting opposite, placing the cups and saucers on the table.

Daisy shook her head. There was a moment's silence as she watched him scoop half a teaspoon of sugar into his tea.

'The news doesn't look good,' he said.

'I know, so what does it mean for the country?' She was pleased to be skirting around the real issue for the time being.

'The next in line is the Duke of York,' said Max, who knew about things like this. 'But can we talk about that later. There's something I want to tell you. I should have told you long ago,' he said gravely. 'It's about my wife.'

Dread weighed heavy on Daisy's shoulders, and she leaned back in her chair. Now the moment was here, she didn't really want to know. What if she couldn't bear the truth? What if Max had done something terrible, like walk out on his family?

'Margarita was a colleague. She came from Spain,' he said, gathering sugar grains into a little pile from some that had spilled onto the table. He didn't look at her, Daisy noted. 'We were on the same assignment in Europe, both far from home and feeling a little lonely.' He looked out of the window to where the moon looked like it was sinking into the River

Mersey. 'We went for a drink. One thing led to another... It was two people giving each other comfort.'

'Do you want any more tea, love?' called the waitress from behind the counter. 'Only we close in half an hour.'

'No, thank you,' said Daisy, a little irritated at being disturbed, knowing how difficult this must be for Max. He shook his head, to silently say the same thing.

'I came back home, we remained friends, and a few weeks later I received a letter from Margarita telling me she was expecting my baby.' Max shrugged at the inevitability. 'I had no choice, we were both Catholics, but besides that I could never leave her in the lurch with a child to bring up on her own.'

'I suppose not,' Daisy said softly, waiting for him to continue.

'Her life would not have been worth living. I had to do right by her.' Again, Max paused, the memory was too painful to put into words, but he felt he owed Daisy that much, at least. 'I returned to Spain. We were married in a little church. On a hot summer afternoon. At the foot of a mountain on the Iberian Peninsula.' His faltering words seemed difficult to say out loud. 'Six months later, she gave birth to little Poll.'

'Does she still live there?' Daisy asked the question even before she thought about it.

Max shook his head. 'Spain is not the safest place to raise a child.' He paused. 'I had an assignment in London, so had to return to England. Then, when I went back to Spain, Margarita said she couldn't keep the child. She had a roving soul, you see, she was never cut out to being tied down.'

'What about your daughter?' Daisy asked, so wrapped up in his story she had left her tea to go cold.

'I brought her back home and asked my sister to look after her when I was away.'

'And Margarita?' asked Daisy.

'She was killed crossing a busy road.'

'How awful,' Daisy whispered, looking across the table to where he was watching her.

'She climbed mountains, went undercover in some of the most dangerous cities, she was fearless but was killed crossing the road.'

Daisy put her face in her hands, her stomach churning. 'And you've brought up little Poll ever since?' she asked, realising Max had tried to do his best by his daughter. 'She must miss you when you go away.'

'Yes, she does,' Max answered, 'that's why I spoil her so much on my return, and why she has me wrapped around her little finger.' He chuckled, and his mood suddenly lifted. 'She knows I can't refuse her anything, and on my last leave she asked if I could work from home like other daddies... I agreed.'

'So, you won't be going on long-range assignments in future?' Daisy's heart skipped a beat.

'Not if I can help it. I've applied for work on a local newspaper,' he laughed. 'You can't have excitement all your life, it's not good for you.'

'I wouldn't know,' said Daisy, 'I've never been any further than Southport in my whole life.'

The head waitress give a little cough. Daisy and Max turned to see her standing by the counter in her hat and coat, and they both spluttered like naughty schoolchildren, apologised, and left. They had not noticed the time fly; they were so deep in conversation.

'Are you working tomorrow?' asked Max and Daisy told him she was. 'Do you think you'll have the energy to come and have tea with me and Poll?' he asked, and Daisy told him she would love to. 'I want her to meet you properly.'

'Really?' Daisy felt her spirits rise and she could not hide the smile that refused to be contained as her racing heartbeat caused a wonderful warmth to radiate throughout her body.

'I will meet you at the station,' said Max tenderly. 'Is that all right with you?'

'Perfect,' said Daisy, 'but it would help if you let me know which station.'

They both laughed again. Max told her he would meet her at Hall Road train station in Blundellsands.

'Blundellsands?' Daisy could not hide her surprise, she had never thought to ask where he came from, thinking Max lived locally. 'I... I didn't expect...' She didn't imagine him to have a house in one of the most exclusive areas along the Mersey coastline.

* * *

Daisy could not remember her journey home. When she got off the train at Marsh Lane station, she turned right, rounding the corner at the public house and crossed the road to pass through Little America, so-called because of its street names. Washington Street, Vermont, Delaware, Nevada, Jersey, Carolina, and Florida Streets were laid out in rows of terraced houses before she reached Beamer Street.

Daisy was walking on air. She could hardly believe she was going to Blundellsands tomorrow to have tea with Max and his daughter. What a treat. Although she knew she would not have much time to get ready – unlike Bridie, who would need a whole day off work to pamper herself if she was going on a date.

Going on a date! The words reverberated through Daisy's head. No. She mustn't think like that. She was having tea with a friend and his family. That's all. Although she was a little apprehensive about telling Mam.

The house seemed unusually quiet when she closed the front door and walked up the lobby. As she reached the parlour door, she could hear a low hum of voices. One was the deep voice of a man.

'Oh, hello, Daisy, love,' Molly said when Daisy entered the front room.

'Hiya, Mam,' she said, surprised to see Mr Casey, the pork butcher, sitting on the sofa. He stood up when Daisy entered the room and held out his hand. She took his hand and shook it. A small crease of confusion pleating her forehead. 'Nice to see you, Mister Casey,' Daisy said politely.

'Mr Casey brought me some pigs' trotters he had left over. The shop closes early on Wednesdays,' said Molly. 'Wasn't that good of him?'

'Thank you, Mr Casey, that's very kind.' Daisy knew her mother and Percy were very fond of a pig's trotter, much to her sister Bridie's revulsion, she would baulk in disgust at the thought of eating one.

So when Bridie opened the parlour door and saw the pigs' trotters she hurried out, slamming the door shut. Daisy went to see what the commotion was because it was obvious Bridie was not pleased at the sight of the pigs' trotters.

'Bridie, what's the matter?' She could see her sister had been crying.

'I can't tell you here,' said Bridie. 'Come into the kitchen.'

'Is it the pigs' feet?' asked Daisy as Bridie recoiled, quickly running upstairs to the bathroom. Daisy followed.

'Bridie, are you feeling ill?' Daisy called through the opaque-glazed half of the door. 'Maybe it's something you ate.' Noises came from the bathroom that made Daisy's heart race.

* * *

'What!' Daisy cried a little later when Bridie followed her into her bedroom. She could not believe what she had just heard in Bridie's whispered announcement. She asked Bridie to repeat it.

'I'm going to have a baby.' Tears streamed down Bridie's beautiful face, now red and swollen from crying.

'No!' Daisy could not contain her shock. 'Have you told Mam?' Then, thinking quickly she realised Mam would be the last person Bridie would tell. 'Of course you haven't.'

'I can't tell anybody.' Bridie, not realising she had inadvertently denounced her older sister, backtracked, saying quickly, 'Except you.'

'I have to think.' This revelation was huge, and Daisy knew her mother would expect her to take the reins, organise what needed to be done.

'Henry can't marry me.' Bridie could barely get the words out through her sobs.

'Can't or won't,' Daisy said as anger seeped from every pore and she thought for a moment. 'I know you don't want to hear this, but I'm glad he won't marry you.'

Bridie's puffy eyes widened. She could not believe her sister's treachery.

'I'm being honest, Bridie, Henry Beamer is no good for you. You must believe me.'

'He said he loved me,' Bridie cried, 'he said he would always love me.'

'The only person he loves is himself,' Daisy said through gritted teeth. She would never tell her sister about his treacherous love affair with his own stepmother, or the depths to which he would sink. 'He is cruel, greedy, self-centred. You are better off without him.'

'How can I bring up a child on my own?' Bridie cried. 'I'll be the talk of the washhouse.' Daisy knew her sister was right. If the news got out, she would never get over the shame of it. Especially when the news came that the father was a fifth columnist, a traitor to his own country. Her sister was better off without him.

'Leave it with me,' said Daisy, 'I'll see what I can sort out.'

Moments later, she was knocking on Mary Jane's door.

31

'Poor Bridie,' said Mary Jane. 'She must be terrified.' Having gone through a similar situation, she could put herself in Bridie's shoes and give first-hand advice. 'The less people who know, the better it will be for her.'

'I can't see that happening,' said Daisy. 'You can't keep anything quiet in this street.'

'I do believe you are wrong on that score,' said Mary Jane and they both smiled. She knew her friend had more secrets than she could shake a stick at. And only by choosing her friends very carefully did Mary Jane's secrets remain hidden.

Daisy knew Mary Jane's eldest daughter, Hollie, was born out of wedlock in their front room, when the residents of Beamer Street believed wrongly that her husband was Red, who had killed his brother Paddy back in Ireland.

But that was before, Cal, a man who also had secrets of his own and loved Mary Jane with every fibre of his being and asked her to marry him after Hollie was born. Daisy had been at the birth, and she was one of the first people, after Cal, who held the new-born babe. They were two halves of the same whole, Cal and Mary-Jane. Good, kind, and trustworthy.

As far as anybody in Beamer Street knew the Everdine clan were just an ordinary family who had done quite well for themselves. Hard-working and courteous, the family had always been discreet. And Daisy would trust them with her life.

'I have got to do something to help Bridie,' said Daisy. 'This news will be the finish of me mam.'

'She's a lot stronger than you give her credit for, Daisy,' said Mary Jane. 'If it hadn't been for Molly, I don't know where I would be now. She was a godsend and my saviour when I needed her.'

Daisy thought back to the days when she was younger and her mother depended upon her, but that didn't mean she was unable to make her own decisions, she knew.

'Molly was a strong woman because she had to be,' said Mary Jane, 'you couldn't do everything for her. But that's not to say she didn't appreciate what you did do. The sacrifices you made. But she's a big girl now and she's got Percy.'

'It's been a night for revelations.'

'As I say, Dais, not everything needs to be on the front page of the *Echo*.'

Mary Jane yawned discreetly behind the back of her hand, and Daisy knew she had outstayed her welcome. They both had an early start tomorrow.

'I'm sorry I've kept you up, I'll see you in the morning. I've got a lot to think about.'

* * *

Daisy alighted from the train at Hall Road and smiled at the array of coloured pansies hanging in baskets and troughs along the platform. A far cry from the soot-encrusted station where she had boarded the train.

She looked around, and apart from a waiting room and the ticket booth, there was nobody about. Daisy felt a moment of panic. Had she got off at the right stop? Was this the station Max meant? She wasn't sure of anything any more.

A railway employee, in his muffler and peaked cap, trundled along the platform. 'You look a bit lost, my dear,' he said in a broad Lancashire accent, so different from the thick catarrhal tones of the dockside dwellers.

'I am supposed to meet someone; this is Hall Road?'.

'Aye, this is Hall Road, and you'd be meeting Mr Galant, I suppose?'

Daisy was taken aback. How did he know?

'He's just gone to the cigarette machine outside the station. He told me to let you know.' The older man smiled, his weather-beaten face as brown as a nut. Daisy, not a natural country dweller, realised how pale she was in comparison.

'Daisy!' Max called, waving from the other end of the platform. He was holding the hand of little Poll, who, with childlike innocence, whooped when she saw Daisy, pulling her hand from her father's.

'Hello, Aunt Daisy,' Poll said, not in the least bit shy. 'Daddy said you were coming for tea.'

'Let Aunt Daisy get her breath, Poll,' Max said, leaning over to kiss Daisy's cheek. Immediately she felt her face grow hot. Where she came from, people only kissed each other goodbye, not hello.

'It's fine,' Daisy said as Poll slipped her small hand into her gloved hand, and it felt like the most natural thing in the world.

'We're not too far,' said Max, 'but I brought the car anyway.' He led the way to the black Austin Seven motorcar. Opening the door, Daisy thanked him and climbed into the passenger seat while Poll fired questions left, right and centre.

'Do you live by the seaside?' asked Poll, leaning on the back of Daisy's seat, looking for all the world like she was going to climb over any minute.

'Not by the seaside as such,' Daisy answered truthfully, 'but I do live by the waterside.'

'So, you can't build sandcastles with Daddy,' she said, completely accepting the fact she was part of her father's life, even though Daisy had not yet come to accept it herself.

'We don't really have any sand where I come from,' said Daisy, 'although, it's not a far walk to go and see the big ships in port.'

'Are there a lot of ships to see?' asked Poll, full of vibrant enquiries.

'If your daddy will let you, we could go and see them one day,' Daisy offered.

'Can we go next Sunday?' The child was eager to get to know Daisy by the look of it and she laughed.

'All right, if your daddy doesn't mind, we can go and see the big ships next Sunday.' Then, turning to Max, Daisy said, her voice full of wonder, 'You can tell her parents are journalists, she's got lots of unanswered questions.'

'I agree,' said Max, 'Poll has a very enquiring mind.'

* * *

The afternoon tea went well, and both Daisy and Max were entranced by some of the little girl's questions and enquiring thoughts. It was soon time for Daisy to leave. Little Poll seemed genuinely disappointed.

'Will you come and see me again?' Poll asked. The day had

been specially prepared in her honour, which, as far as Daisy was concerned, was true. She found the child a breath of fresh air. Lively, fun and made her forget her troubles about Bridie.

'Shall we take Daisy home,' Max asked, 'or shall we keep her here forever?'

'Keep her here forever,' Poll squealed with delight, throwing her small arms around Daisy's legs and Daisy found it so easy to laugh out loud. She hadn't had so much fun since her own brothers and sister were small. Coming here had given her a chance to believe 'what-if?' as she had done years ago.

'We will take Daisy all the way home, and we might just catch sight of a big ship,' Max said as they scrambled into the car. Then he whispered, 'All she needs now is a kitten and all her dreams will have come true.'

'What do you mean?' asked Daisy.

'You,' he said in a serious tone she didn't hear very often. 'She has done nothing but talk about you since she met you in town a couple of months ago.'

'Daddy kept saying you would come and see us one day,' Poll said matter-of-factly, 'but I was beginning to think you would never come. It has been so long.'

'Well, I'll have to make it sooner next time,' Daisy answered, wondering if she should be building up the child's hopes like this, but she was so caught up in the joy of the day she couldn't stop herself.

* * *

When she arrived home, Daisy saw her mother sitting in the chair by the unlit fire in the kitchen. Molly was twisting a damp handkerchief into an almost unrecognisable screw of material.

'Mam, what's the matter?' Daisy said, but before Molly replied, she knew the answer.

'It's our Bridie,' Molly answered, 'she's... she's... in the family way.' Molly looked up when Daisy said nothing, her eyes like gimlets. 'You knew, didn't you?'

Daisy went over to her mother, and she knelt by her chair as she had done as a child, patting her mother's hand. 'Aye, Mam, I knew, but only recently. I did not keep it from you deliberately.'

'When did you find out?' Molly asked, and Daisy was saved from answering when the parlour door opened, and Mary Jane came into the front room.

The three women silently acknowledged each other and Mary Jane, with no need to be invited, sat down on the sofa.

'You knew too.' Molly's voice held a note of accusation. She hated being the last to know. 'She's my daughter, she should have come to me first.'

'It doesn't matter, Mam.' Daisy's tone was tender, like she was talking to somebody who didn't quite understand what was going on. 'We'll make it all right, you'll see.'

'How?' Molly asked, her voice harsh. 'How can we make it anything but what it is – a shambles? If your poor sainted father were here now, I don't know what he'd do.' Molly seemed to sag under the weight of her troubles and Daisy did what she always did, she went and put the kettle on. A few moments later, she brought a tray of tea things through.

'Is Bridie upstairs?' she asked and when her mother nodded, Daisy called her down. 'You can't deal with this on your own,' she told her younger sister. 'We will stand by you. You always have a place in this house no matter what you've done.'

'I have a suggestion,' Mary Jane offered, 'and please tell me if you don't want to go along with it, but I took the liberty of telephoning my brother this morning.'

'Mary Jane's brother is a doctor,' Molly told Bridie, who was well aware of the fact.

'All three brothers are, Mam.' Bridie still had the spark of defiance in her.

'Well,' said Mary Jane, 'it just so happens he is in need of a housekeeper, and when your time comes, he and his wife will take good care of you.'

'You mean cook and clean for your brother and his wife?' Bridie could barely believe what she was hearing. Before she'd told Henry about the baby, he had promised her the earth. He said they would live abroad. Have riches above avarice. He did not bargain for children though. She had watched the dream slip from his eyes to be replaced by disgust. He'd called her a mantrap. A whore. He'd reacted like a man possessed. He had ordered her out of his car to walk the rest of the way home.

'Beggars can't be choosers, Bridie.' Molly's voice was harsher than any of them had ever heard before. 'Mary Jane knows what she is talking about in a situation like this.' Daisy held her breath. Surely Mam wasn't going to spill the beans about Cal not being Hollie's father? 'Mary Jane's brother will look after you and you can keep in touch by the telephone.'

'But Henry might change his mind,' Bridie cried, 'and when he does—'

'And when he does, I'll run him down the bloody path myself!' Daisy answered. 'Believe me, Bridie,' she said, 'you have had a very lucky escape.'

* * *

When Daisy left the office on Monday, she was surprised to see a crowd had gathered on the corner of Beamer Street and she slowed a little, her natural curiosity getting the better of her. There was always something going on in the neighbourhood, but this was different. This wasn't children playing in the street or women jangling on the corner. There was a police car outside Beamer's factory.

Unable to resist, knowing her mam would want every detail, Daisy watched the scene with heightened anticipation. What had gone on at Beamer's? she wondered. Even Mary Jane was out looking. In fact, all front doors, which were always open, now had somebody standing on the front step, gawping up at Beamer's.

'What's going on?' Daisy asked Mary Jane, who shrugged.

'You know as much as me, Dais,' Mary Jane answered. 'But if what you told me about Henry Beamer being at the charity fundraiser has got anything to do with it, he will be in big trouble. You mark my words.'

Moments later, it appeared Mary Jane was right as she saw Henry being brought out of the large soot-covered, red-brick building with handcuffs attaching him to a senior-looking police officer.

'D'you think they've found out what he's been up to?' Daisy asked, knowing Henry had his sticky fingers in a lot of unsavoury pies. Daisy hoped their Bridie would let the scales fall from her eyes so she could see what Henry Beamer was really like.

'He'll have been up to no good, I'm sure,' said Mary Jane, knowing that it was old news Henry was a little too fond of his father's wife and was impatient to see the old man off. 'Do you think he's been caught with his hand in the till?' asked Mary Jane and now it was Daisy's turn to shrug her shoulders.

'Either that or he's done his father in for his inheritance.' Their imaginations were running wild and what they didn't know they invented. A pleasant pastime for the women of Beamer Street. 'Oh hello,' said Daisy, 'he hasn't done his father in – or the stepmother,' she said, watching as Mr Beamer and his wife Phoebe were brought out in handcuffs and bundled into the back of a waiting black police van parked up outside the factory. 'I wish I'd been a fly on their wall,' said Daisy. 'Wait till I tell Mam. It's a wonder she's not out here with the rest of us, to see what all the commotion's about.'

They watched as the van started up and left the street, and as each woman went back to her own house, Daisy could hear them talking in hushed tones.

* * *

'You'll never guess what you've just missed, Mam,' Daisy said, taking off her coat and hanging it up on the hook in the hallway. She removed the bucket hat she wore over her sharp, glossy, bobbed hair and pushed open the kitchen door. 'Oh hello, I didn't know we had a visitor,' she said, surprised to see Max sitting at the kitchen table having a cup of tea with her mother.

'You look bushed,' said Max, getting up without preamble and kissing her cheek, but Daisy didn't feel embarrassed at his show of affection, she liked it, and she wanted the world and her mother to know she and Max were in love.

'Max has got news.' Molly knew full well Max had more than a soft spot for her eldest daughter. Daisy deserved to be happy. She had taken on so much responsibility at a young age. And had never been as carefree as the others when she was growing up, always there to pick up the pieces when something or someone got broken, their hearts, their hopes, and dreams. Daisy had always been a shoulder to cry on, and she did it without complaint.

Molly had never wanted a life of spinsterhood for her eldest daughter; she wanted her to have a life and a family of her own. Daisy had hardly gone dancing like the other girls did. Not that she was short of offers, because Molly knew she had been asked out many a time. Sometimes, she would go on a date to the pictures or some such, so it seemed right when she took up with Harvey – even getting as far as an engagement. But it wasn't to last. Molly knew Max was the only man for their Daisy.

'I've just got back from London,' Max said. 'Questions are being asked in the House.'

'In what house?' asked Molly, her brows pleating.

'The House of Parliament,' Max answered.

'They let you into the House of Parliament,' Molly was most impressed. She didn't know anybody who had been inside there before.

'One of my sources informed me... well, never mind all that, but to cut a long story short, I went to London on business, and I heard the prime minister being asked if he was aware of functions being attended by the German Consulate in Liverpool.' Max didn't want to say too much, but the outcome may concern the family, Bridie especially.

'You met the prime minister!' Molly gasped. 'I think any minute now I might need the smelling salts.' She was sure she was going to faint clean away. But not before she got all the news.

'I watched the proceedings from the press gallery; they

wouldn't let me sit next to Neville,' Max said drily. In his capacity as an investigative reporter, he was privy to a lot of things Joe Public never got to hear about, especially those important enough to be included in the Official Secrets Act.

'Neville who?' Molly asked.

'Neville Chamberlain,' Max smiled when he saw her wide-eyed look of surprise. 'He said many Germans attended the fundraiser we catered for,' Max told Daisy, whose face paled, her heart hammering in her chest.

'Does that mean everyone is in trouble?' Molly interrupted and Max patiently shook his head before continuing.

'Uniformed Nazis are holding meetings, not only in Liverpool, but all around the country,' Max continued, 'but in Liverpool this is tantamount to asking for trouble when the news gets out. Liverpool people won't stand for Nazis or Fascists in their backyard.'

'Good for them,' said Molly, 'I can't abide fascists.' She hadn't realised Henry was a fascist.

'That fundraiser we catered for,' Max said, 'was hiding a much more sinister purpose.'

'Never!' Molly gasped, her cup paused between saucer and lip. This was better than the spy novel she'd been reading. And it had practically happened under her nose. 'Ina King will never top this,' Molly gasped. 'Not in a month of Sundays.'

'What do you mean, Max?'

Max looked around to make sure the coast was clear and lowered his voice. 'The fundraiser was also being used to recruit Nazi supporters from across the country to spread anti-Semite propaganda.'

'What! Here? Never!' said Molly. 'I can't believe there are such people in Liverpool.'

'We don't have to look very far,' said Max. 'People we speak to every day, could be Nazi sympathisers,' he said gravely. 'People like Henry Beamer.'

Molly's hand flew to her mouth. Suddenly she had trouble swallowing. What about Bridie! Would she be in trouble too?

'That's what I was going to tell you,' Daisy said. 'I've just seen Henry, Phoebe and her husband being carted off in handcuffs by the police.'

* * *

'You mean Henry is a Nazi?' Molly asked the next morning as the postman dropped an official-looking envelope onto the mat in the lobby. 'And he's been here, in my house, courting my daughter. Oh, my good Lord... What about poor Bridie? She'll be arrested too!'

'Mam, calm down.' Daisy thought her mother was going to burst with the shock.

'Apparently,' said Max, 'Nazi sympathisers have been operating in lots of countries since Hitler got into power. They have been recruiting members for the German Labour Front ever since. The consulate has been suspected of undercover activities for some time. Some of the officials were acting as intermediates, and it has been rumoured they have been buying extremely sensitive material.'

'What kind of material?' Molly felt her blood turn to ice.

'Maps of the docks. Local factories. Hospitals, including the Mersey Infirmary, which would prove very dangerous to local people in time of war.'

'Never!' Molly gasped. 'Who would do such a thing?'

'Do you think Henry might have something to do with

Hitler?' Daisy asked Max. This was something you read about in the Sunday papers. It didn't happen in Beamer Street.

'Someone has been talking with the German Secret Service,' Max answered, unwilling to name Henry as the man the English authorities had been keeping a close eye on, 'and this man has at least one co-conspirator in London.'

Max knew Daisy's unsuspecting observation during the fundraiser; was the spur he needed to record undercover activities and bring them to the attention of the people who needed to know. Unbeknown to Daisy, he had photographed Henry from a balcony, taking a bung from Karl in return for some files, which, Max suspected, were the plans of Beamer's Electricals and the surrounding dockside area. Henry had also been suspected of setting up meetings to sell information but had, up until the fundraiser, managed to avoid being caught. However, the evidence spoke volumes in the case of Max's photographs, and he knew those files, which Beamer had sold to the Germans, could prove very dangerous in the event of war.

'What about his father?' Daisy asked. 'Surely he can't carry on trading with an arrest hanging over his head.'

'He was the brains behind the whole operation,' Max told them. 'Wilhelm Beamer used his wife to act as a go-between to carry out the work he is now unable to do, and he encouraged his son to be her wingman, although I suspect he became a bit more than that.'

'You mean he has been two-timing my daughter.' Molly, a simple woman who was naive in the ways of the world, was most indignant her daughter had been deceived in such a way.

'Mam, he's been doing much worse things than two-timing our Bridie.'

'And what about our Freddy. He'll lose his job because of this!' Molly's face grew pale. Jobs weren't easy to come by these days.

'The powers-that-be will put someone in charge of the factory.' Max knew Beamer's Electricals was in a prime spot being so close to the docks, and the work done there would be of national importance should trouble in Europe escalate, especially now when peace was on very shaky ground. 'I'm sure it will all be sorted without any pandemonium,' Max said. 'In fact, I don't think anyone will even notice.'

But Molly was having none of it. She had been through one war, she'd heard stories. She knew how the land lay. They'd just heard about the crackdown on alien informants on the wireless.

The kettle whistled, shrill and oblivious, as Molly stood frozen in front of the wireless. The voice crackling through the speaker repeated the name she'd recently heard. Wilhelm Hausemann, trading under the name of Beamer on the banks of the River Mersey. Charged with treason. Awaiting trial. The words felt like something out of a story meant for someone else's life.

Molly turned slowly, the light catching the flour dust smeared across her apron, remnants of an unbaked pie. Her hands trembling slightly, she reached to shut off the wireless, silencing the news she'd just heard as Bridie came through the back door, cheeks flushed from the cold weather.

'We've just heard.' Molly's voice was a whisper, and Bridie froze where she stood. Her lips parting, her heavily mascaraed eyes searching her mother's face. She knew it was too late for denial. The truth sat between them, heavy and unavoidable.

'I didn't know, Mam. I swear. Not until... Not like this.'

Bridie's eyes brimmed with unshed tears, but Molly didn't reach for her. Her gaze was fixed on the table, where the envelope still lay. Official, unforgiving.

'The father of your unborn child. A traitor.' The word hung in the air like an accusation. Molly's voice wasn't angry. It was something else. Something hollow. Full of fear and trepidation.

'They don't know what they're saying. It's all hearsay. Henry. He's not...'

'Stop. Please.' Molly's chair scraped against the tiled floor as she sank into it, her hands clasped in prayer. The clock ticking loudly in the silence. 'You always saw something in him. I thought it was hope. I thought he'd be the one to lift you up. Not drag us down.'

'He's not what they say he is, Mam.'

Molly's jaw clenched. A storm bubbled inside her, fierce, barely contained.

'Then he can prove it. But you, Bridie, you need to decide what kind of story you want to tell your child.'

Bridie stood in the doorway, framed by the ebbing light of the day. Outside, Bootle was quiet. Inside, everything had shifted.

* * *

Molly grappled with the weight of the truth, needing someone who wouldn't flinch under its burden. Turning down the short, narrow street, she pushed open the high, wrought-iron gates of Saint Patrick's churchyard and walked the narrow path past the weatherworn gravestones. Clutching her coat tight against a rising wind, her footsteps were slow, deliberate. She wasn't one for confessions, not even to God. But tonight, she needed someone who knew her when choices were simpler.

She dipped her fingertips in the cool stone font of holy water before kneeling down, the leather kneeler cold and smooth beneath her. She saw Father Egan gathering hymn books from the long wooden pews. He was older now, she thought, his hair thin and starkly white against the black cassock. With a slight stoop, his face was now carved by years of listening in the confessional box.

'I didn't come for absolution,' Molly said, her voice dull and flat. She hadn't stepped foot in this church since her first husband, Bert, was taken from her back in 1916.

Father Egan didn't turn. He lay the hymn books down softly at the end of the pew, then rested his hand on the altar rail.

'A bit of quiet, perhaps?' he said in that gentle tone barely above a whisper. 'For a truth too heavy to carry alone.'

Molly let the silence stretch. The soundless church smelled of incense and wax polish, reminding her of her youth, memories of better days. 'I'm worried about Bridie. The future. And the child she's carrying.'

He nodded, waiting.

'Her man has been jailed.' Molly didn't mention a name. 'For treason.'

Father Egan looked up. There was no shock in his eyes, only the sadness of a man who'd seen too many families torn. 'And your faith?'

'Still cracked. Like the good plates I never use. But still there, I suppose.' She got up off her stiff knees and sat in the front pew. He joined her.

'Sometimes our children choose the storm, Molly,' he said. 'Sometimes the storm chooses them.'

'And I'm meant to stand by her while she sails straight into it?'

'You're meant to keep the shore in sight. So, if the tide turns, she knows where home is.'

Molly let his advice sink in and she swallowed hard, her fingers tracing the edge of the polished oak pew, where generations before her had prayed.

'I want her child to be born into something that still resembles hope.'

'Then start there. You don't have to forgive him. But you must protect what's yours, like those plates. Keep her safe and don't let him take your hope with him.'

'This is something I'd rather keep behind my own front door,' said Molly, able to comprehend what was being asked of her. 'This kind of news is meat and drink to the folk around here – they thrive on a bit of something out of the ordinary. Thrive on it.' Her hands fluttered like birds in flight, the words landing with finality.

* * *

Max glanced out of the rain-speckled window, watching the evening mist curl over the rooftops like smoke from a long-extinguished fire.

'This is all very hush-hush, Molly,' Max reminded her when she got back from the church. 'You must tell nobody.' His knuckles whitened around the teacup, its rim trembling against the saucer.

'That, I can promise,' Molly said, her voice softening. She knew people were going to find out soon enough. 'And to think, I'm the one keeping secrets these days. I won't tell a single soul.'

'Well, I say good riddance to the whole family of them,' said Daisy, 'I knew from the minute I saw him, that Beamer was trouble.' She wrapped her cardigan tighter, warding off the chill that wasn't just in the air. His name left a bitterness at the back of her throat. 'They'll get what they deserve.'

She glanced towards Bridie's empty chair – the worn cushion still bearing the faint shape of her sister's absence. Daisy's eyes lingered. In the hallway, she heard a distant echo of Bridie's humming. And she realised nobody could keep her sister down for long.

Beamer did her no favours, Daisy told herself. And even as she thought it, she knew Bridie's future was hanging by a thread.

* * *

'I've organised the boat tickets for Bridie,' said Mary Jane a few days later. 'The best thing she can do now is get as far away from here as she possibly can.'

'Thank the Lord, Beamer kept her name out of it,' Molly whispered, making a hasty sign of the cross, 'otherwise she might've been arrested too.'

'My brother Connor and his wife will look after Bridie,' said Mary Jane, 'and when the time comes, they will make sure her baby is well looked after, having never been blessed with children of their own. But there is just one thing...'

'What's that?' asked Molly, hoping Mary Jane was not going to pull the rug of security out from under her youngest daughter.

'I took the liberty of telling Connor that Bridie is a widow. Cashalree is a small village, and it doesn't take long for tongues to wag.' Mary Jane ignored the look of doubt on Molly's face. 'I said she lost her husband, who was taken suddenly whilst working on the docks.'

Molly, Daisy, and Mary Jane were silent for a long moment.

'Strictly speaking,' said Mary Jane, 'it was a kindness he was taken.' She was fully invested in the make-believe story, and Daisy wondered if she was, in some imaginary way, reliving her own past. She did her best to stifle a smile. Owing to the gravity of the situation, this was no smiling matter, but it did not go unnoticed that if Mary Jane could find a way to stretch her elasticated principles, she would not let the opportunity slip by.

'The threads that bind us are strong, and one day we will all be reunited.' Molly wiped a stray tear from her eye, and Daisy knew she would have to think of something quickly if she was to prevent her mother from coming apart at the seams.

'We should have a leaving party for Bridie,' Daisy said, 'we'll invite everybody in the street. It'll be much easier for her to go if she's busy among friends, instead of dwelling on what could have been.' If there was one thing Daisy could not bear, it was goodbyes.

'Bridie won't feel she's leaving home; it'll be like a long holiday.' Molly brightened when her youngest daughter entered the room with Mara.

'Are you looking forward to your big adventure?' Mara asked. 'You will love it, I'm sure.'

'I am now,' said Bridie, 'I can't change anything, so I might as well look on the bright side. And what about you, Mara?'

'I have a deep respect for Miss Treadwell,' she told Bridie and Molly, 'for her compassion and authority.' She saw in her employer a gentle strength. The lady almoner was a woman who commanded respect without even raising her voice, but after the fundraising night's fiasco, which would be plastered over every newspaper when Henry Beamer went to trial, Miss Treadwell felt she had no choice but to resign.

'I wish I was coming with you,' said Mara, 'but there is so much work to do at the hospital and Miss Treadwell is up for retirement, even though nobody expected she ever would.'

'Do you think you'll take on the job?' Bridie asked and Mara shrugged. Who knew what was going to happen. All Bridie did know was that they had swapped places. Who'd have thought she was going to live in Ireland and Mara was going to live here. 'I'm not as disappointed about going to Ireland as I first imagined,' said Bridie. 'I'm excited at the prospect of living in a new country.' Although, she was ashamed of the reason she must leave. Henry had been working with the Germans for years, building their trust, passing dock secrets. 'He had the audacity to write me a letter from Walton Gaol,' said Bridie, her face flushed a deep pink, 'that's where he's awaiting trial.'

'What did he say?' asked Molly, doubting he would ever be a free man again – if he didn't hang, that was.

'He said he loved me from the moment he met me,' said Bridie. 'But if a man can lie to his country, he can lie to anybody.'

'You'll love Ireland,' said Mary Jane, trying to ease Bridie's thoughts from the terrible truth while still proud of her homeland, made even more enchanting by her absence.

'Is this you not mentioning your homeland again,' Cal said with a grin as he came into Molly's kitchen and pulled out a chair, joining the women who had gathered to swap information. He knew his wife loved to talk about the old country and having someone like Mara to share stories with. The hard part was trying to stop her.

The loving sight lifted Daisy's spirits. Molly and Percy had a good marriage too, but unfortunately, Bridie was not going to have such a wonderful experience, but, forever the optimist, Daisy prayed everything would work out just fine in the end.

Her thoughts wandered, thinking how nice it would be to have a perfect marriage. Mam had Percy and would not go through this trying time alone. When the news about Bridie dimmed her spark a little, Percy was there to cheer her up.

'A farewell party is just what Bridie needs right now,' Daisy said, already thinking what food she was going to organise.

* * *

The day before Bridie was due to leave for Ireland, friends and neighbours came to wish her well at regular intervals, all stopping for a cup of tea and a bite to eat. The girls from the salon had even had a whip-round and bought Bridie a pair of functional wellington boots tied together with a pink ribbon.

'It rains a lot in Ireland, that's why we have such verdant green fields,' said Mara, who would miss her friend dreadfully.

'You'll be surprised how often you'll be wearing those,' said Mary Jane, who had rarely worn wellingtons since she left Ireland.

The house saw a constant stream of people and Bridie didn't have time to dwell on morbid thoughts of unpatriotic shenanigans or a swinging rope.

'If I'd known I was going to be this popular, I'd have left home sooner,' Bridie laughed, knowing everybody thought her very daring to go and work as a housekeeper for a doctor in Ireland.

'You did leave once before,' laughed Daisy. 'Remember London?'

'How could I forget,' Bridie answered, knowing Karl was in cahoots with Henry.

She had told none of the neighbours about her predicament about carrying a traitor's illegitimate child. Her mother could do without the shame. She had brought them up to be honest and proud. Two words that Bridie felt she had no right to utter.

The party was tiring for Bridie and Molly advised her to try to get some sleep, or she would be tired travelling tomorrow.

'I doubt I'll be able to sleep,' said Bridie. Then, for the first time she forgot about herself and put her arms around her mother. 'I am so sorry about all this, Mam.'

'These things are sent to try us,' Molly said, pragmatic as always. 'Today's news is tomorrow's chip paper.'

'You are the best, Mam,' Daisy laughed, knowing her mother had a saying for every occasion. 'Have you checked your ticket for boarding time, Bridie, just so they don't go without you?'

'I haven't even looked at it,' Bridie said, too upset to bother. Then, taking the ticket from her bag, her eyes widened, and her jaw dropped. 'It's a first-class ticket!' Bridie was thrilled as she showed her family the ticket.

'You'll be like queen of the sea,' Daisy laughed, knowing this was right up Daisy's street.

'The ship is sailing to New York and stopping at Cobh,' said Mary Jane, 'that's where Bridie will disembark and be met by my brother, Connor.' She recalled the ferry boat that had brought her over here all those years ago and realised just how lucky she had been to meet Molly and her family. Now it was time to repay the compliment.

Molly, with a tear in her eye, and for the first time she could recall, was speechless.

'You are not just neighbours,' Mary Jane answered, 'you are more, even, than friends, you are my family here in England, and I am proud to send one of my sister's home on such a fine liner.'

'The ship will be stopping in Ireland for a short while to

take on people travelling to America,' said Bridie, 'then continuing her voyage to New York.'

'Now don't you go hiding until the ship leaves Ireland and stow away,' Daisy laughed.

'Don't be giving her silly ideas,' said Mary Jane, half wishing she were the one making the journey. 'You are going to have such an adventure.'

'With a mop and bucket?' Bridie answered drily, knowing she was being taken on as a housekeeper even though she had never been over-fond of housework in her life.

For a fleeting moment, Daisy saw the familiar, rebellious Bridie shine through, and she knew her younger sister would be just fine in her new home, if she could get used to the quiet of the countryside and the lack of dance halls.

* * *

The following morning, Bridie, accepting the error of her ways, could not wait to put as much distance between herself, Henry, and his forthcoming trial as possible. She didn't want to know what the outcome would be. He was a traitor to his country, but, more importantly to Bridie, he had been a traitor to her. And she could never forgive that.

Her family piled into Max's car and headed to Princes Dock. Molly loved being a passenger in a motor car, and there were none so luxurious as the one Max owned.

After the boom years of transatlantic voyages, most people on Merseyside knew that all shipping companies were faced with financial troubles when the great crash occurred in 1929.

'Times were bad for Cunard,' Max informed them as they headed towards the dockyard in his car. 'It got so bad the two former rivals, Cunard Line and White Star Line had to merge to stay afloat, if you'll pardon the pun, so the new company became the Cunard White Star Line.'

'Your daddy is a fountain of knowledge,' Molly told little Poll, who was sitting in the back seat of the car, the journey doing nothing to curtail her ten-to-the-dozen chatter, while Bridie, sitting on the other side of the little girl, had never been so quiet, Daisy noted from her seat beside Max.

Max told them, to try to take the look of worry from Daisy's eyes. He knew she would miss Bridie, even though they were usually at loggerheads with each other.

A massive crowd gathered beneath the ship's towering bow on the river and Poll squealed with delight at the sight of the huge liner.

'I'm in good hands then,' Bridie said, knowing she could not change the situation, so she might as well try to enjoy it. However, her breath hitched in her throat when she caught sight of the luxurious interior. 'It says here in this brochure this design is known as *Art Deco-style*.'

'It most certainly is,' said a steward, who had come to proudly show them around the ship. Everyone oohed and ahhed, inhaling the opulence and grandeur of polished wood and new leather.

'I do believe if you had not been a journalist, you would have made a first-class seafarer like our Davy,' Daisy told Max, equally proud her brother, after all his studying, had passed his exams and was now a master of his ship. Like most families on Merseyside, there was at least one member who went away to sea.

'Look after Mam. I'll visit, I promise.' Turning away quickly, Bridie did not want her sister to see the tears in her eyes.

'You've landed on your feet this time,' Daisy called, if not a little envious, then certainly proud of the fact her sister would arrive in style to her new home.

'This way, ladies and gents,' said the steward, dressed in his crisp white shirt, dark jacket, and peaked cap, showing them off the ship before she sailed.

'I never thought I'd see the day when I waved one of my brood off on a luxury liner,' said Molly, completely ignoring the reason why Bridie was now waving her headscarf from the ship's rail to the crowd below. 'Don't forget to write,' Molly shouted, quite forgetting she had always told her children it was common to yell outdoors.

32

'This is the biggest ship I've ever seen, Daddy,' said Poll, proudly looking at the picture postcard of the ship which Daisy had bought for her. 'Have you ever travelled on a ship this big?'

'No, not really,' said Max, 'but we may do one day.'

'Come on, little one,' Molly said, holding out her hand after a shopping trip, 'let's see who can reach the car first.' Molly loved being chauffeured around the shops in Max's car.

'Me! Me!' cried Poll and started running towards the car, thrilled with the new-found ready-made family, which Daddy had found just for her. Or at least that was what he said last night when'd he told her he was going to ask Daisy to marry him.

'Do you mind, Poll?' Max had asked his daughter, knowing that, for as much as he adored Daisy, and had done from the moment he'd set eyes on her, he could never be truly relaxed about marrying her if Poll was not happy. However, he was ecstatic when she said she would be thrilled if Daisy would come to live with them.

'Shh,' said Max, 'we mustn't spoil the surprise.' After all,

Daisy might not want to get married. He knew how independent she was, and how much her business meant to her. And what about her life in Beamer Street? Would she want to leave her friends? There were so many reasons for her to say no, but he didn't want to burst his daughter's happy bubble, nor did he want to think of his own reaction if Daisy turned him down.

* * *

'Daisy, have you heard the news?' Betsy called when Daisy entered the office and began to take off her coat and hat, the young girl's voice was charged with excitement, like electricity crackling through her body when she was unable to keep still.

'What is it, Betsy? What's happened?'

'Dad got his job back in Beamer's, well not his job, exactly, a better one. A charge-hand, he'll be one of the bosses, giving the orders and...'

'Well, good on him.' Daisy was as thrilled as Betsy, knowing his hard work had stood him in good stead with the new bosses at Beamer's. 'He deserves this, after everything he's been through. I bet your mam is made up.'

'I know,' Betsy answered. 'Mam said she was knocked bandy with the joy of it.'

'Well, it's good to know the factory is in good hands.'

'Mr Everdine put in a good word for him; he said Dad was too good at his job to be a janitor, looking after houses.'

'Well, there's nothing wrong with janitors, but your dad is a good electrical engineer, one of the best; he is doing what makes him happy.'

'It's all thanks to you and Mary Jane,' Betsy said, 'and we'll be forever grateful.'

'What did we do?' Daisy was baffled. She hung her hat and coat on the curly black coat stand.

'You both gave me a chance on the day when it looked like we would never have any prospects again and all hope was lost.'

'Never stop hoping,' said Daisy, 'it's a very powerful emotion and should never be rejected or ignored.'

* * *

Back home that evening, little Poll looked very solemn for a five-year-old as she stretched and kneaded the dough Molly had given her.

'Has Daddy asked you anything, yet?'

'What kind of thing?' Daisy asked, watching Poll, dressed in a huge white overall and an over-large baker's hat clipped to her curly hair, mirroring Molly's actions with the dough at the kitchen table.

'You know,' Poll said evasively, and Daisy shook her head. She loved having Poll around, she was like the child she never had, always interested in what was going on around her.

'No, I'm sorry, Poll, I don't know.'

'You do.' A smile spread across Poll's cherubic face and, pretending not to listen, Molly could not resist smiling back. 'You know, the wedding thing.'

Daisy was quiet for a moment, and her heart lurched while Molly immediately stopped rolling the dough.

'The wedding thing?' Her tone was tentative; she dare not even contemplate the thoughts running wild through her head. 'The wedding thing.'

Whose wedding thing? Not hers, surely. Daisy and Max had never mentioned marriage. Especially not in front of Poll. She wanted to run her own business. She couldn't just give it up, as would be expected of her, to look after Max and Poll.

'No, Poll,' Daisy said, keeping her voice as casual as possible, 'Daddy's never mentioned any wedding thing.' At least, not to her.

What if he wanted to marry somebody else and Poll had got the wrong end of the stick? Daisy felt her hackles rise. Over her cold dead body!

'If he did mention the wedding thing,' Poll asked, 'would you say yes?'

'I don't know,' said Daisy, 'we'd have to wait and see.' He'd said it to pacify Poll. Daisy knew the little girl's dream was to be a bridesmaid, dressed in all her finery and looking like a princess. Everybody had a dream, it seemed.

When Daisy had first met Max, he'd told her that he loved her. It was in a jokey kind of way, but he had said it all the same, and the feeling she experienced was the next best thing to elation Daisy had ever known.

They had talked at length about the future when they were young and carefree, she about her business expectations and he about his yearning to be a correspondent in exciting times, but they had never discussed what they both wanted for each other. Daisy only realised this now. She had never given it much thought before. But now she could think of nothing else.

* * *

When Max arrived to collect his daughter, the late-afternoon light spilled through the front room nets in flower-patterned shadows on the wallpaper.

'Fancy a drink?' Daisy asked, her voice light, too light. She wasn't much of a drinker – never had been. A single glass could loosen words she'd spent weeks trying to bury. She poured two small sherries, hands slightly unsteady, and passed one to Max. He took it, eyes soft, studying her, trying to read something between the lines of her quiet smile.

What she wanted to say couldn't be said stone-cold sober, not this thing that had grown between them, steady and patient, like ivy finding its way around old brick. Tonight, she needed a nudge. A little courage.

The silence ripened between them until Max cleared his throat. His voice cracked slightly, the sound oddly loud in the small room.

'Will you marry me?' He said it like it had lived inside him for too long, waiting for just the right sliver of quiet to slip out.

Daisy stared for a heartbeat. Then two. Her chest fluttered in messy, aching ways.

'I thought you'd never ask,' she whispered. Her sherry forgotten, she flung her arms around him, knocking his glass off balance. It landed with a soft clink on the rug, but neither of them noticed. 'Yes,' she said, her voice thick with joy. 'Yes, yes, yes.' Outside, a chill wind rattled the old windows, but inside, the world finally felt warm, still, and perfect.

33

July 1936 was a busy month for Max, news-wise, and Poll was happy to stay with Aunt Daisy and Nanny Moll, as she now called them, and they were thrilled she was such a huge part of their lives.

'I can't remember what I used to do before Poll came into our lives,' said Molly, thrilled she had something other than the departure of her youngest daughter, Bridie, to dwell upon. Poll was a lively, inquisitive child who was interested in everything and everybody. And Molly could not think of a child better suited to joining her family.

Poll was like the daily newspaper when she entered the house, telling Molly everything that was going on in the street, all the local information gleaned from unsuspecting new friends. This child was like a gift from the gods to Molly, who loved to know what was going on, aware that children rarely spoke their minds in front of adults. Poll was no such child; having been surrounded by adults all her life, she conversed as they did.

'She's a ray of sunshine after a storm,' Molly told Daisy.

'There's a twenty-year-old head in that five-year-old body. There's never a dull moment.'

'What time are we going to town, Aunt Daisy?' asked Poll, excited with dreams of being fitted for a new bridesmaid dress, it was all she could think of now Aunt Daisy and her daddy were so much in love. 'We could look for your wedding dress. I could help.' Poll dreamed of Daisy walking down the aisle in a cloud of white satin and lace.

'Who said I'm getting married,' Daisy asked, surprised. 'When and if I ever marry I'm wearing a suit, or, as some call it, a two-piece costume, a pleated skirt and fitted jacket.'

Poll pulled a face. All her dreams of a frothy white dress shattered into little pieces. 'But you can wear a skirt and jacket, any time,' Poll said, her disappointment written all over her face. 'Why do you want to wear a skirt and jacket?'

'I can't imagine myself in a long white frock, with a veil,' Daisy explained. 'The last time I wore anything like that was when I made my first holy communion when I was seven.'

'I bet you looked a treat,' said Poll, checking her teeth in the mirror, hoping her new tooth would grow before the wedding.

'Mam wouldn't let me eat or drink anything in case I spilled something on my new white dress,' said Daisy, omitting to tell Poll the dress went into the pawnshop the very next day, 'and I had to sit on a stool in case I crushed the fabric.'

'Sounds heavenly,' Poll sighed, her hands clasped to her, swinging from side to side.

'It was a lot of trouble,' Daisy answered, 'while everybody else was out playing and having fun, I was stuck in the parlour on a stool being gawped at by the neighbours.'

Poll giggled. She had never met anybody as wonderful or as funny as Daisy, whose ready quips made a change from the dour character of her Aunt Grace, daddy's sister, who never let her play outside with her cousins, in case she fell over or got run over. Whereas here in Beamer Street, where cars rarely ventured, everybody played in the street, even very young children. She loved it here.

'But nobody would make you sit on a stool on your wedding day,' Poll reasoned, and Daisy could see her point.

'Let's wait and see,' Daisy answered, knowing that Poll fitted into the household very well indeed.

'Wouldn't you rather have a nice white gown?' asked Poll.

'Do you know something, young lady,' said Daisy, 'I think I would like that – you've changed my mind.' Daisy had a feeling this wouldn't be the first time.

34

In the quiet moments, Mara would help the nurses dress wounds, spoon broth to patients, read a passage of a book or newspaper aloud, or just generally help out on the charity ward where she could let her thoughts roam freely. She found a sense of purpose, knowing in the eyes of the old, infirm, and forgotten, she understood the echoes of a nation, fractured, weary, but still worth caring for.

Her interactions with patients were tender, fragile things, built on silences, fortified by acts of care, threatened by truth. Mara's bond began as an added duty, but over time, the wards became one of the few places where she felt truly grounded. At first, Mara approached the patients with quiet efficiency. She listened more than she spoke, offered gentle hands and a steady care. Yet even in the early days, so Doctor Montgomery told her, patients sensed something different in her, a steadiness, a dignity. Some call her 'the wee nun' – not because she was religious, but because of the solemn grace she brought to suffering.

As Mara spent more time among those same faces –

injured dockworkers, malnourished children, widowed mothers – she saw reflections of her own grief in theirs. Without intending to, she began to offer small glimpses of herself. A soft Irish lullaby for a feverish child, a joke shared with a man missing a foot, a memory of Mayo when a patient mentioned sheep in the mist. These moments weren't planned, and they surprised her. But she built faith and something even rarer – affection.

Before long, patients came to her for her company. She became a confidante, one who never gossiped, her silence felt like a refuge. They told her things they couldn't tell the nurse, the doctor, or even their own kin.

And as they opened up, something shifted in her thoughts and in her heart. She realised that bearing witness, offering a quiet dignity, was what her father might have missed. *This* was the republic she could believe in: one of mercy, not martyrdom.

Over time, she realised, she had stopped seeing herself as a guest in Liverpool, or as a fugitive from her past. Her relationships with the patients transformed her from a hidden soul into someone fearless enough to have her own thoughts and ideals.

The patients she interviewed for admittance into the hospital received excellent care and she wished she could allow all of them access to the healing services. She was attentive, precise, but could not be seen to favour one patient over another.

Her work ethic was unmatched. Mara arrived early, stayed late, volunteered for tasks no one else wanted – laundry, lifting, bathing the dying. It was both an escape and a penance. If she was constantly in motion, there was no time to dwell. And if she were indispensable, perhaps no one would question why she was truly there.

But still, her eyes never quite settled. She was always watching. Windows. Hallways. Doorways, as though expecting someone or something from her past to walk in.

In the early evening of that chilly day in the dockside hospital's charity ward, Dr Monty collected Seamus O'Flanagan's body. They immediately saw something in each other, and shared stories of the past remained their joint secret. She spoke in low tones, of a father who vanished, a name abandoned, a token passed by the dying man.

She did not cry, nor ask for pity. But her voice wavered when she reached the part about not knowing who her father truly was. Hero. Killer. Ghost. Maybe all three. Dr. Monty listened silently, the professional demeanour slipping from his features like chalk in rain and replaced with an expression she could not gauge. When she finished, he let out a breath.

'You know,' he said, 'I spent six months convinced my brother was alive in Belgium. I wrote him letters every week, even after the telegram arrived. Madness, really. But somehow, silence felt worse.'

Mara blinked, surprised, she'd never heard him speak like this.

'You've got ghosts,' he added gently. 'So, do I. The thing about medicine... we borrow bits of the dead to keep the living going.'

She had stared at him for a long moment. Then, very slowly, she handed him the two halves of the brass fob she carried at all times from her apron pocket, allowing him to see it. The first time anybody had seen it since Seamus O'Flanagan's death. He took it carefully. Respectfully.

'Thank you,' he said, 'I can mend the two pieces for you. Would you like that?'

Mara nodded, and for the first time in years she felt no urge to retreat. Their relationship had unfolded from there, friendship turned to romantic tension, but above all, the unspoken understanding.

Dr Monty, the name only she ever used, became her quiet co-conspirator, the one person who knew the truth and neither imagined nor recoiled from it. He didn't pry when Mara began to seek him out, not to talk, necessarily, but for the comfort of being near someone who saw her *and stayed*. They shared tea late in the evening near the records cupboard, where Mara corrected his Irish pronunciations under her breath. Saving him a slice of soda bread from the pantry, pretending she had made a mistake. He pretended not to notice.

Then, one day, when a favourite patient died in her arms, Mara witnessed the removal of her friend from the ward. The utmost reverence with which Dr Monty carried out his duty, with dignity and respect for the dead woman, made her heart swell. *This is how every living soul should be treated*, she thought, gaining a new regard for the man who had become her quiet friend over the last few months. When she despondently returned to the staffroom later, she found him waiting, holding out the cup of tea he had made for her.

No words. Just being there for her. Their implicit interaction was always on the edge of something understood. They didn't touch, but when they both reached for the same folder, their hands accidentally brushing, Mara could not ignore the electric spark that lingered.

'I'm finished for the night if you would like me to walk back with you,' Dr Monty offered one rainy evening, and Mara felt a whizz-bang shoot between her ribs.

'Is it my umbrella you're after?' She smiled that easy smile and he returned it with a low chuckle.

'There's no fooling you, Mara,' he answered, glad she hadn't refused.

They paused near the waterfront, and she spoke a line of an Irish poem, too softly for him to understand. He didn't ask for translation. There was no need. There were no words that could ever equal the hauntingly beautiful tone of her voice.

'For medical observations,' Dr Monty said when he gave her a small medical book. The first few pages were blank, but later, she found he'd written a single line:

'*The heart remembers what the mind chooses to forget.*'

'Why have you given me this?' Mara asked and Dr Monty told her it would be something to remember him by when he moved to another hospital in Plymouth. Mara was silent for a long time. Then quietly, she asked, 'Will you write to me?'

'No.' He shook his head and was silent for a moment. Mara felt her world implode. She did not think she could feel like this twice in a lifetime. First her father, then...

'I am only going to accept the posting if you come with me.'

Mara wanted to ask him to repeat what he'd just said, but she knew she'd heard right. 'I can't go,' she said, 'I'm needed here, especially now. Miss Treadwell is retiring. The patients know me, the staff...'

'In that case,' he said with a finality of one who brooked no argument, 'I shall stay too.'

'But what about your career?' Mara didn't know whether to be disappointed for him or delighted for herself. She plumped for delighted when he said:

'What good is a career when you can't be with the woman you love?'

'Oh, my word,' Mara gasped. 'Is that what the King meant when he gave up his throne, do you think?' The papers were full of the news of a constitutional crisis when King Edward had proposed to an American divorcee, Mrs Simpson.

'I do believe I know how he feels,' said Dr Monty.

'It's been an eventful year, I'll say that much,' said Mara, still trying to come to terms with the news Dr Simon Montgomery loved her. They became known as the quiet duo, with sharp instincts and high standards.

Over time, their relationship became a calm point in the chaos of illness and grief.

Their attraction bloomed into love and remained a sacred kind of intimacy that transcended labels and gave Mara a sense of anchoring she never expected.

35

DECEMBER 1936

'Daisy, come and listen to this!' Her mother called from downstairs and, applying a smear of lipstick to her generous mouth, Daisy rolled her eyes. What now? But there was something in her mother's tone. Daisy knew her mam was worried. And when Molly was worried everybody knew about it.

Coming out of the middle bedroom, Daisy saw the front door was wide open and as she made her way downstairs, she noticed a huddle of women around the wireless. Peggy, Mary-Jane and more.

'Have you heard the news?' Molly said. 'The King has given up the throne because he cannot marry the woman he loves. She is a divorcee!'

Daisy's eyes widened, she felt as if she had been hit over the head, stunned. Making a sound like she was blowing out a candle, she listened to the news on the wireless, and knew the voice belonged to the King. Recalling him attending the charity fundraiser with a tall American woman. Was she the woman for whom he had given up the throne?

* * *

Daisy never thought she'd see the day as she sat waiting for Max in the tearoom at the Pierhead.

'Turn that wireless off,' called the older waitress to her younger assistant, which brought back memories of working here, rain, hail, snow, or sunshine, waiting on customers who had just arrived or were leaving the port.

'The news is all about the King and that American divorcee. Disgraceful, I call it!' the indignant waitress called over to Daisy in the almost empty teashop. 'I've never heard the likes of it in all my born days. I'm sick of the sound of him. He wants locking up.'

Someone turned off the wireless and Daisy sighed. The news was depressing, but at least it drowned out her thoughts of how her sister might be faring in Ireland.

* * *

When Mara came home from the hospital, she was surprised when Daisy handed her the letter from Ireland. The note inside said:

Dearest Mara,

You have listened to my cares and woes constantly and never spilled one deplorable secret. Please don't tell Mam or our Daisy that the money I donated to the hospital fundraising dinner came from Karl's office safe. He doesn't need it where he is going, nor Henry. I'm sure you have much more deserving cases to spend the money on, especially now you are the lady almoner.

I could not let Karl or Henry get away with treating me in

such a deplorably shabby way... and I couldn't keep the
money. That would have been dishonest. Let's just say, I
relocated the cash to where it will be most needed. Have a
wonderful Christmas,

   Your good friend, Bridie xx

* * *

It was a cold December morning between Christmas and New Year 1936, when an official-looking man arrived at the hospital in a long black coat, fedora hat and highly polished shoes and asked her assistant for Miss Mara O'Murchu, his voice clipped, eyes alert.

Mara glimpsed him in the corridor before he saw her. Her blood ran through her veins like ice water. She knew that face. She'd seen him on the train that day she came to Liverpool and met Bridie at the station. She knew he'd been watching her and in her haste to get away from him, she had tripped and fallen on the platform, and he'd disappeared into the crowd.

He'd stood beside her father once, years ago, arms crossed, a glint of steel beneath his smile. A field courier then. But now? Now he looked... official. And dangerous.

He claimed to be with a Catholic charity liaison group visiting Irish patients. His papers were in order – *too* in order, Mara thought. Something about his crisp vowels set her teeth on edge. She turned and walked away without a word, heart hammering against her ribs like fists on a coffin lid.

She found Dr Monty alone in his laboratory. He looked up as she entered and immediately froze. 'Mara... you look like you've seen a ghost.'

'I need you to do something for me,' she whispered. 'Don't ask questions. Just listen.' Her hands trembled as she pressed a slip of paper into his palm, *a patient list*, with a name circled in red. Jake O'Flanagan. 'If anyone asks about him, say he was a patient, discharged last week. Say you signed it. Do *not* mention me.'

Dr Monty's brows knotted. 'Mara... what is this?' It wasn't like Mara to be so formidable. Her demeanour was one of tranquillity, which took the unfamiliar by surprise when they tried, fruitlessly, to get free medical help when able to pay.

She shook her head. 'Please. Just do it.'

He didn't move. 'Tell me what I'm covering up before I sign my name to it.'

'Someone's here from Dublin,' she said quietly. 'He knows who I was. And he's looking for someone I promised to protect; he was just a young boy of seventeen, he knew my father. Someone who doesn't need Dublin's justice but Liverpool's mercy.' She waited. Would he retreat? Report her? Walk out?

He nodded once, eyes never leaving hers. 'Then we protect him.'

A breath escaped her – half relief, half disbelief.

But he wasn't finished.

'I'll do this,' he said, 'but we don't keep secrets like this again. Not from each other. You trust me?'

She stared at him for a long moment. Then, with trembling fingers, she unclipped the brass fob from her chain and placed it in his hand.

'I do.'

* * *

It was just after dusk when Mara saw the man again. She was leaving through the staff door behind the dispensary, coat collar drawn up against the wind. The awful smell of fish, blood and bonemeal being loaded onto a ship permeated the night air. The dockers preparing the ships for the night tide. He stepped from the alley, Seán Flaherty, former field courier turned official in priest's clothing.

'You're a hard woman to find, Mara O'Murchu,' he said in a practised voice that was deceptively forgiving.

'I didn't ask to be found,' Mara replied, not slowing and not looking back.

He caught up and walked beside her.

'Don't worry. No public scene. I simply need a name. There's a man here – an agitator. Veteran of Athenry. Loyal to your father when he was just a lad, or so he claimed. He's been writing to Dublin. Stirring things.'

Mara paused, her breath steady, though her heart spat sparks.

'I don't know who you are talking about,' she said, 'this is a hospital, not a political debating centre.'

'O'Flanagan?'

'Long gone,' Mara bartered.

The priest's smile was glacial. 'So, he *is* alive?'

Mara's gaze didn't waver. 'He was ill. A patient. That's all.'

He stepped closer, a velvet voice with a heart of steel. 'You owe your father's cause more than that. O'Flanagan's letters endanger what remains. Names, dates. He's unpredictable.'

'And you're frightened,' Mara said quietly. 'That the truth might outlive the lie.'

He leaned in. 'I don't want trouble, Mara. But protecting that man could make you... *difficult* to explain, should the need arise.' His remark landed like a match tossed into dry grass. But Mara didn't flinch.

'My name isn't yours to explain,' she said. 'And if you come near here again, I'll make sure *your* name is known in every veterans' hall from here to Sligo. You forget – *I* know what you carried. What you buried.'

There was a lengthy silence, he was weighing up his options. Then he offered a cool nod. 'Be careful, Mara. Mercy makes poor armour.'

As he disappeared into the mist, Mara stood alone, shaking, but not from fear. Something had shifted. Her voice had found its edge. She turned towards the hospital, not away.

The moment sealed her quiet transformation from secret-keeper to protector. Her identity was no longer something she wished to hide; it became a source of purpose. She told Dr Monty of her intentions and made some hasty arrangements that would take Jake O'Flanagan to safety.

* * *

Dr Monty hadn't heard the news first-hand from Mara. He'd heard it from a porter in the loading yard. 'Some fellow in a fancy coat was sniffin' around the wards, asking if the lady almoner was still in her office. Said he knew her from Dublin.' Dr Monty's heart skipped a beat. He didn't say anything. But that night he waited in the staff library until Mara arrived for her usual hour of quiet filing.

'You saw him, didn't you?' he said.

Mara looked up, the weight already in her eyes. She nodded once.

'I handled it,' she said. But her voice was tired, in a way it hadn't been before. 'Yes, Jake O'Flanagan left, but not as a fugitive. His was a quiet act of courage, for both our sakes.'

* * *

After his conversation with Mara and the shadowy visit from Father Seán Flaherty, Jake understood the clock had begun ticking. He was not naive – he knew what quiet men in long coats were capable of, especially when they come armed with tidy papers and unfinished vendettas. So, with Mara's help he left early the following morning, before the hospital bell rang for breakfast. Jake left a note for Mara tucked into a cardboard folder on her desk:

You gave me breath when I had none left, as your father once did, and he paid a high price for doing so. That's more than most men get once, let alone twice in a lifetime. Time to move before ghosts catch up. May the wind be always at your back and the Lord accept you ten minutes before the divil knows you're dead.

No goodbyes. Just one last kindness. In vanishing, Jake shielded her from any responsibility.

Weeks later, a letter forwarded without a return address. A mention of a dockside chapel in Glasgow, where the new groundskeeper kept the keys but never told his surname. Mara read it with a faint, bittersweet smile. He was safe.

And because of that, something in her quiet grief lifted. A redemption. For, her father, a man who chose healing over heritage and paid the price for a good turn.

Mara recalled her conversation with Bridie when they first met on that eventful day last year at Lime Street Station.

Women don't have to serve any more, haven't you heard? We're emancipated now. We can do anything we want to do... The words now gave her the courage she needed to post the letter she had written to her mother. She would stay here on Merseyside and help those who needed her most. There was much work to do on the dockside. Then there was Monty. Her quiet strength.

* * *

MORE FROM SHEILA RILEY

The next instalment in the gripping, heart-wrenching Beamer Street series is available to order now here:
https://mybook.to/BeamerStreet5BackAd

ABOUT THE AUTHOR

Sheila Riley wrote four #1 bestselling novels under the pseudonym Annie Groves and is now writing the second of two saga trilogies under her own name. She has set her series around the River Mersey and its docklands near to where she spent her early years.

Download your exclusive bonus content from Sheila Riley here:

Visit Sheila's website: http://my-writing-ladder.blogspot.com/

Follow Sheila on social media:

- facebook.com/SheilaRileyAuthor
- x.com/1sheilariley
- instagram.com/sheilarileynovelist
- bookbub.com/authors/sheila-riley

ALSO BY SHEILA RILEY

Reckoner's Row Series

The Mersey Orphan

The Mersey Girls

The Mersey Mothers

Beamer Street Series

Finding Friends on Beamer Street

A Safe Haven on Beamer Street

Family Ties on Beamer Street

Binding Threads on Beamer Street

The Dockside Sagas

The Mersey Mistress

The Mersey Angels

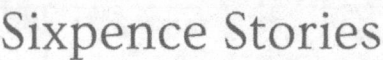
Sixpence Stories

Introducing Sixpence Stories!

Discover page-turning
historical novels from your
favourite authors, meet new
friends and be transported
back in time.

Join our book club
Facebook group

https://bit.ly/SixpenceGroup

Sign up to our
newsletter

https://bit.ly/SixpenceNews

Boldwood

Boldwood Books is an award-winning fiction publishing company seeking out the best stories from around the world.

Find out more at www.boldwoodbooks.com

Join our reader community for brilliant books, competitions and offers!

Follow us
@BoldwoodBooks
@TheBoldBookClub

Sign up to our weekly deals newsletter

https://bit.ly/BoldwoodBNewsletter